COME TO THE EDGE

By the same author
The Colonel

COME TO THE EDGE

David Hart

HUTCHINSON
LONDON   MELBOURNE   AUCKLAND   JOHANNESBURG

© Copyright David Hart 1988

All rights reserved

First published in Great Britain in 1988 by
Century Hutchinson Ltd
Brookmount House, 62 – 65 Chandos Place
London WC2N 4NW

Century Hutchinson South Africa (Pty) Ltd
PO Box 337, Bergvlei, 2012 South Africa

Century Hutchinson Australia Pty Ltd
PO Box 496, 16 – 22 Church Street, Hawthorn
Victoria 3122, Australia

Century Hutchinson New Zealand Ltd
PO Box 40 – 086, Glenfield, Auckland 10
New Zealand

ISBN 0 09 173619 6

Printed and bound in Great Britain by
Butler and Tanner Ltd, Frome and London

Come to the edge
We might fall
Come to the edge
It's too high
COME TO THE EDGE
So they came
And he pushed
And they flew.

Christopher Logue

This book is dedicated to you, Citizen.

ONE

COME TO THE EDGE
from *Ode to the Dodo*,
Christopher Logue,
reproduced by kind
permission of Jonathan
Cape 1981.

MY ROOM is rectangular, white and silent. My bed has a white enamel frame and sensible metal springs. High up, on the south wall, there is a square, metal-framed window, too small for me to jump out of even if the reinforced glass could be broken. I cannot jump out, but the sky can and does float in whenever I want it to.

Two unoriginal landscapes hang on the south and east walls. One depicts a field of corn in the foreground, with trees in the background. The other, trees in the foreground and many fields of corn in the background. Both scenes are overlooked by a summer sky.

There are two hard chairs and one reasonably comfortable, upholstered one that I deny myself and reserve for visitors. Oh yes, I still practise self-denial as others exercise their bodies. And with just as much pleasure.

For the rest, there is a bedside table with a small cupboard underneath, a washstand with an unbreakable, blue, plastic water-jug and an equally unbreakable, blue, plastic beaker. My toothbrush and toothpaste sit happily in the beaker waiting to be used.

Not my razor. I do not have a razor any more, not even a safety razor. The authorities, in their utter ignorance of my character and disposition, fear that if I had access to a sharp enough blade of any kind I might try to do away with myself. Instead, a razor is brought to me every morning. I shave under the closest supervision. As soon as I have finished, the razor is taken away.

The light is attached to the ceiling, out of my reach. It is controlled by a master-switch in the ward-orderly's office. At seven every morning it is switched on. At eleven every evening it is turned off. Day in, day out, winter and summer, it never changes. The authorities have no sense of diurnal variation.

No doubt, the authorities think that it was they who decided to send me here. It was I who decided to come here. By my actions most carefully calculated I made sure that the judge had no alternative but to send me here. Similarly, I have no doubt that the authorities think that

I am confined here at their pleasure. Nothing, of course, could be further from the truth. I would only be confined if I wanted to leave. I have no intention of leaving.

Let the authorities have their little delusions. Deluded is disarmed.

* * *

Alexander, my keeper, presents another example of the difference between the way things appear to the authorities and the way that they are. Alexander is employed to keep an eye on me. He is in charge of my security and supposed either to sit beside my bed and engage me in wholesome conversation, this hospital is run according to modern practice, or, if my conversation is too tiring, to sit outside my room and spy on me stealthily through the Judas-hole, as a weasel spies on a rabbit.

The roles are, in fact, reversed. He is the rabbit and I ... well, I will come to that.

Alexander has a soft spot for me. I saw and continue to see to it that he does. I made an arrangement with Alexander soon after I arrived here. Not, of course, financial. I used a much more reliable currency. I made myself so appealing, so apparently helpless, so much in need of sympathy that Alexander gave his love to me without question, quite suddenly, one empty Monday afternoon after he had fed and watered me.

Like all but the rarest and highest gifts of love, this one had to be earned. And what an earning! I had to alter my appearance, to soften the sharper edges of my aspect, to transform all of myself from one who appears strong to one who appears weak. I, who am usually so fastidious, allowed particles of food to get stuck in my moustache. I, who always keep myself clean, allowed saliva to dribble down my chin onto my bedshirt. I, the possessor of a superb, predatory stare, was obliged, in order to win Alexander's love, to put a look into my eyes that was, quite simply, pathetic. Alexander was quite taken in. Charitable love blossomed.

Charitable love is all very well. But it was insufficient for my purposes. I was looking for more. I needed worshipful love. It didn't take me long. Once the gates of the heart are opened and the victim's sympathy is engaged, engineering the transition from compassion to worship is comparatively easy. With a skilful *son et lumière*, using carefully calculated facial and bodily expressions and a few well-chosen syllables, day after day, I worked on Alexander until he came to consider me to be close to the divine.

And that's how it's been ever since. Alexander has soft blue eyes. His gaze doesn't penetrate. He can't see through a brown-eyed bird like me. So he worships me.

Alexander would never admit it, of course. But it is quite evident from his every word and gesture that I am the object of his most tender and devout thoughts.

Of course, Alexander's love is unrequited. It could not be otherwise. A weaker man in my position might well have thrown in the towel and abandoned himself to Alexander's daily-offered affection but I will not. Indeed, I could not. Such surrender would be the end of me.

PEOPLE SAY THAT I look like an eagle. Not without reason. Although I have a head, two arms and two legs, there is something unmistakably aquiline in my aspect. My gait is ungainly, like a grounded bird. I am very thin. I am very tall. The length and curve of my nose resembles more a beak than any human organ. The long, swept-back, streamlined brow is most unusual in a man. The mane, flowing aerodynamically back from the brow, gives the impression more of feathers than of a head of hair. My eyes . . .

I will tell you the truth about my eyes, Citizen, but you won't like it. In your childish way, you'll think that I'm boasting. But if I don't tell you, you won't be able to understand my career.

Career? Most people who know me do not think that I've had a career at all. Career is a grand word signifying success. In the eyes of others my life has not been much of a success. I will go further. Every one who knows me, without exception, thinks that my life has been a miserable failure. I did badly at school. I have not managed to acquire any property. Indeed, the property that I inherited is mine no more. I have no home that you would call my own. I have abandoned my woman and my child. I have not made money. In fact, I have lost money. I have not achieved honour. I have not achieved dishonour. I am not even notorious. Apart from a day or two of mentions in the newspapers and on the television and the radio, soon forgotten, few people have ever heard of me.

Nonetheless, I count my life a success, as will become clear.

Dov's eyes. They are brown, haughty, unblinking. And that's not all. Dov's eyes are not windows into his soul. When you look into his eyes you do not see the customary sparkling, friendly complicity of another man. Instead, you see the implacable gaze of uncounted years of evolution. When you look at Dov, Citizen, he does not lower his eyes, instead he looks back without inhibition, without compunction, without complication.

Most people spend most of their lives with their eyes more or less closed. And when they are open they see almost nothing, merely the bare essentials to avoid collisions and other immediate dangers. Most people might as well be blind. Raise you hand unexpectedly to a man and his first act is to close his eyes. As soon as danger threatens, people close their eyes. That is the way members of a crowd avoid personal danger. They close their eyes and rely on numbers for their safety.

Every member of a crowd, when faced by an attacking predator, says to himself, he can't kill more than a few of us, I'll be safe. And he reassures himself in this way even when a hundred have been taken and there seems to be no end to the killing.

A free spirit is not prepared to entrust his survival to a crowd. When danger threatens, he opens his eyes wider to see better exactly what it is that threatens him.

A crowd cannot tolerate those who look and especially those who see. To see is to rebel. To see, the seer has to abandon his friendships, his loyalties, his responsibilities. He had to abandon all of his attachments and focus all of his attention and all of his will on everything that falls beneath his gaze. Dov has the gaze of an eagle. He is a seer.

SINCE I HAVE decided to tell you something about myself, Citizen, I shall begin with a description of some, at least, of my ancestors.

My ancestors. Names and characters, babbling, jostling, each struggling to master his fate, to dominate those around him, in the ghettos of mediaeval Europe, in small hamlets and forest forts. Faces and names spreading out through great periods of early time like an ever-opening fan. Back to men and women who lived in caves in the hills overlooking the desert, implacable in their will to survive, utterly ruthless, killers with no conception of civilisation, blindly pursuing their brutal aims. Further back to the first grunters and gatherers emerging over forgotten millennia from the waters, striving to satisfy their insatiable will to life.

The Darwinian view. Genesis, on the other hand, would take me back, generation before generation, until the lines begin to contract and arrive, at last, at one man and one woman who lived in the Garden of Eden.

Imagine paradise. Imagine all those fruits and flowers in their mythical superabundance, all that sickly plenitude. I've never seen why you get so excited about it, Citizen. I've never seen why you're prepared to die in the name of your vision of paradise, father, son and holy ghost, fighting other citizens who have their own vision of paradise and their own solution to the puzzle of being.

Why stop with the Bible at Eden or with the empiricists at the emergence of life from the seas? Why stop in the thick, bubbling, planetary soup of the solar system in formation? Why even waste time with the nebulous cloud of gas spinning slowly in its place that agglomerated into the sun? All universally common and relatively insignificant events. Man's inspiration for life, man's will to live is older, very much older.

And so are the genes. Those immortal molecules, projecting from the unending past out into the infinite future. When they decide that *homo-not-always-so-sapiens* is no longer a suitable capsule for their living, man will disappear.

* * *

So much for my blood. What of my patrimony.

The family fortune, the fortune that I am supposed to have inherited and dissipated, was founded by my Jewish great-great-great-grandfather.

Things were not good in Krotoschin at the end of the eighteenth century. They got worse as the nineteenth century began. Though comparatively rich, Isaac decided to move on. He converted his property into gold, packed up his more portable possessions, gathered up his family and servants, those who wanted to go with him, and set his eyes on England.

The battle at Austerlitz formed the first obstacle to the party and provided the most dramatic adventure. Isaac was pulled up short by the French rearguard. His family, his servants, horses and chattels were impounded.

Isaac stepped carefully down from his carriage and permitted the mud to soil his shiny black boots. He looked at the French officers, at their battle stains, at their impatience. He realised that if he was to proceed he would have to pay. And he knew that he was not negotiating from a position of strength. Presently a bargain was struck. A number of louis d'or changed hands. A receipt was given by the French officer in the name of his Emperor, Isaac was a punctilious man, then, as the sun glistened on the braid and the frogging and the fine blue serge of the officer's uniform, Isaac and party were escorted across the field without a scratch, even though the battle was in progress.

To you, Citizen, an ordinary gawper, such a crossing would be inconceivable. To you it would be unthinkable that a battle meadow, a field of smoke and fearful noise and devastation, a field of pieces of men and blood-stained mud could somehow, at the whim of a French officer, be parted as the Red Sea once was in Moses' desperate haste and crossed without so much as the staining of a well-pressed trouser.

It was. My father had the receipt to prove it.

Isaac and party moved away from the noise of the battle. The ladies removed their scented handkerchiefs from their noses. The horses settled down.

Calm but poorer, day after day, the party traversed the plentiful French fields until they reached the north coast. There, they took ship.

After an uneventful channel crossing, they had had enough of events, they landed at Dover in unhurried, untroubled England.

The King's Officers were courteous. It was clear that these were people of quality, capable of speaking English, capable of reading, capable of writing, capable of offering a few pieces of gold to the officers as a token of their gratitude for the friendly welcome that they received.

Like most immigrants, they made their way to London. Unlike most, they bought a fine house in Houndsditch, bedrooms for each member of the family, smaller bedrooms for the six servants.

Once settled, having nothing but contempt for what they considered to be an extraordinary cult of amateurishness among the business classes in England, Isaac and his descendants, up early in the morning, found little difficulty in stretching out their hands and adding substantially to their capital.

By the second generation, Nathaniel had amassed sufficient means to lift up his eyes and look out of the city into the countryside.

He looked at the countryside, at the towering hedgerows and deep, secret lanes, at the patchwork of flowery meadows and fields of waving corn, looked until he found and purchased a fine English estate in an unfashionable county, close to the east coast, close to the shallows of the grey, North Sea, close to the yellow-horned poppies that grew in abundance at the foot of the sand-cliffs.

At the heart of the estate was a fine house, built in the reign of Queen Anne, of red brick with cut-brick coigns, pediment and frieze. The front had a central bay of three windows surrounded by two bays of two windows each. The roofs were steep, the chimneys numerous, the windows regular.

The house stood on an eminence commanding its wide lawns and its rose-beds, its laurel shrubberies and its sweet-scented lilac plantations, its two lakes, fish rising, its large, treeful park.

* * *

Nathaniel begat Jacob. Grandfather Jacob was the possessor of a good eye. He first cast it on my grandmother out hunting on the twenty-fourth day of November, 1903.

A bright morning. Frosty air. Many leaves, golden, rust, crimson, still clung to the trees. Autumn had been mild.

Grandfather Jacob was galloping out of the Nursery Wood in a cloud of rising, wheeling rooks, galloping past the friendly oaks and elms, galloping south towards the park when the ground unexpectedly rose right up to him and broke his nose. He was so astonished that he abandoned all attempts to retain consciousness, rolled over, and lay quite still on his back.

The chestnut mare that he had been riding was as surprised as he, because he was considered by all, including his horses, to be a good horseman. The mare recovered from her shock more quickly than her newly-unseated rider. She took leave of Jacob with a gentle snort and, delighting in her unexpected freedom, set off at a fast trot in the direction of her comfortable stable. As far as the mare was concerned, the day's hunting was over.

Jacob lay on his back on the damp, mossy ground. Dimly he felt the cool morning air on his face. He could hear no sounds. Wondering where he was, he decided to open his eyes and make a brief reconnaissance.

The light that flooded into his slowly-returning consciousness was illuminating a woman of quite extraordinary beauty, to him then and ever after, a woman who was bending down over him, taking an intimate interest in him.

Careful Jacob closed his eyes again to give himself time to consider his position. On the one hand, his nose hurt. On the other, he had just caught a glimpse of a lovely young woman. On the one hand, his posture was acutely embarrassing. On the other, the young woman who was bending over him had undoubtedly displayed concern for his well-being.

Emboldened by the shock of his fall and the lowliness of his physical circumstances, realising that, for him, there could be no more going-down, newly-careless Jacob opened his eyes again, lifted his arm, grasped the arm of the woman and, putting her feelings to a most strenuous test, pulled her down towards him and kissed her.

I imagine the touch of their usually inhibited lips.

That one kiss, as is the way with kissing, led to many kisses. Many kisses, as was the custom of the times, led to marriage.

Jacob begat Albert, my father.

MY MOTHER TOOK to her bed to conceive me. She took to her bed to bear me, what a trouble, and there she remained, a dark-eyed beauty who lived in her bed, dark hair always perfectly arranged auburn, around skin always perfectly arranged alabaster, around bones perfectly proportioned. Her face was traversed in the appropriate places, perfectly to the north by two horizontal lines of soft, dark black brow and, further down to the south, exactly where you would expect to find them, by two horizontal, softly-curving lines that made perfectly etched, dark-red lips. At the equator of this arrangement there were two small holes for her nose, which, when viewed in profile, straight, not too protruding, was perfectly shaped, according to the fashion of the times.

My perfect mother lay in her bed in a large, light, pale blue room with three great windows looking south over the front lawn to the park. A glistening, sunlight-splitting chandelier hung from the centre of the ceiling. Three large, deceitful mirrors, surrounded by carved-wooden architraves, were attached to the wall opposite the bed.

The mirrors had been touchingly installed by Grandfather Jacob to flatter his wife's generous figure. On the few occasions that my mother left her bed and passed before them, they performed the same deceitful role for her. But unhappily. My mother, if she had any physical imperfection, was a little too thin.

The room smelled of the passing of the seasons, of her several perfumes, adopted, discarded, adopted again, of freshly-laundered linen, of the nap of the old, pale-blue carpet, of the coal-fire that sparkled in the grate, every day, winter and summer.

My mother lay, in a mood of determined disillusion, between fine linen sheets, changed every day at ten in the morning precisely, the moment that she chose, every day, to bathe. She and her bad temper lay protected from engagement with any but her own interior world by the tens of yards of pale blue silk curtains that surrounded her and ran from the distant roof of the bed, yard upon yard to the floor, billowing out like the ramparts of a great fortress, proud, disdainful, distant.

Sometimes the curtains were completely closed, dour and forbidding, at other times the curtains were cracked open so that my suspicious mother could spy out through the open door into the passage.

In this way she monitored movements in the house, gathered intelligence, oversaw her family and household.

Most of the time she remained morosely silent. Occasionally, she would shout a warning, an instruction, a criticism, a demand.

The household was adjusted to her condition and great precautions were taken not to disturb her.

* * *

Except by me. Sometimes I penetrated her silken castle. As, for example, on the day of my birth.

I was born in my mother's bed at four-thirty on a misty winter afternoon. The nights were drawing out again. The earth was full of the excitement of spring impending.

The midwife thought that she saw feathers on the head of the boy-child who struggled so readily from his mother's womb. She was drunk. Perhaps that is why she thought that she saw the feathers. My mother later said that she also thought she had seen feathers. But she was full of morphine, a notoriously hallucinogenic drug.

Some enter this troubled world and let out a great shout of triumph. Others struggle from their mother's womb and howl. I did neither. Instead, I opened my eyes.

The midwife who was holding me up so that my mother could inspect me was uttering banalities. Look at the little sweetie. What a fine little man you've made. I ignored her banalities. I opened my eyes, found my eagle's gaze and lifted myself without effort above myself, above my mother, above the midwife, higher and higher until, looking down, I could see everything.

I saw my mother's state of mind. Her self-indulgence. I saw her fear of the world. I saw, especially her fear of me. I saw the midwife's loneliness. Her weakness. Her failure to find solace in alcohol. And I saw myself, newly-born, astonishing, capable of anything.

My unblinking stare had such intensity that it held my mother fast. She couldn't move her limbs. She couldn't move her features. She couldn't move her vocal chords. Nor could she take her eyes away from mine. She was paralysed.

Presently, I looked away. My mother shuddered. Her body shook like the first few convulsions of a wet dog shaking water from its coat.

My father and the doctor arrived, a few moments later to see an odd-looking, thin boy-child, with something of a knowing look that the doctor knowingly ascribed to wind.

I saw blue. The blue curtains of my mother's bed, a mimic of the sky. And flesh-pink. My mother's flesh. I also saw her black hair lying on the pillow. But I paid no attention to that. I quickly realised that it was the darker pink of her nipple, sitting on top of a warm, bulging hillock of friendly-looking flesh, that I wanted.

I waited until my father had taken the doctor off to his study so that they could toast my arrival, the one to steady his nerves and help him come to terms with the new and confusing feelings that fatherhood brings, the other to satisfy his habitual craving.

I was sufficiently fastidious, even then, to want to be presentable for my mother and so I waited until the midwife had washed me. Her rough hands of many washings, my skin of new sensations. I waited until the midwife offered myself, newly scrubbed, to my mother. Even then, I waited for what I considered to be an entirely reasonable time for my mother to take the first step, to do her duty and feed me. But she did not.

After a few moments of declining expectation I was forced to accept that, without prompting, my mother was not going to make any attempt to do her maternal duty. Accordingly, I filled my lungs, threw my head back and let out a howl. The content of this my first *communiqué* was clear. I wanted to be fed.

But the howl produced an unexpected result. My mother shuddered again. Perhaps she had begun to realise that motherhood brought responsibilities as well as the pleasures so often advertised.

I howled again, louder, concentrating on the responsibilities. And I had discovered, after the first cry, that firing off howls drove away the desire for milk. For a moment. When the desire returned, I simply howled again, again and again until the midwife realised through the mists of her drunken stupor that I had to be fed. She lifted me up towards the heavens, hoping that by showing me to my mother once more she could coax her into feeding her new-born.

But she was beaten to it. Before the midwife could complete the formalities, the fine little man needs his milk, the boy is wantin' his feed, at the apogee of her lift, I wriggled free of her and threw myself into the air. In so far as I had an intention, it was to glide elegantly down onto my mother's breast.

My flight was brief. And in a downwards direction. It ended with an undignified crash-landing on my mother's belly.

I swallowed my pride, recovered what, even at that stage, I felt I could legitimately consider to be my poise and made a shy at crawling. I lunged forward. Fell. Picked myself up onto my hands and knees again. Lunged. Fell.

This sequence was repeated many times as I struggled bravely against gravity, friction and untrained muscles, slowly over my mother's prostrate body towards the distant hillock of her breast.

Eventually, after heroic efforts, I arrived at the summit. There, I tried to clamp my lips around the hoped-for source of life-giving sweetness. But the moment that my mother felt my toothless gums pressing her flesh, the moment I applied the muscles of my throat and mouth to sucking, before I could get a single drop of milk into my mouth, she shuddered again.

Her shudder was so forceful that I fell from her body onto the bedclothes, from the bedclothes onto the floor, from the floor into the hurdy-gurdy of a life of constant, joyous struggle.

NEITHER OF MY parents were paying much attention to their business when I was conceived. Nor did things improve as I grew older.

I forgive them. For my sake. If I did not, their inattention would provide me with a lasting excuse for my behaviour. I have never made excuses. For myself or for others.

So, you can see, Citizen, that I do not feel sorry for myself. Indeed, it is for you that I feel sorry. I was conceived an individual. I was born an individual. I will die an individual. I have no need of you.

You, on the other hand, need me. You feel yourself compelled to join with others and form a crowd. As soon as you crawl off your mother's tit you join the crowd of your family. At school you surrender a little more of your individuality and join the crowd of your schoolmates. Later you surrender again and together with a surrogate mother, join the crowd of your own family.

I could never do that. Instead, I rejoiced and still rejoice in my highest solitude.

You join crowds because you feel lonely and afraid. But in the heart of a crowd you still feel lonely and afraid, especially when the hubbub ceases to distract, in those silent moments when you are forced to face the unblinking benign indifference of creation. I feel sorry for you.

And you repay the compliment. You feel sorry for me. You get up out of your comfortable chair and tell yourself, it's not Dov's fault he's a rebel. He must have been born that way. Some of you, the more soft-headed, turn to your walking companion and exclaim, oh, yes, I know him. The odd fellow with those mad eyes. The one who never joins in. It's such a shame that nothing can be done with him. But he's too much of a simpleton, too much of an innocent for this world.

Simpleton. Innocent. A nice distinction. Lying in the eyes of the beholder. And those of you who don't go so far still regard me as an outsider. Outside your world. Outside your way of looking at things. Out.

Dov knows what you think. All of you. I can see it behind your eyes. Other people's feelings are always clear to me. And their intentions. Often before they are aware of them. Even when they put on their best disguises.

* * *

I saw through my mother's best disguise when I was five.

I see my mother now. A grey silk scarf knotted gaily, a little too gaily, around her lovely neck. Immaculate that day in her city-best grey flannel suit, with black pigskin city-shoes and matching bag. She had gloves in her hand as though she intended to go out.

Tentative, watery sunlight, slipped in through the windows and played on the pale panelled walls and on the carefully carved cornices.

My mother appeared at the head of the deep-red, deep-carpeted stairs, at the end of a morning that had, until then, been like every morning. Her dramatic and entirely unexpected appearance took the whole household by surprise.

Maudie the maid was the first to see her. The unexpected glint of the rings on my mother's fingers glistening at the head of the stairs caught the girl's eye as she worked bottom-up on her knees two flights down cleaning the brass carpet-rods.

'Oh, Madam.' She tried to stifle her surprise.

She remained on her knees as her employer began her formal descent and she was still kneeling when she was struck by the expensive scent that my mother had too-liberally applied to herself. Had Maudie been upright the oncoming wave of scent might have knocked her off balance and sent her bumping head over heels down the stairs.

My crazy mother descended the stairs like an actress at the climax of a tragedy. She paused at the bottom, for maximum dramatic effect, lost on Maudie, then walked with her most stately step and most studied nonchalance on through the hall in the general direction of the domestic offices. As she walked she fixed on her face a peculiar, distant smile that stank of sacrifice.

By the time I had received the news of this quite unexpected appearance, my pantomime mother had entered the lofty old kitchen and begun to launch a series of complaints about the conduct of the house.

I rushed in to witness this extraordinary phenomenon.

Two large windows. Two white-china Belfast sinks beneath. A fat, warm, grandmother of an Aga stove opposite. A huge, scrubbed, wooden table in between.

Warmer than other rooms, furniture not formal, floor not minding being dirtied, except immediately after washing, this friendly kitchen was the only room in the house that welcomed me entirely without complication.

As did its inhabitants. Wendy, the housekeeper, whose territory it was. She provided me with a certain measure of maternal love. Within her capacity. Not heroic. Often fussy. Old Austin. The groom who lived in. He offered his services as an overacting, music-hall uncle. Maudie and Daphne the housemaids.

These were my friends. The kitchen was their territory.

My mother walked elegantly from drawer to cupboard to drawer, inspecting the state of things, criticising the cleanliness of the pans, complaining about the condition of the linen, the unscrubbed appearance of the kitchen table, the coating of friendly grease on the utensils.

Wendy nodded and bobbed and apologised. Old Austin looked for an excuse to leave the room. The maids looked away.

'I've never seen anything like it.'

'Yes, Madam.'

'Anybody would think there wasn't a housekeeper here at all.'

'Yes, Madam.'

'You know I can't abide dirt.'

'Yes, Madam.'

'See to it, then.'

'Very well, Madam.'

My mother wondered if there was anything else that she should criticise. Wendy wondered what else she could say. Together they wondered.

Eventually, my mother crossed to the stove, leaned a little too nonchalantly against the shiny chrome safety-rail, drew breath and upon the exhalation, which was slow and deliberate, allowed her glance to fall on me.

I approached, excited by this extraordinary appearance. She was better. She was up and about. She was showing signs of being a mother like other people's mothers. She was throwing her weight about.

Dov offered her his kindest, most grown-up smile, hoping that she would understand how pleased he was to see her.

I should have known better.

A breeze from outside came in through the open window and filled the silence inside with its own solitude. Each individual in that place was momentarily overcome with an irresistible sense of isolation. The sunlight departed.

Moments passed. Presently, I saw that there was not to be a returning smile on my mother's unpredictable lips. Instead, she stood, her back to the stove, staring at me without expression, towering over me, unreliable, dangerous.

Dov's smile faded.

I had no idea what was going through my mother's mind. I remembered the tone that she had used to address the staff. I saw Wendy's astonishment, old Austin's evident discomfort. Maudie's confusion. Daphne's downcast eyes.

At first, I had been impressed by my mother's unaccustomed authority. Now it came to me that my friends needed my protection. I realised that their position as servants rendered them helpless in the face of her aggression.

I realised that my mother should not be at large in the house upsetting everyone, threatening the habitual smiles. She belonged back in her bedroom.

I would have to try to force her to go back. I was the only one who could do it. How to get her there?

I had been keeping my eyes away from her. With a great effort I lifted my eyes and looked straight into hers. She stared back, smiling, now. But not a friendly smile. A superior curl to the edges of her lips.

Born of fear, although I didn't realise it then.

I did not smile. Instead, with great effort, I stared at her, an unblinking, unremitting, primal stare.

I stared and I willed. My mother's smile departed.

'What are you staring at?' The faintest traces of hysteria at the edge of her voice.

I stared. She laughed. More tremors of hysteria in the sound.

'Why are you staring at me like that?'

Dov kept staring. A five-year-old boy looking up at his mother's face in the gloom far above him.

'Are you getting a crush on me?'

I kept my mother's increasingly hysterical words away from me so that they became sounds in the distance, words from another mother in another room, lit by the light of another spring.

Silence. I stared and I willed. Slowly my will began to tell. Slowly she turned, began to retreat.

Dov willed his mother out of the kitchen into the pantry, step by deliberate step. He willed her slowly past the china-cupboards, past the ironstone dinner service, past the delicate porcelain tea service, past the green, baize-lined silver cupboards with the rows of neatly arranged silver, past the canteen of silver cutlery. Looking at nothing, seeing nothing, as though mesmerised, she stepped from the pantry through the panelled door into the hall.

Dov willed her slowly along the panelled hall, step by step on the deep-red carpet, past the green velvet-covered love seat, past the two pictures of hunting scenes, past the small oak table with twisted legs, through the arch with its carefully-carved architrave, round to the foot of the stairs.

Dov willed her right foot up onto the first step, then her left foot, then her right, up and up, step by step Dov willed her up the stairs, tread by tread, her hand on the highly-polished oak banister, his hand on the banister behind her, she looking over her shoulder at him, transfixed by his gaze, step by weary step, slowly up, past the carved-wooden figure thought to be Cardinal Wolsey, past the family portrait done when Victoria was Queen, past the paintings of horses and grooms.

When she arrived at the top of the stairs Dov willed her along the landing. Her head turned right round over her shoulder, her eyes fixed on his, step by mesmerised step, past the watercolours of summer meadows and fields, past the set of carved mahogany hall chairs, beneath the small, glass lantern, step by step on the deep-red carpet until, at last, she came to the door of her bedroom

There this *ersatz* mother stopped, made one final, supreme effort to resist her son's will. Dov pressed. Mother resisted. Dov pressed harder.

Suddenly her face crumpled without warning or shame into a terrible grimace. All beauty gone, an ocean of great tears rolled down her rumpled cheeks.

MY EARLY CHILDHOOD was not without maternal affection. Wendy was kind, Maudie was friendly and Daphne, the German maid, provided much of what my mother did not. She became my informal nanny.

She had been engaged as a maid and had no especial training with children. But it came about, my mother in her bed, Winnie too shy, Maudie too young, nobody else available, that Daphne stepped in without a word, nursed me when I was a baby and nannied me when I was a boy.

I formed a close friendship with Daphne until she betrayed me.

Daphne was sturdy, blonde, kind. She had a pretty German face with a small, upturned nose and a small square chin. She wore a brown housecoat with a clean, white, starchy apron bound to her with two long white bands that began over her bosom, ran up over her shoulders, down the other side, crossed at her back, circled round her slim waist to the front, crossed each other again, returned to her back where finally they were tied in a large, flirtatious bow just above her delightful behind. She covered her legs with thick, brown stockings, summer and winter. Her shoes were flat and sensible.

Daphne's first duty in the morning was the opening of the curtains throughout the house. I always accompanied her. I delighted in the gentle return of day-time consciousness, in the melody of the early birds, in the respectful, patient silence of the still sleeping house.

And I delighted especially in the way that the light came boldly into each room when Daphne opened the curtains. Each room would suddenly be transformed from a place of enforced darkness into a palace of new light.

In every room I made Daphne wait until I was ready, until I had absorbed all the dim shapes of the furniture into my memory. Then the sudden transformation created by the light was all the more exciting and complete.

Sometimes I stood in front of the window, my back to the curtains, looking out into the room so that I could try, when the first shafts of light came in, to race my eyes along in front of them and reach a table or a chair or a section of wall before they did.

I never succeeded. The light always got there first. One moment I could just make out the flat, polished surface of the sofa table, the walnut bureau, the mahogany card table, the next it was a blaze of glimmering, shiny wood, fixed in form and location.

Daphne and I would meet in the kitchen. She would be finishing her tea, her hands round her mug, holding it close to her face, enjoying the warmth of the steam. When she was ready she would put the mug down, nod to me. In silence we would wander into the darkened hall and the curtain-opening would begin.

Daphne always began her round on the ground floor and ended on the top floor. On the top landing there were four great windows covered by huge red damask curtains that were operated by a clever system of pulleys and cords. One morning, as Daphne stood before the first window and leant over to reach the cord, I found myself throwing myself down onto the floor.

I didn't know why.

I lay on the friendly red carpet for a moment looking up towards Daphne. Then I began to roll over and over towards her. As I rolled I realised that I was trying to catch a glimpse from below of Daphne's sturdy legs, trying to catch a glimpse of the inexplicably exciting gloom of her thighs.

I knew what I was trying to do but I still didn't know why.

She remained at the curtains just long enough for me to roll into position and catch a glimpse of the darkness under her skirt. Then she looked down and pretended to have just noticed what I was doing.

She smiled shyly. Paused flirtatiously for an instant, then walked away.

Day after day that summer, in the earliest mornings, Dov followed Daphne around the house as she opened the curtains. Day after day, on the top landing their game would begin, she delaying her tasks, spinning them out, stretching the time it took her to draw the four sets of crimson curtains on the four great windows, stretching her lovely body to reach the window cords.

After a few days I realised that, far from objecting to my rolling on the floor in the vicinity of her skirt, she wanted me to do it.

And I did, day after day until, not entirely unexpectedly, she stood quite still one early morning so that I could crawl right into the exciting palace of her skirt and close all the doors.

A strange, faintly acrid smell. Two great trunks rose up in the dim light and disappeared into the obscure, exciting gloom.

Without thought, Dov's fingers begin to undertake further investigations.

At first, Daphne didn't move. But after a few moments, to my surprise, she began to tremble and murmur. My fingers advanced further into warm, damp parts. The trembling increased until, suddenly, she was overtaken by an uncontrollable shudder. She let out a long, low moan, bent down, picked me up and held me close to her.

* * *

I felt excited throughout that day as I wandered along the garden paths, as I watched Bernard, the gardener hoeing the onions, as I chatted to old Austin, as the life of the estate continued its regular ways. I was the possessor of a secret that I shared only with Daphne, an exciting secret, a secret that transformed me.

Late in the afternoon I wandered into the kitchen. The staff were sitting at the kitchen table having tea. Instead of their usual, uncomplicated welcome, they refused to look me in the face. I could see that they were disturbed. To my surprise, I saw that they were angry too. Although they began to say the usual things in the usual way, their eyes did not follow their words.

'What's the matter with you all?'

I shouldn't have asked. I knew at once, from the way that Daphne was staring at her tea-cup.

'You shouldn't have done that.' Winnie spoke. 'It's not right.'

Daphne suddenly stood up, rushed out of the back door into the yard.

'You've upset the poor girl.'

This was entirely unexpected. Daphne had been a willing partner in our game. She was much older than I. She was the responsible one. Somehow, responsibility had been transferred to me. As though I were an adult. Besides, it had never occurred to me that I had done anything wrong.

Nor has it ever since.

Dov stood and grinned at Winnie.

'It's not funny.'

Bravado widened my grin. I stared at Winnie. Eventually she lowered her head, looked at her tea.

At this, I strolled out demonstrating as much unconcern as I could muster.

* * *

The following morning Daphne handed in her notice.

My father was astonished. He asked her for an explanation, an uncharacteristic request. She offered him none. Instead, lowered her head and blushed in confusion. Her blush embarrassed my father so much that he muttered an apology and strode out of his own study, leaving her alone and confused.

You might think, Citizen, that by keeping silent, Daphne was being loyal to me. That she was determined to keep to herself the experience we had shared. You might think it but you would be quite wrong.

Daphne had already betrayed me to the other staff. That she said nothing to my parents did not detract from that first act of disloyalty. Her decision to leave our household just as she and I were beginning on an exciting journey of exploration was an even greater act of disloyalty. Her leaving without any satisfactory explanation greatly increased the suspicion felt by all members of the household that I was in some way responsible for her departure. A third act of disloyalty.

IT'S HARD to order these recollections. I can only look back when Alexander's blue eye stops staring at me with tender accusation and fades away into the velvet darkness of night.

There is so much I could tell you about my early childhood, Citizen. I could tell you about the games I used to play with old Austin, about the formal dinners we used to share in the staff sitting-room, behind the kitchen. I could tell you about the red and white chequered plastic tablecloth, the lines of squares converging towards infinity as they ran away from me, and, unaccountably, so old Austin insisted, converging towards what must have been the same infinity as they ran away from him.

I could tell you about the day that I filled a brown paper bag with water and balanced it on top of the kitchen door so that it would fall on Maudie when she opened it returning from the outside laundry.

I can see Maudie now. A basket of newly-washed linen held to her. She opens the door, as expected, and the bag falls. Unexpectedly, it misses its target and falls onto the floor behind Maudie's smartly retreating heels.

I could tell you of the surprising and fearful joy that overcame me when, one May night as I lay in my bed, the song of a nightingale appeared out of the darkness and tumbled into my bedroom through the open window. I could tell you of the faintly white voice of the mallard's wings that I heard, every autumn, as they came to the lake to feed on water-swollen acorns. I could tell you of the sound the hares made as I watched them limp carefully through the newly fallen snow.

I could tell you, Citizen, of all these things and many more but why should I? My childhood was not a happy one and in any case it came to an abrupt end when my father sent me to a boarding-school in the Thames valley.

Dov's father did not send him away hoping that his son would achieve greatness. He was a father too modest to consider any son that he might have capable of greatness. He did not send me away hoping that I would fulfil his unrealised ambitions. My father never discovered an ambition, certainly not consciously. He sent me away to a boarding-school when I was nine because he himself had been sent away to a boarding-school when he was nine.

My father had not taken the trouble to visit the school before committing me to its care. He had selected it after a brief conversation with an acquaintance in his club, some eight months previously, on one of his rare visits to London.

Perhaps that is why the school buildings seemed so large, cold and unfriendly when our car turned into the gateway and rustled along the grey, tarmac drive. The house had been built by a retired Victorian engineer who expressed his eccentricity and his bachelor way of life in the unsympathetic arrangement of the vast numbers of yellow bricks, in the unexpected and unfriendly bay windows, in the ugly, low pitch of the countless slated roofs, in the gloomy ivy that seemed slowly to be sucking the life out of the buildings.

There were wrought-iron fire-escapes shooting out from unexpected windows and running in uncomfortable squares down to the ground. There were bricked-up windows and painted-out windows. The front door was pompous but scruffy. Unnumbered entrances and exits by careless boys had robbed the steps and the door and the door furniture of their proper shapes.

Masters were lined up to receive the new-boys. Tall, short, fat, thin, well-dressed, scruffy, they shook hands and smiled at the parents and made half-hearted attempts to provide a welcome to their new charges. I looked at them, at their eyes. I realised at once that these men were being friendly to impress the parents, not to welcome the children.

An older boy was selected from the waiting pool by a gruff command. He approached and, without any pretence of friendliness, grimly showed father and son along the red tiled passages to the new-boys' dormitory.

A white-painted room with a bare wooden floor. Two over-large sash windows looking out onto a playground. Ten iron beds were arranged around the walls. Each bed had a depression in the centre of its longitudinal axis caused by the repeated pressure put on the metal springs by previous childish bodies.

I contemplated these shapely memorials to unknown strangers for a few moments. Then the notices forced themselves on my attention. Notices everywhere proclaiming this to be out of bounds, this to be for football boots and not for slippers, this to be kept open at all times, this to be kept locked shut.

I had never before experienced the oppressive effect of such notices. Their peremptory commands assaulted me. Commands issued impersonally, by their nature pointing to an authority, unseen, unknown, immeasurable.

An authority that I knew I would have to challenge.

I unpacked my overnight bag and sat on my allotted bed listening to my father making desultory and unconvincing attempts to comfort me.

'The smell reminds me of my place.'

'I thought it was closed down.'

'You'll soon make friends. Congreve will be a good sort. I think I knew his father.'

'Was he at school with you?'

'Old Dotty Congreve was. Good cricketer. If it's his boy, you'll get on fine with him.'

It wasn't as it transpired.

'You'll soon settle in. After the first couple of nights.'

'I'm sure I will.'

'Don't be afraid to blub if you're homesick. Most do. I did.'

I had no intention of blubbing.

'It's natural.'

New-boys were casting furtive glances at each other. Parents were trying to smile convincingly.

Dov sat on his bed and stared at his father. He was tall to me but not when compared to other men. He had a bald pate surrounded by very soft, black hair. His nose was a prototype of mine, not so long. Otherwise, he had high cheekbones, a sculptured upper lip, a firm jaw, large vulnerable ears.

At first glance he looked strong. But his eyes were weak, without penetration. No great personality proclaimed itself through them.

I sat on my bed and stared at this weak man. Suddenly, I too, was overcome by weakness. I stared at my father's so vulnerable ears and realised that this parting was traumatic for him. I had never, for a moment, thought that it would be.

My astonishment did not rest there. As I looked at my father it suddenly came to me that I longed to comfort him. I wanted to touch him. I wanted to put my arms around him. I wanted to tell him that I knew how to look after myself, that he needn't worry about me.

While other parents were offering comfortable words to their sons Dov was contemplating putting his arms around his father's thin shoulders.

My father must have sensed it and feared that the spate of emotions about to flood over both of us would overcome him. He stood.

'Well, my boy. Good luck.'

I felt that I had to say something. I couldn't let him leave without one last attempt. With a great effort I managed to speak.

'Don't go.'

The words forced themselves out of me. Too loud. Most of the parents and boys in the room heard. They began to stare at this odd couple, misunderstanding entirely.

I had not pleaded with my father for my own sake but for his. I wanted to explain to him that he needn't be concerned for me. I wanted to convince him that exactly opposite to the convention, it was I who was concerned for him and that I was ready to comfort him.

He misunderstood entirely. I felt hopelessly confused. The sympathetic glances of the other parents added to my confusion.

My father should not have misunderstood me. After all, he had never received any kind of appeal from me before. Not even in the most extreme moments of my childish needs had I ever for a moment allowed myself the luxury of asking my father for help.

Outside, the sound of boys running on wooden floors, boys shouting greetings, boys arguing, car doors shutting.

My father's face began to contort. He began to tremble. He made a great effort to control himself. Suddenly, he turned on his heel, stepped smartly out of the dormitory.

Dov sat alone on his bed listening to his father's departing step until it was masked by the intrusive and unfamiliar noise of other boys and their parents busily arranging their more conventional partings.

THE FIRST OF the school authorities I confronted was the English master. He taught in a small green wooden hut with a black tin roof, in the garden, well away from the other classrooms. The reasons for this segregation became clear to me at our first meeting.

We were sitting at our desks, eyeing each other as new-boys do. Some chatting, many silent, some blubbing for their mothers, all waiting for the arrival of the first of our masters. Presently, a strange crunching sound came to our ears. An uneven, dragging step. A creature of some kind was approaching. The class fell silent.

The sound arrived outside the classroom door, stopped. The new-boys waited in mounting fear and expectation. Suddenly the door was flung open so violently that the handle banged against the wall on which it was hinged and fell to the floor. We stared out at the garden. There was no-one to be seen. We waited. In a moment, a deep voice appeared and floated into the room.

'Wily and cunning is the Ogre.'

The new-boys froze. More moments passed. Suddenly, a huge figure appeared in the doorway. Green-tweed golfer's suit. Giant legs surrounded by yards of tweed. Huge calves swelling beneath long brown woollen socks. Brown, leather shoes with nail-studded soles.

He entered the classroom with a far-away smile on his enormous lips, crossed to the platform, dragging one of his feet.

The new-boys stared at this vision in absolute silence.

'Silence,' he bellowed as he mounted the platform. The new-boys' silence deepened.

He strode to the blackboard, took up a piece of chalk and wrote. SILENCE.

'You,' he said, pointing to a fair-haired boy in the front row. 'Can you read?'

The boy was about to open his mouth to speak but the English master stopped him.

'No, don't speak. I have already demanded silence. Nod your head if you can read. All of you.'

The new-boys nodded their heads.

'Good, then there will be no excuse. You have read this command.' He pointed to the blackboard. 'Obey it.'

He sat down and stared at his class. Slowly a vacant look came into his eyes. His jaw sagged a little and the tip of his huge tongue slipped onto his bottom lip. His chin sunk slowly to his chest.

* * *

I have always had a deep-seated aversion to any form of restrictive clothing, even if it is necessary, for example, to keep warm. I would rather be cold and free to move than warm and restricted.

The school rules were very particular as to dress, appearance and tidiness. My school shirts, as it transpired, were too small, the collars too tight. I wore them with the top button undone, the knot of my tie, so I thought, hiding this imperfection.

But the English master spotted the gap. He asked for an explanation. I offered him none.

Why should I have? What could I possibly have said that would have satisfied him? It was clear to me that the master had no intention of accepting any excuse I gave him, however reasonable.

He was standing in front of the blackboard when he first noticed my collar. His right hand was raised, a piece of chalk between his fingers. He remained in this pose and stared at me, a smile at the corners of his unnaturally thick lips, a frown on his prehensile brow. I stared back. He asked for an explanation. His tone was unnecessarily triumphant. I could see that he was a man who lost control of himself easily.

'If you don't say something you'll be in trouble.'

'The collar-button was undone because I don't want to die, Sir.'

The class laughed. I was surprised and gratified.

'If I closed it the school would have much more trouble with a corpse on their hands, Sir.'

The class laughed again. I was greatly encouraged. 'I thought that we were studying English, language and literature, Sir. Not young men's fashion.'

This produced further laughter which the master was unable to stop, even by screaming for silence at the top of his voice.

I saw that the class was slipping beyond his control. So did he. I held up my hand and the class fell silent. This infuriated the master even more. I saw my opportunity and delivered my mortal blow.

'I don't want to be a shirt-maker when I grow up, Sir. In fact, I don't want to be a shopkeeper of any kind.'

This threw the class into hysterics. And the English master.

'You will go and report to the headmaster for rudeness, insubordination and wilful disruption, immediately,' he screamed at the top of his rage.

The class fell silent at this invocation of the headmaster. The English master scribbled a note, folded it, handed it to me.

* * *

I was still glowing with the pleasure of the laughter that I had created as I wandered along the empty passages towards the headmaster's study clutching the English master's note. The school was almost silent, only the monotonous droning of masters lecturing their classes, the occasional roar of anger or snatch of laughter.

Presently, I came to the headmaster's study. I stopped, wondered if I should go in or simply wander out into the grounds.

It was a lovely September day. The smell of newly-cut grass came into the passage through the open door. Sparrows chattered in the ivy outside.

After a few moments I knocked on the door of the headmaster's study. A muffled voice invited me to enter.

I stepped into a long low room, with a bay window looking out onto the playing-fields. The other walls were lined with books in glass-fronted cases. The furniture was old and broken down.

Presently the headmaster lifted his skull-like head. I looked at him calmly, smiled.

'Ah yes, it's Dov, isn't it?'

'Yes, Sir.'

'Good. Yes. I presume you've been sent to show me good work. Well done, my boy. It is encouraging when new boys shine so early in the term.'

He opened a brown wooden pot that sat on his desk, took a sweet out of it, handed it to me.

'There, Dov, well done.'

I took the sweet and handed him the English master's note. I watched his expression veer from approbation to perplexity, to self-annoyance. It finally came to rest at anger. Presently, he flew into a rage, just like the English master. At the top of his rage he took a cane from the umbrella stand in the corner beside his desk and told me to lower my trousers and told me to put my face in the cushion of the faded, black-leather chair and told me not to make a sound, however severe the pain.

A mistake, Citizen, to obey. I see it now. I should simply have refused to bend down. Then what? The headmaster would have been helpless. He couldn't have assaulted me informally. He couldn't have cuffed me or boxed my ears. Even then such things were not permitted.

Unfortunately, these reflections did not come to me that day.

IN THE HALL outside the headmaster's study stood a large fireplace with a white marble chimney-piece. A white eagle sat in the centre of the pediment, on a carved branch. A large, disdainful eagle, it held an irresistible fascination for me. Every time I waited to be beaten, I stood and stared at it. Everytime, it stared back and gave me courage.

Dov emerged after a particularly bestial beating one October afternoon. I glanced at the white eagle in the mantel. It seemed to be staring at me with more purpose than on previous occasions. Suddenly, the bird shook itself. No mistake. It shook itself.

I watched, fascinated. I willed it to shake itself again. It did. Then it raised its eyebrows as though to ask if I was afraid.

Dov was not afraid.

It was a surprisingly warm day. The sparrows in the ivy outside the open door were chattering as though it was still summer.

Satisfied with my reaction, the white eagle shook itself again with greater vigour. Its determination was absolute. I waited and watched, delighted. In a moment, its shoulders emerged from the stone like a chick breaking out of its egg. Then it lifted its wings, one by one, stretched them out, held them hunched for a moment. I laughed with delight.

Watch this.

Wings still outstretched, the white eagle lifted its left talon, clasped and unclasped it, stretched it out, replaced it on the stone plinth. It repeated the movements with its right talon, then settled itself.

Moments passed. The sunlight poured into the passage. The sparrows in the ivy outside had fallen silent.

Suddenly, the white eagle opened its beak, emitted a clear, soft whistle. Then with perfect action, it opened its wings and slowly began to fly towards me with great, sweeping beats of its sparkling white wings. It seemed to be coming down a long tunnel, slowly covering vast stretches of ground. Eventually, unexpectedly, it enfolded me in its warm, mobile silence.

Then, as slowly as you can imagine, Citizen, we turned, together, towards the open door, drifted outside.

I felt the summer sun on my back as I lifted without effort into the uplifting air, up and up, the air warming me as I flew across the school buildings, as I glided over the blue-slate roofs, over the yellow-brick chimneys.

I saw the black-painted, iron fire-escape curling down the outside of the principal building, past the dormitories on the first floor, past the headmaster's private sitting room, past the assembly hall, over the ivy and the yellow bricks, down to the lawns. In a thought I flew down the staircase, round and round down towards the ground. At the first floor, I stopped, hovered for a moment, then lifted up backwards, yes, backwards, Citizen, without effort, up and up until I was above the roofs once more, above the rusty old lightning conductor, above all the discipline imposed by the school authorities, higher until I was far above it all, higher, I had no fear of heights, higher and higher, circling, drifting, climbing.

I looked down. In the kitchen garden, gardeners. One was bending down pulling radishes, shaking the earth off them, putting them into a small wooden seed-box. The other was pushing a wheelbarrow full of vegetables up the path towards the kitchen. It occurred to me that they would be astonished if they looked up. None of them did. I wondered what would happen if they did. Was I invisible? If they saw me, would they die of fright? Would they, like most adults, pretend that they hadn't seen me, even if they had?

Dov noticed that the other birds were flying away from him in fear. Pigeons and rooks, sparrows and starlings, all were flapping wildly to escape.

I flew on towards the boundary fence erected to keep the children in.

Not me any more, I thought, as I flew over the fence chasing a pigeon, tumbling, rolling, climbing in the summer air, free to dance up on the warm, rising thermals, to slide gently down over their edges, to glide forward until I slipped into another warm bank of rising air, free to turn and roll and climb and dive, free to be wherever my eyes willed me, without effort, free as only an eagle can be, as fast as only an eagle can be, covering enormous tracts of ground without effort.

* * *

The headmaster was the first to discover that the white marble eagle that had sat so patiently on its branch in his mantel for so many years had suddenly opened its wings and flown away.

He didn't see it like that, of course. He stood outside his study, the door open, stared at the mantel. His mouth, also, was open.

After a few moments, he shouted for the other masters even though classes were in progress. Masters appeared, looking worried. Boys soon followed, looking pleased. The monotony of school routine had been interrupted. The school matron and the housekeeper both appeared. They all stood before the mantel and stared at the yawning hole where the white eagle had been, at the chips of broken marble that lay on the stone floor.

The headmaster pulled himself together. Masters and boys were despatched to all points to search. Maids were summoned, sent to search their cupboards. Gardeners and the school carpenter were called, sent to search the grounds. Masters shouted at boys. Boys shouted at other boys. Soon the school was in uproar.

The searching was fruitless. Eventually, the headmaster sent us all back to our classes and called the police.

Exactly as any other frightened citizen would. By calling for the police he was calling for a larger and more secure crowd. Safety in more numbers.

My contempt for him increased.

Two policemen arrived with knowing looks later that afternoon. One carried what looked like a salesman's black briefcase. They went straight to the scene of the crime.

Boys crowded into the hall to stare at their uniforms, to watch them at work. Their gestures, their speech, their large feet, their rough hands, all spoke of another, tougher world.

The briefcase was opened and proved to contain a small tin of white powder, a small, rubber bulb with a brush attached, a magnifying glass, two pairs of white gloves, a Polaroid camera.

The officers performed their task as though it were a religious rite, inspired, no doubt by the many expectant, childish eyes. They put on their gloves slowly. One opened the tin carefully and began to paint the white powder onto the mantel. When this was complete the other blew it off with the rubber bulb. Together they examined their work through the magnifying glass.

They discovered such a plethora of childish fingerprints it quickly became apparent that this line of enquiry was too fruitful to lead to any useful intelligence.

Then they took a series of photographs of the mantel.

This didn't help them any more than the fingerprints had.

The headmaster suggested a conference in his study. The school was sent back to work.

* * *

The headmaster summoned a school assembly later that afternoon.

Every person in the school, masters, other staff, boys, was herded into the great, dusty, assembly hall. High windows. Parquet flooring. Smell of polish. Dust rising from the floor boards.

The two policemen took the platform. Stood importantly. Allowed the boys to stare at their uniforms for a few moments. Presently, the sergeant spoke.

'There is no question in my mind, I simply do not believe that any of you boys is responsible for this extraordinary crime. Nor do I believe that the staff are involved. We are treating it as an outside job.'

He explained that he had never seen such a strange mutilation. Special stone-cutting equipment must have been used. At least two men must have been involved because of the estimated weight of the object. Further enquiries would have to be made.

The entire school stood in the assembly hall. Much greater silence than usual at school assemblies. Boys paying much more attention. Sunlight floated into the room through the high, circular window behind the platform.

The sergeant continued to speak.

His attempts to make unmysterious that which was clearly mysterious had exactly the opposite effect. The boys were beginning to realise that the disappearance of the white eagle was no longer a cause for celebration. A disturbing feeling was entering into what had, until then, been a secure world. A world of rules, regular hours, goals to be attained.

A fairy-tale world for which Dov had nothing but contempt. A dream-world Dov had now learned to disrupt.

I WAS PHYSICALLY mature, in all aspects, before the end of my thirteenth year.

I made this discovery with the unwitting help of a small, slow, deliberate tortoise that had decided to cut its shackles and set out on a voyage of discovery. A decision it was to regret, at least until I rescued it.

By then I had graduated from the prep-school to the public school to which the prep-school was attached.

Yes, Citizen, the school authorities were not at that time prepared to admit to a failure and expel me, although they would have dearly liked to.

At the far end of the playing-fields the boys were encouraged to cultivate small gardens. The school authorities hoped in this way to teach their charges the rudiments of an ancient branch of civilisation.

'As with Timur the Lame,' the headmaster had said, announcing his decision, 'as with Barbur his descendant, so it will be with you young conquerors.' Boys sniggered. The headmaster smiled tolerantly. He had been in a fine humour that sun-filled day as he announced his decision that we should be cultivators as well as scholars.

It became school policy that boys should be encouraged to grow flowers and learn the Latin as well as the English names. *Coreopsis tinctoria*, *Delphinium grandiflorum*, *Iridacae*, *Lupinus*, I remember were among the permitted species; all varieties of *Cannabis*, of *Digitalis*, of *Papaver somniferum* and of *Nicotinus*, were very strictly proscribed.

No great hardship. Most boys grew vegetables, so that they could obtain the nourishment that they knew that their growing bodies needed and did not get from the school food. Those that felt adequately nourished sold their produce.

During the second season of cultivation a mysterious attacker struck the boys' brassicas and legumes. As soon as the warm, soft darkness of night had fallen and the leaves had lowered their defences, night after night, unprovoked attacks were made by an unknown agent. The next morning great sections of leaves had been nibbled away.

The culprit was eventually discovered. A tortoise. Despite his nocturnal habits, he was tracked to his cleverly concealed lair underneath the potting shed.

No one knew where he had come from or where he was intending to go.

* * *

The shell lay cowering on the grass in the middle of a circle of boys. Huddled inside, the frightened tortoise listened to the several and terrible deaths that were being planned for him.

'We can get a hammer,' Spotty Smith said, 'from the gardener and break the shell. Then we can get at him.'

'If we drop it on that stone,' Wetty Davies said, 'from high enough, it'll break anyway.'

'A spade'll do the trick,' Montague mi. said. He was too tough to have a nick-name. 'Just clout it hard with the sharp end of a spade.'

'I don't know why you don't just put your hand in and pull its head off,' Spotty Smith suggested.

The tortoise, cowering inside his shell, listening to these proposals for his future, was as white as a tortoise can be.

'It'll bite your hand off. They've got razor teeth.'

Something came upon me. I decided to intervene.

'I'll look after it. If I feed it, it won't attack the vegetables.' I wasn't sure why I had spoken. 'There's no point in killing it.'

'Why not?'

'There's no point. That's all.'

Eventually I persuaded the other boys to release the tortoise to me.

I bent down, picked it up. It was surprisingly heavy. I peered inside. I could just see the leathery skin and the shadowy outlines of its head in the darkness.

The other boys returned to their gardening. I carried the tortoise to the games master who was on duty that afternoon. He suggested that I go to the gardener's cottage, which was out of bounds, and ask if the gardener would look after it.

As I stepped through the wicket gate into the gardener's own garden, the relieved tortoise under my arm, I saw the gardener's daughter walking among the lupins and the hollyhocks. Grania was her name, I knew. Even though I had never seen her before, she was well known throughout the school. Many senior boys had expressed their devotion to her beauty.

I approached along the tidy path between the delphiniums and michaelmas daisies. She wore a poppy-red dress, close at the waist. Her slim, girlish legs were bare. Her feet were also bare. She had long, shining, brown hair, tied into a pigtail which reached almost to her waist.

She watched me approach with the absolute self-confidence of a young girl who knows that she is attractive.

I stopped before her and stared in silence. The more I stared at her the less confident I was. Not because I was afraid of her. Something entirely unexpected was happening in my trousers.

After thousands of years of complex civilisation, after tens of thousands of years of evolution of every kind of concealment and subterfuge the simple physical signal of sexual attraction has not been eradicated.

Not in my case, in any case.

'Are you looking for my father?' she asked eventually.

I explained that I was quite happy to transact my business with her. She smiled. A lovely, welcoming smile. It caused a further commotion in my trousers.

'What's that you have under your arm?'

'A poor tortoise.'

'How sweet. Poor thing. It must be starving.'

'Actually, it's not. In fact, it's been eating too much. The cabbages in Davies' garden. And Smith's. And Montague mi.'s. Montague mi. is the worst. It's very partial to his lettuces.'

Dov had intended this speech to be heroic. It was, in fact, garbled and too rapidly delivered. She stood smiling at me with an expression of wry amusement.

'They were going,' I went on, 'to kill it. I'm rescuing it.' I allowed a little righteous anger to flush my cheeks. As I hoped, becomingly.

She probably thought that it was a blush of embarrassment.

'Oh,' she said.

'Exactly.'

'Oh. That's kind of you.' She smiled again.

Her smile made me realise that she was much more grown-up than I, that she had more experience of this kind of conversation. And her looking at me had a continuing and quite extraordinary effect in my trousers. An effect that she watched with ill-concealed amusement.

'I'll have to ask Father,' she said eventually, as though she had made up her mind about something important. 'Unfortunately. But I'm sure he'll agree.'

She smiled, creating and quickly sealing a special conspiracy between the two of us.

'Where shall we keep it? They live in boxes, don't they?'

She walked over to an old brick and tile shed, covered in honeysuckle and roses. I followed.

'There might be a box in here.'

There was no door. We both had to bend down beneath the great rose-bush that grew all over the entrance to crawl into the warm darkness. I smelt the freshness of her skin as I crawled in beside her.

Our eyes soon became accustomed to the faint light. The shed was full of old pots, broken tools, old seed-boxes. Hanging higher up, on pegs, two old sieves for preparing seed-bed soil. A hoe. A rake. A rusted garden fork.

'Look,' she cried, 'there's a wooden box. Over there in the corner. That'll do.' She reached over for the box, past me. Her hand brushed against my chest. Rested for a moment.

'Well, go on, then. Pass it.'

I reached down, handed the box to her.

As she bent down and slowly lowered the tortoise into the box Dov's attention was entirely focused on her. Her hair, her eyes, her lips, her skin. These were the world and she was the centre. He wanted to take her away from her parents, who were, in his imagination, so jealously guarding her. He wanted to take her away from the school authorities, who were so jealously restricting him. He wanted to transport them both to a place where the world would belong to them exclusively.

I tried to kiss her.

'No. Don't. Don't.'

But she put her arms around me, kissed me, more and more passionately.

We kissed and moved closer. Her body gave off exciting scents. We kissed again and somehow moved even closer. Eventually words broke into my consciousness.

'You can't do that. No. Please don't.'

But there was no stopping me, and, despite her words, she didn't resist.

A FEW DAYS AFTER I had spent those moments of pleasure in the gardener's potting shed with his unexpectedly randy daughter, the headboy sought me out in morning break.

Archie Moore was a well-developed seventeen-year-old, slim, fair-haired. His beard had been growing and been shaved for two years. He was without spots of any kind. He was always tidy.

We were both crossing the parade ground, I in a south-westerly direction from the Art Schools, he in a north-easterly direction towards the Fives Courts.

Pink candles glowed on the chestnut tree that stood beside the path.

He approached with a small group of admiring boys, stopped when he caught sight of me.

'I wonder if I could have a word with you in my study. Shall we say at two-thirty?'

What could I say? Although Archie Moore had made a polite request it was not meant to be a request at all but a command. He was, after all, headboy. His word was law. I mumbled my assent.

A few hours later I walked up the long flight of stone steps to the great front door of the principal school building. The Corinthian columns seemed to close behind me as I stepped across the portico and went inside. I found my way up to the first floor, along to Archie Moore's study.

A small group of small boys was waiting outside his door, fags, ready to conduct the headboy's business, slavishly to obey his whims, to laugh at his jokes, however bad, to jockey for position and favours.

Fags know a great deal of their master's affairs and have some influence over his decisions. For this reason the headboy's fags were a privileged species and were treated as such by their contemporaries.

They were a year younger than Dov. This did not prevent them greeting my appearance with a host of facetious remarks and jibes. I ignored them, waited quietly.

Although my outside was calm, my inside, it has to be confessed, was not.

I was kept waiting for fifteen minutes. Intentionally. It was part of the pre-interrogation softening up.

Forcing a boy to wait for an unknown reason outside the study of the headmaster or of the headboy before punishment is the most common and most ferocious form of mental torture practised by school authorities. The boy sits and examines his conscience. Even if it is clear nonetheless he worries. Is he going to be beaten or simply let off with a warning? Will he be beaten in another's stead because of a mistake of identity? Could he have committed a crime of which he is unaware? His mind races over these and countless other possibilities until his resistance is severely weakened.

One of the headboy's fags eventually looked at his watch.

'You can go in now. Remember to knock.'

Archie Moore's study was very different from most senior boys' studies. The room was the same size. The school furniture was the same. The curtains and chair-covers were in the same gaudy bad taste. But there the similarity ended. All other boys' studies were untidy. A jumble of dirty games clothes, work books, work papers, magazines, newspapers, gaudy posters exhibiting as much of the female form as each particular housemaster permitted, football boots, family photographs, photographs of a girl-friend.

Archie Moore's study was very tidy. There were work-books. There were clean and dirty games clothes. There were magazines and newspapers. There was even a poster of a girl in a bikini. He wouldn't have wanted to be thought in any way abnormal even if he didn't at that time, have much of an interest in the female form. All had been wrestled into and was contained in a rigid orderliness that was subtly disturbing.

'Come in. Stand over there.' He indicated a spot on the rug. I stepped to the appointed spot. He stared aggressively at me, saying nothing.

'You wanted to see me?' I wasn't going to let him take the initiative.

'You know why you're here?'

This was a common approach, designed to get the accused to blurt out some confession, often to another crime than the one for which he had been summoned.

'I'm afraid not.'

He adopted a more conciliatory tone which I didn't trust at all.

'It will go much better for you if you own up. You know that. It's always like that. I admire boys who've got the guts to own up.'

'To what?'

I had intended to speak aggressively but somehow my question came out in a plaintive tone. He seized on this first sign of weakness.

'I am investigating the affair of the tortoise.'

So he had discovered. It couldn't have been worse.

'It would be better if you told me all about it.'

'Very well.'

I began at the beginning. I told him how the boys' gardens had been attacked by an unknown assailant. How the tortoise had been discovered. How some of the boys were intending to kill it. I told him that I was an animal-lover and had decided to go to its rescue.

At this point I examined him with great care, hoping to detect a ray of sympathy, a sign of relenting. My hopes were not fulfilled in the least. He stared at me without moving a muscle. Not even his eyes showed the slightest flicker.

I continued haltingly, my mouth drying, to explain how I had taken the tortoise to the games master, how the games master had given me permission to take it to the gardener for safe keeping. At that point I stopped speaking.

'Go on.'

'There isn't any more really.'

'Did you see the gardener?'

'No.'

'Oh?'

'No.'

'Who did you see?' He was bearing down with terrible inevitability on the one point in the affair that I hoped to conceal.

'His daughter.'

'Ah. Did you ask the games master for permission to visit the gardener's daughter?'

'Well, no.'

'I see. Go on.'

'Nothing else really.'

Silence fell. Archie Moore stared at Dov. Dov stared back. The interview was as humiliating as it could be. I felt a great pressure to confess. I had as great a determination to keep my counsel.

'It will go much better for you if you tell me everything.'

It was at this point that I began to make mistakes. I put on my best adult voice and posture and launched a counter-attack.

'Look, don't you think that this is all a bit unreasonable?'

'I think it is worse than unreasonable to interfere with a girl who is not only the daughter of the school gardener, not only from a different class, but who also happens to be under-age. Interfering with under-age girls is a criminal offence. You're lucky that her father spoke to me and not to the headmaster. You would certainly be sacked and might even get sent to prison.'

I was surprised. I had never for a moment thought that I had committed a crime. An offence against the school rules, certainly. A crime, certainly not. I had not given a moment's thought to the question of her age. She was certainly sexually mature.

'You have two choices. You take a beating from me and we'll keep the matter to ourselves entirely or I speak to the headmaster. If I speak to the headmaster you will certainly be expelled. If you are expelled, not just you but your family will be in disgrace. They will suffer for your crime. Think about it. You can have five minutes.'

He picked up his tidily folded copy of The Times and began to read.

When I had recovered my poise I began to reflect. Expulsion held no fears for me. In fact, I couldn't think of anything better. I would be able to go home. I would be done with this ridiculous school and the ridiculous rules and regulations to which I was unable to conform. And I had no feelings of guilt. Standing there in Archie Moore's study considering my few moments of pleasure with the gardener's daughter in her father's potting-shed, I did not feel that I had done anything wrong. Rather I felt that I had been adventurous, bold, resolute, at least in expressing my natural inclinations. Adventurous, bold, resolute: qualities that the school authorities professed to admire.

And I knew then, as I know now, that my natural inclinations were entirely healthy. Not only were they healthy, they were shared by many of my fellow students. Not simply towards women in general but especially towards the gardener's daughter. Many boys were quite open in their admiration for her.

Dov was about to tell Archie Moore that he should speak to the headmaster if he felt he must when his tongue took charge.

I have still, to this day, no idea what overcame me. Perhaps I had been put off balance by the skilful interrogation. Perhaps I had not yet sufficiently prepared myself for expulsion. Perhaps Archie Moore had persuaded me, temporarily, that I had done something wrong. Whatever the case, to my horror, I heard my tongue whisper the fateful words.

'All right, I've made up my mind. I'll take a beating.'

It didn't stop there, my traitorous tongue. It didn't loll back, satisfied with its appalling work. Dov was just recoiling from the first treachery when his tongue committed another, even more heinous act of treason and plunged to new depths.

'Thank you for keeping this away from the headmaster. It's very decent of you.'

Yes, Citizen, that is what my tongue said. I heard it as though from far away. Nonetheless I heard it distinctly.

As distinctly as, a few moments later, I heard the swish of the cane and felt its athletic bite on my bare buttocks. As distinctly as I saw the look of smug pleasure on the faces of the fags who were waiting outside the headboy's study when I limped out.

IT IS TIME, Citizen, for Dov to interrupt his school days and take a holiday at home. It is summer. An especially hot summer, as you will see. The summer when I finally disposed of my mother.

As Dov entered his first manhood, middle-class England was experiencing a period of timely moral turmoil. The hollow conventions that had governed public morality for more than half a century were lifeless, like blown birds' eggs on display in a dusty glass case.

There was never any likelihood that England would re-examine its morality immediately after the last war as the other Europeans did. Victory, for an ancient state, makes too many spiritual demands. The moment the conflict is resolved the victor, overcome with relief, discovers that the passionate hatred for his enemy that has so recently inspired him has suddenly, mysteriously transformed itself into love.

Whereas, in the past, a victor laid waste to the territories he conquered to remind his enemies of his anger, in this weak century, in this century of democratic longing for peace at any price, much of the victor's energy has been devoted to restoring the fortunes of the country he has so recently devastated, to rebuilding his former opponent's institutions and industries.

While the newly defeated has watched his country being rebuilt out of the spiritual and material resources of his conqueror, he has been given an opportunity to re-examine his own morality, the morality that led him to defeat. And he has. He has seized the opportunity to adjust his morality to the new realities of the times. In this way his national institutions have been given new vitality.

The victor has not been so blessed. Victory has expended his spiritual reserves beyond the possibility of moral revolution. He has not been able to adjust his morality to the times. Decline, moral and material, has set in.

It wasn't until the sixties, almost twenty years after the war, that

England undertook a thorough examination of itself. As soon as it did, unexpectedly, shockingly, ordinary, public morality, like a dead fish floating in a sluggish river, hit an eddy and quietly turned on its back.

The social waters were first troubled by artists. Unexpected buds of social liberation appeared in the nation's cultural life. Writers, painters, musicians stormed the capital with their sparkling visions.

Political cabaret appeared in clubs and on late night television shows. Satirists flourished. 'Roll over Beethoven,' the new troubadours sang. And he did. 'Fuck,' the television personalities commanded. And viewers did as they were told. Those that could.

For a few summers of unexpected cultural sunshine, England basked in the glow of old morality swept aside even though the necessary destruction had not been replaced by any new construction.

In this heady air the unthinkable was thought and the undoable was done.

* * *

Dov embraced the new licence with relish. He began, beneath the relentless blaze of the sun of that first summer of new social breath, to think the unthinkable. Eventually, he began to approach the doing of something that was undoable.

Looking back to fourteen-year-old Dov. Looking back to the unthinkable thoughts that entered my head that day and subsequent days, to the undoable act.

Sun-browned grass as dry as a doormat. Trees as still as rocks. Skylight unrelenting. Fields waiting for harvest, patient, silent.

Dov's father had gone away to stay with friends in Scotland for a few days. Dov was bored and restless. My body wanted to get on with it and finish growing.

As I wandered aimlessly through the unmoving landscape, watching the kestrels hanging motionless in the air, as I felt the heat of the sunbaked brick-paths on my bare feet I found that I was thinking about my mother lying alone in her bed protected by her will and the habit of the household. My mother shouting unexpected and shocking commands, whispering whimpering requests, shooting glances out through cracks in the bed-curtains. My mother's face, her brown eyes, her tall brow, like mine, her pretty nose, her straight mouth, her small breasts, her slender arms, her limbs that were such a mystery to me.

As each day passed I found, increasingly, that I could not think about anything for long but my mother, her face, her limbs, her graces.

I lay in bed on the long summer nights of my adolescence troubled by the demands of my sex. I lay in my bed, night after hot night, restless, inquisitive.

'Oh Dov . . .'

A female voice in the night. The long summer light slowly fading. An adolescent boy lying in his bed listening to the wood pigeons in the poplars.

> *Two coos, taffy.*
> *Take two coos, taffy.*
> *Take two coos, taffy.*
> *Take.*

They always end on the first syllable. Unless they perceive danger. That night there was evidently no danger for the wood pigeons.

'Oh Dov . . .'

Oedipus claimed that he was innocent. He claimed that he had no idea that Jocasta was his mother. The gods didn't believe him. They punished him and they punished his children.

Oh, Oedipus, woundedfoot, how devastating the attractions of a mother can be. Of course you knew that she was your mother. How could you not recognise the flesh that was your flesh, the breath that was your breath, the skin that was your skin?

I know exactly how you felt. Your father had wounded your feet. Mine was too weak to do that. Your father tried to do away with you on Mount Cithaeron. Mine tried to do away with me by ignoring me. I know exactly how you felt.

You have always claimed that what others called your sexual crime was innocently committed. So it was. But not so innocently that you didn't know what you were doing. It was another kind of innocence. The innocence of thinking that what you were doing was not wrong even if it was against the laws of society.

I too approached my mother out of that anotherkindofinnocence.

You wanted to free yourself from the tyranny of parental authority. I too wanted and always want to free myself from the tyranny of all kinds of authority. You acted to free yourself. So did I.

'Oh Dov . . .'

There is an age when the rages of a young man's sex begin to master him, a glorious age when the will to make life, the accumulated will to survive of all of his ancestors is speaking through his sexuality, when his will for immortality through another life is at its most determined. If a young man at such an age is left alone with his mother, if the weather is unusually hot and oppressive, if the unthinkable is becoming newly thinkable everywhere around him, if he is, in any case, by character and inclination, unafraid of experiment and devilry of all kinds . . .

'Oh Dov . . .'

From the day that my father had left the house, as I passed my mother's room in the morning, in the evening, I saw that she was looking at me in a new way, with interest, with excitement.

And her tone of voice had changed subtly, when calling to me, when asking me to visit her, when giving me instructions to pass on to the maids. No longer sharp and self-pitying, her voice had become warm and enticing.

'Oh Dov . . .'

I found my mother's new tones even more of an assualt as night after hot, restless night unfolded its tedious hours. Dov began to realise that his mother had to be overcome. How else could he be free? Free in himself. Free from her claim on his affections. Free from the spying watch she kept on the passage. Free from the guilt he felt about her being so different from other mothers. Free from the new tone in her voice. Free from the terrible frustrations of his adolescent sexual urges.

'Oh Dov . . .'

She must have sensed my frustrations and begun to feel unexpected frustrations herself. She must have been thinking of my body as much as I had been thinking of hers. She must have been hoarding the fragmentary glimpses she collected as I passed and re-passed her room every day.

'Oh Dov . . .'

His mother's mocking authority was rising to a crescendo, teasing him, insulting him, caressing him in a way he could not shake off.

'Oh Dov . . .'

The voice floating out from her bed, which seemed, that night, like a cloudy palace of uncountable ramparts, like a blue, billowy fortress. Each curtain a wall to be scaled, each fold of material a ditch to be leaped over.

'Oh Dov . . .'

Dov had never heard such tones in his mother's voice before that extraordinary night when the restless summer heat reached its greatest oppression and he slipped into his mother's favours at last.

'Oh Dov . . . Oh my Dov.'

THESE REFLECTIONS ARE taking their toll of my resources. Alexander is looking increasingly worried. I tell him not to be, meaning it but, of course, instead of taking my words at face value he interprets them and finds in them grounds for even greater concern.

Exactly why most human relationships are so arduous. Even when one expresses himself clearly the other will often do everything he can to avoid taking the expression as though the meaning is to come from the face of the words. He will seek to interpret, to impart his own colour, to try to seek out hidden meaning. Most human conflicts arise from just such incomprehension.

As, for example, the conflict that I experienced with the school authorities. Incomprehension? In my case? You will say, in your conventional way, Citizen, but Dov was just a rebel. Nothing complicated about that. The school authorities had no option but to try to beat him into conformity. It's not the fault of the school that he was the kind of rebel who cannot be beaten into anything, who, the more he is beaten, the more he refuses to conform. What were the school authorities to do?

Some of Dov wanted to conform. I had some of the attributes of the co-operative animal. A very skilled school might have been able to get me to conform. That I was sent to an unskilled school, that the school authorities had no idea how to deal with one such as me, that my desire not to conform, always strong, was encouraged by the school authorities' crass efforts, all these form the first concrete example of the kind of sacrifice that I have made for you, Citizen.

Yes, sacrifice.

I lie here wondering how to acquaint you with the sacrifices that I have made for you. That, after all, is one of the reasons that I am telling you my story. Not so that you will be grateful to me. Your gratitude would probably kill me, as it has killed so many others.

Suffocated them with adulation. Dazzled them with honours. Overcome them with the sheer pressure of success. But my story will be of no value to you if you do not accept that I have struggled all of my life, not for my sake, but for yours.

You are suspicious, Citizen. I know. You have a right to be. Most men who make such claims do so for their own purposes. I offer my story to you so that you can judge for yourself if some, at least, of my actions have been magnanimous or if they have all been selfish.

Even if you judge some of my actions to have been magnanimous, we are not out of the wood. You, Citizen, are, after all, a member of a crowd and magnanimity is frightening to a crowd. If members of a crowd witness a magnanimous act, they become suspicious. They ask themselves, why has he done such a thing? There must be a reason that we cannot, just now, see. He must have done it for his own, selfish reasons. Nobody would do such a thing unless there was something in it for him.

There was nothing in it for me. Absolutely nothing. There never has been.

* * *

Each day, the conflict with the school increased. My detachment from the authority of the school, from the authority of the vision of the world that the school tried and largely succeeded in imparting to most of its pupils, was becoming complete.

Oh, yes, most of the little brats conformed. They always do.

My detachment expressed itself particularly on the question of exams. I realised, almost as soon as I realised anything about school life, that exams were not so much designed to elicit the extent of the examinee's intelligence, ability or knowledge but rather to be a marking system for the performance of the school. On the day of the exam, for example, some brilliant candidates might be feeling nervous or ill or simply uninterested. Their results would be bad. On the day that he was marking the examiner might be feeling bilious, or take a dislike to a boy's name or to his handwriting. His marks would be low.

The more I reflected on this the more I came to regard exams as a charade in which the examinee co-operated with the school authorities in a corruption designed to deceive others. I knew the extent of my knowledge and understanding and had no wish to display it to my masters. Not simply out of a tendency to rebellion. Whenever I sat an exam I could never quite overcome a sense of conforming to an act of extraordinary hypocrisy, a kind of empty, pointless, ritual dance designed to call up gods long since dead.

And successful results, advertised by the authorities as so desirable, did not fulfil their promise for me. Indeed, the more successful I was, I was never very successful, the more disappointed I felt when I discovered that a good result bought none of the satisfactions offered or implied.

Exams were not difficult. They were not journeys of discovery. They did not leave indelible impressions on the mind. They were simply conspiracies between a boy and the school, designed to con his parents into believing that he had permanently acquired certain packages of knowledge. In truth, what he had acquired, if anything permanent, was not knowledge but rather a collection of strange totems called facts. Forced to learn in parrot fashion, like a parrot, he had no understanding of what he had learned.

Fact: the square of the hypotenuse is equal to the sum of the squares of the other two sides. In Pythagoras' imaginings. Square upon square. The mad stuff of reality bordered by squares imposed on it by his imaginings. But only in his and others' minds.

Fact: Canute was unable to persuade the sea to keep to itself. Even if he had wanted it to, which he didn't. Accordingly, it wetted his feet. The mad stuff of time refusing to stop for a king. Could it have? The question could not be asked. Not in any discussion of the facts. The master would be unable to answer it and so would regard it as an attack on his authority. Science now teaches us that time can be slowed or accelerated by motion relative to gravity. If it can be slowed, presumably it can be stopped.

All facts are finite. By masquerading as truth, which is infinite, facts deceive. Facts, especially scientific facts, are nothing more than man's imposition of patterns on the unpatterned phenomena he observes.

Facts lead people, young and old, to see the world as a package of hard, immutable things which it is not.

* * *

Eventually, on a summer Saturday, I decided, unilaterally, to change the rules of the exams that I sat.

The maths master sat at his desk on a raised platform, his eyes pointing generally in the direction of the boys he was invigilating. His mind's eye, however, was far away, re-examining the latest Jaguar that he had inspected that morning in a car showroom outside the school.

He had spent twenty minutes discussing a two-seat coupé, two occasional foldaway seats behind, with an excessively polite salesman.

The discussion had an unreal quality. Both knew that the maths master had insufficient means to buy a Jaguar or any car, for that matter. Both pretended otherwise. The maths master played out this charade in order to increase his self-esteem. It is harder to understand why the salesman was prepared to join in. Perhaps he took pity on the maths master. Perhaps he thought that he needed to practise his sales technique.

The maths master thought, with great satisfaction, that the salesman had been taken in. The salesman succeeded in convincing the maths master that he was as important a customer as any.

Many relationships, some enduring, are based on similar deceptions.

The maths master sat at his desk dreaming of a gleaming black Jaguar. It negotiated hundreds of picturesque corners. It purred along countless straight roads, all more or less resembling the road from the school to his parents' house in Gloucestershire. Not only did the Jaguar glide through his imagination. A suitably attractive female companion appeared beside him. Less defined, nonetheless as real, she provided him with a number of admiring gazes and tender smiles. She lit cigarettes for him as he drove. She even brushed her hand against his knee. By accident, of course.

Presently, both the girl and the Jaguar began to lose their charm. Doubts about the likelihood of his ever meeting the girl or managing to afford the Jaguar began to assail him. The images became blurred.

The maths master sighed, took out a copy of the exam paper that his wretched pupils were struggling to answer and hurriedly scribbled the answers alongside the questions. He always scribbled the answers alongside the questions, in this way, no doubt to facilitate marking.

This habit had not escaped my attention. Nor had another of his habits. After scribbling out the answers, he usually fell asleep.

I intended to show my classmates that rebellion could hang in the air as an eagle on his wings, silent, superb.

When I was sure that the maths master was sleeping deeply enough I stepped silently up from my desk, floated onto the platform.

The other boys all stared in frozen amazement. As I had expected. The class became silent.

I hovered behind the maths master, read the answers from his crib and memorised them. Then I wheeled round and floated silently back to my desk.

Ignoring the other boys' pathetic surprise, even the few glances of admiration that one or two of them were beginning to permit themselves, I quickly copied the answers down against the appropriate questions on my paper.

When I had finished, I threw down my pencil with a loud click and stared vacantly out of the window. The sound of the pencil dropping onto the wooden desk-top woke the maths master. As I had intended. He wiped the dreams from his mind and scanned his class. He spotted Dov looking pleased with himself.

'Finished already.'

'Yes, Sir.'

'Too easy for you?'

'Oh no, Sir.'

'Can't you do them?'

'Yes, Sir.'

'I see,' he said, seeing nothing. He wandered over, picked up my exercise book. His expression slowly changed from annoyance to surprise.

'Very good.'

'Thank you, Sir.'

'A sudden transformation?'

'Sir?'

'Not usually so successful.' His puzzlement was increasing.

'Sir?'

'Always thought you were bright. Taken a sudden interest in the subject, have you?'

'In the subject, Sir?'

'Mathematics,' he said with exasperation. He was easily exasperated.

'Oh, I see, Sir. Not especially, Sir.'

'You may go,' he said. 'As a reward,' he added. He looked at the large clock that hung on the wall opposite his desk. 'Ten minutes early.'

I slowly packed away my pencils and instruments. I put my exercise book in my desk with great deliberation. Then I stood and walked quietly to the door.

* * *

The other boys caught up with me in the subsequent break, including Hautbois.

'That took guts.' We were walking along the path to the playing-fields to watch a house cricket match.

'Not really.'

'Oh come on,' Hautbois said, 'it was terrific. What if he had woken up?'

I considered. Did I want a friend? Did I want an ally? If so, why not Hautbois? Until now, even though he had shown that he was ready for a friendship, I had not allowed myself to warm to Hautbois or to anyone else. Having friends was a complication. They made demands. They had to be looked after. The advantages might be great for those who felt happy as members of a crowd but for an outsider a friend could cause great difficulties. But I had already decided that it was cowardly not to try to make a friend, at least one, once. Besides, I felt full of strength, enough strength to have a friend and remain absolutely independent. If I was to have anyone as a friend it was Hautbois. I liked him. His silly desire to ingratiate himself with his fellows made me feel sorry for him. His gawky, uncomfortable frame and concerned expression evoked feelings of tenderness that, at first, surprised me.

* * *

Our friendship blossomed. It was not long before the first fruits appeared. It occurred to Hautbois that Dov's nerve could be turned to advantage. He suggested that we consider selling to other boys the answers to the maths questions that I was continuing to obtain and had begun to share with Hautbois. I agreed, more to please my new friend than myself. I had no interest in money then, just as I have none now. But I was keen to escalate my rebellion against the authorities, just as I am now.

Discreet enquiries were made. Soon, for a modest payment, each member of the class was being surreptitiously supplied with the answers to the papers set by the somnolent maths master.

The boys were not the only beneficiaries of this enterprise. The maths master, looking at the rapidly improving results of the Upper Fourth, began to think that he had achieved a teaching breakthrough, that his methods, so long ignored by other members of the staff, had begun, at last, to bear fruit. Some of his colleagues had mocked his methods. A few had mocked him. Now they would have to eat humble pie.

His regular daydream changed. Gone was the Jaguar. Gone were the twisting roads. Gone the breeze flying through his over-long hair. He saw himself as headmaster of his own, admittedly minor, public school. He saw grateful parents offering him large cash rewards, unsolicited of course, as their sons were converted from dirty, idle, thick-skulled boys into tidy, hard-working little fellows capable of administering what remained of the Empire, very little, and possibly, such things had been known, of restoring England to its former greatness.

All went well for a while. Hautbois and Dov had both been unpopular.

For different reasons. Dov out of disdain for the conformity of his fellows, Hautbois because he had tried too hard to make friends. Now that both of us were able to assist our class-mates to much improved maths results popularity appeared, as surprising as the first blush of spring.

Even though we both swore each and every of our customers to utter and absolute secrecy, rumours of our service began to spread around the school. Eventually, word came to the ear of the headmaster, as word does, even in a badly-run school, that one of his maths masters was assisting his pupils to cheat, or if not assisting, then certainly conniving.

The headmaster had smelt a rat when the maths master had been able to boast in the common room, one summer afternoon, that his class had all achieved over ninety per cent in their last paper. His colleagues were astonished and disbelieving. He ignored their reactions. It was clear, he said triumphantly, that his methods, so often scoffed at, were beginning to pay off.

The headmaster decided to take the Upper Fourth for maths himself and discover to his own satisfaction the full depth of the new understanding of this subject that had so suddenly been achieved by the otherwise unremarkable pupils of this class.

A few well-chosen oral questions were offered. Not one of the pupils was able to answer, with any degree of certainty, the simple problems that had been posed so recently and with such successful results in the examination papers.

Worse, many of the boys, stuttering and mumbling, looked at me hoping, wildly, that I would be able to give them guidance. The headmaster noticed their pathetic looks and the direction of them.

Further investigation.

After a careful examination of the papers that the class had completed since the beginning of term, the headmaster discovered that several careless mistakes made by the maths master had been faithfully copied by his pupils.

So those were his methods. There could be no doubt. The man had allowed his pupils to cheat, assisted them to cheat, connived at their cheating. What difference did it make? Whatever his action and motives the result was the same.

The headmaster dismissed the maths master, with effect from the end of the term, so that the work of the school, he said, would not be disrupted and its reputation prejudiced. The maths master was astonished. And he remained astonished as the headmaster went on to tell him that I would have shot you out immediately, but I have to think of the reputation of the school.

Rumours quickly spread throughout the school of an unnatural influence that Dov and Hautbois, Dov particularly, had managed to exert over the unfortunate maths master, who, in this scenario, as well as in others was cast as an innocent, other-worldly, clever man who had been corrupted by two rather odd adolescents into providing them with answers that they were supposed to work out for themselves. The form of corruption that it was thought had been used ranged from pecuniary to sexual, although not much credence was given to the latter since nobody had ever considered the maths master to have any sexual inclinations of any kind whatsoever.

In either case, much sympathy was felt for the sacked man. Even by those who had benefited from my efforts.

Yes, Citizen, even by those in my class. I shouldn't have been surprised. A crowd is notoriously fickle. And grasping. It takes and always tries to avoid paying. Even if, as in this case, the price of discovery for all, including the maths master, had been clearly invoiced.

Both Hautbois and Dov were ostracised by their fellows for the remainder of the term. I didn't care at all about the reluctance of the other boys to consort with me. I enjoyed it. I returned to my habitual solitude. Hautbois, on the other hand, was a social animal. His association with Dov in this enterprise had tarnished his carefully-constructed reputation and he had to work very hard to repolish it.

This work took the form of refusing to communicate with me in public so that he would be seen by others to have distanced himself from me and apologising to me in private for each public rebuff so that he would be seen by himself not to have abandoned, for a mess of social pottage, the friendship that he had once so earnestly desired.

By this careful strategy he succeeded in gaining a modest popularity and in salving his conscience.

He did not succeed in preventing his expulsion at the end of the term. I too was expelled.

H AUTBOIS' FATHER took it badly.
A few days after the beginning of the holidays he sent a note to my father asking him to send me over for an interview. I resisted this request. My father unexpectedly broke my resistance.

The sky was wearing its changing colours. The thick, palpable summer air had been silently replaced by the thinner, more transparent breath of autumn.

Wendy the housekeeper appeared at the door to Dov's room, huge, friendly, excited.

'Your father wants to see you in his study.'

I could tell from the tone of her voice that she regarded his wish as extraordinary. It was. He never sent for me. If he wanted to exchange views with me he did so at mealtimes.

'What does he want?'

'You know.'

'Oh that.'

'You'd better go, or you'll regret it.'

'Why?'

'He's your father.'

'So?'

'Go to him.'

'He won't persuade me. I see no point in getting a wigging from old man Hautbois.'

'Go to your father, boy, do.'

'I'm not going to see old man Hautbois.'

How often we waste our efforts staring away from the inevitable with sad endurance, with puny stubbornness. Of course I would go to my father. My father had never asked me into his study before. I was far too curious to ignore this summons. Not curious as to what he wanted to say. I knew. I wanted to see if he would manage to say what he wanted to or if he would lose his nerve. He had never before, as far as I could remember, given me any parental instruction.

* * *

Cool sunlight floated quietly into my father's study, settled on the rows of books that stretched from the floor to the ceiling.

I liked this room. It expressed the good things about my father much more successfully than he was ever able to. The books expressed his love of literature. He never spoke of it. The pictures were very good. Chosen by a man with a painter's eye. They expressed his vision. He never spoke of it. The books spoke of his learning. He never showed it. The Afghan rug was very fine. Its rich colours expressed his warmth. He never spoke with or demonstrated that, either.

Despite the books, the pictures, the warm rug, the room had a sad, gentle atmosphere, as though time had passed it by. When my father went away I spent many secret hours standing on the rug, sitting in his chair, looking at his little watercolour paintings, at his papers so neatly arranged, sitting quietly bathing in his personality. There was no other relationship to be had with him.

* * *

Father sat at his desk shuffling papers. Son entered. Father looked up. Gentle surprise.

'This is a pleasure.' He stood. Walked slowly over to the window. Stood with his shy back to me.

'Wendy said that you wanted to talk to me.'
'It's a lovely day.'
'Yes.'
'Have you been outside?'
'Not yet.'
'The herbaceous is at its best. You should have a look.'
'I thought I might go biking.'
'Ah.'
Silence fell.

My father was wondering how to approach the subject of Hautbois père. He was trying to summon up his energy and courage so that he could issue a parental command. I decided on a pre-emptive strike.

'I don't see any reason why I should go and get a wigging from old man Hautbois.'
'Yes, I know what you mean.'
'I wasn't cheating, in any case. Not in the ordinary sense.'
'What were you doing?'

'It's too complicated to explain.'
'Try.'
'You wouldn't understand.'
'Why don't you try me.'
'All right. Look. There's no point in exams. It's just an excuse for the school. An easy way out. Exams are a way for the school to deceive parents. If they had any guts, they'd report on a boy from their personal experience of him, from their understanding of his personality, talents and learning. That's what teachers should do. Instead they hide behind the easily measured results of exams.'

My father looked out over the park already browning in the summer sun, over the mature and too mature trees, over the few younger trees that he had planted when his father had died.

'We ought to take the dead wood out of that stag-headed oak.'
'Yes.'
'It'll keep going for another hundred and fifty years if it's done properly.'
'Yes.'
'They're like people when you get to know them, trees.'
'Yes.'
'Like old friends.'

The conversation was not progressing as my father had hoped. I was increasingly disappointed by my father's failure to take control of this interview.

'Well I think I'll go for that bike ride.'
'Yes, of course.'

Father looked at son. Hopelessly. He wanted to instruct his boy. He was unsure how to proceed.

'Are you afraid of Hautbois père, as you call him?'
'Of course I'm not.'
'People will say that's why you don't go to see him. People will say that you're a coward.'
'Do you think I am?'
'No. But I might have to change my mind if you don't go.'

I was furiously angry. I felt hot. My stomach felt tight.

I turned on my heel, walked out of my father's study without a word. Without a word, I walked outside to my bicycle. Unthinking, I grabbed it, jumped on. In a moment I was in motion, heading down the drive.

The smell of summer flooded into my nostrils. I ignored it. The warm air rushed past my ears. I didn't hear it. The road rushed past below me. I saw nothing. My father's attempt to persuade me to go to old man Hautbois had infuriated me. Its success had infuriated me more.

* * *

The family Hautbois lived several miles away in a converted mill. Dov arrived hot, angry, out of breath an hour later.

Hautbois, père et fils, were in the garden fiddling with a lawn-mower. The engine was in pieces. Hautbois père was directing operations. Hautbois fils was acting, obediently, as assistant mechanic. Various rubber pipes, cables, springs, bolts, nuts, were spread out on a newspaper on the grass.

There is a discernible atmosphere to all mechanical operations. Those conducted by professionals are calm, orderly, efficient. A pleasure to watch. Those conducted by amateurs vary wildly from greatly enthusiastic to morosely pessimistic. Also a pleasure to watch. But for different reasons.

The Hautbois' lawn-mower operation was rapidly approaching the morose phase. Both Hautbois' expressions demonstrated clearly that they knew that there was no hope that either of these improbable engineers would manage to put all the parts together again in the correct working order.

I leaned my bicycle against the garden hedge.

'You want to see me.'

'Hallo, Dov,' Hautbois père looked nervous. 'Yes, I do. Good of you to come over. Come in.'

He took a rag from his pocket, wiped his hands, threw the rag to Hautbois fils. The little drops of sweat that speckled his bald pate glistened in the sunlight.

We went into the musty, uncared-for house. Climbed the stairs to the first-floor drawing-room. It was clear from the fading white paint, the cracked panelling, the conventional furniture conventionally covered that the room was only used for formal occasions and that no-one in the household had ever found any relaxation in its uncomfortable interior.

Hautbois fils and I stood beside the white-painted fireplace. Hautbois père began to pace. He put on his best barrister's frown.

'I don't blame you, Dov, any more than I blame Christian.' Hautbois fils' improbable first name. 'He's just as much to blame. He was an accessory both before and after the ghastly fact or facts,' he paused briefly, 'in fact.'

Too many facts. By that repetition he demonstrated his lack of confidence even though he was accustomed to stand before a judge and address the court on the iniquity or honesty of criminals and innocent men.

'Christian has proved a most unreliable witness. Perhaps you can explain exactly what happened.'

He stared at me hoping that I would believe in his gimlet mask. I didn't.

'No, I'm afraid I can't help you.'

'Were you cheating?'

'In the eyes of the school, of course we were.'

'Yes, that's exactly how Christian put it. Exactly. Word for word. I detect a conspiracy.'

Hautbois fils looked at me. I looked calmly back trying to give him strength. There had been no conspiracy.

'Since there is a conspiracy,' Hautbois père went on, 'I must assume that there is something to conceal.'

Both his premise and his conclusion were false. I could see from his flushed cheeks that he was warming to his cross-examination.

'It will come out eventually,' he said ferociously.

He wore an old pair of grey flannel trousers, much patched and darned.

'It would be much better for both of you if we heard it now. From both or either of you.'

His shirt was also much darned.

'You were sacked for cheating. Were you cheating?'

'In the eyes of the school we must have been,' I said. 'Otherwise they wouldn't have sacked us, would they?'

'But not in your eyes?'

His once proud brown leather shoes were cracked and down at heel.

'Why not?'

'In my eyes,' I said, 'exams themselves are a form of cheating.'

'A novel line of argument. What do you mean?'

He wore a scout's brown handkerchief around his neck, clasped at the throat by a leather ring.

'Cheating by the school authorities. They con parents into believing that knowledge has been acquired permanently by their dear little ones, when in fact,' I too was warming to my explanation, 'no such thing has happened.'

This was too much for Hautbois père. His entirely conventional and only modestly successful career had not equipped him for such reasoning.

'It is clear,' he said; 'that you and Christian are conspiring to keep the truth from me.'

'No we are not, Father.'

'Don't argue with me, Christian.'

Hautbois père paced in silence. Every now and then he stopped and shot an aggressive glance at Dov or at Hautbois fils or both.

'I don't think you realise how serious this is. Your school careers have suffered a terrible setback.' He turned to me, glared. 'Your father might be rich enough to buy you a place at a decent school so that you can complete your education. I cannot do the same for Christian.'

'I'm not going to another school.'

He stared at me from his inconsiderable height.

'We are pleased when Christian has friends. We entertain them without stint. You have always had free run of our house. You have been entertained here without stint.'

'Thank you very much.'

'Don't mock me,' he said angrily.

'I'm not mocking. Christian is welcome at my house whenever he wants to come.'

More pacing. The musty atmosphere of the room was beginning to oppress me.

'I have given both you boys an opportunity to explain yourselves. Neither of you has done so, satisfactorily. Accordingly, I must rely on the report of your headmaster.'

He glared first at his son, then at me. Countless sleepy judges had been impressed with this technique. The course of the lives of accused men had been changed by it.

'According to the headmaster you set up a complex and highly sophisticated system of cheating in which one would keep watch, usually you Christian, while the other, usually you, Dov, read off the answers over the sleeping maths master's shoulder.'

He was standing as though in court. His right hand in position to grasp his lapel, had he been wearing a coat, his left hand before him, as though holding papers, had he had papers to hold.

'Apparently, the maths master, and I have had plenty to say about this, was given to taking extended naps during his classes.

'The headmaster has confirmed that the man has been sacked for this extraordinary laxity. I told him that the fees these days are not a trifle. I told him that it was simply too bad to employ a master who is incapable of remaining awake during class.'

He looked inquisitorially at me.

'Do you, Dov,' he asked, 'disagree with the headmaster's report?'

'It's one way of looking at it.'

'There is only one way of looking at this matter. Truthfully.'

I was tempted to explain to Hautbois père that there are an infinite number of ways of looking at any event or series of events. He wouldn't have understood. He was dedicated to discovering a peculiar, arid kind of truth that is supposed to lead to justice. That it does often lead to justice is nothing to do with the apparent truths revealed by witnesses in a court. It is to do with the innate wisdom and goodness of the judge or the members of the jury. Or both. If they have such qualities. When they do not, the lot of the accused is terrible.

The sun was blazing in through the closed windows, heating the room like a greenhouse. The room was getting mustier. Hautbois père was sweating profusely.

'Shall I open a window?' I asked.

'Do not interrupt me.'

This churlish reply demonstrated, to me at least, his increasing sense of frustration and impotence.

'The headmaster went on to explain,' he went on to explain, 'in considerable detail, that you sold the information that you had obtained in such a dastardly fashion, for cash. How much was it, in total? How did you divide the spoils? What have you done with the money?'

'Spent it. It wasn't much.'

'I see,' he said, seeing nothing. 'Christian, what have you done with the money?'

'Likewise,' Hautbois fils replied miserably.

'Have either of you given any thought to the career of the maths master who, though negligent, very negligent indeed, was, nonetheless, an innocent caught up in the web of your disgraceful conspiracy?'

The sun shone mercilessly into the Hautbois' drawing-room, accentuating the ugliness.

Dov stood in the sun and realised how much he hated what he saw. He hated Hautbois père. He hated his pretensions. He hated the bad pictures on the walls. He hated the colour and texture of the curtains, the carpet. He hated the ugly furniture. He even, at that moment, hated Hautbois fils. Not only did he hate it all, he was contemptuous.

Dov stood in the hot, sun-filled room overwhelmed by contempt. He realised that something was going to happen, that Dov was going to act.

Watching himself, as though from above, Dov saw his hands wander to his fly. With one deft movement it was open and his hose-pipe was out and leering contemptuously at the assembled Hautbois and their tasteless surroundings.

Hautbois père stood on his spot like a stunned calf. He had no precedent for such a demonstration. Not even the most hardened criminal in the most frequented dock had ever, in his experience, done such a thing.

Before Hautbois père could take a breath Dov gave him further ground for surprise. A fine yellow fountain began to descend in a perfect arc into the centre of the faded carpet.

Hautbois père contemplated this demonstration for a few moments then turned and rushed out of his drawing-room in headlong retreat.

TWO

A LEXANDER HAS JUST asked me if I want to be visited by Reverend Jenkins or by Father Kelly. The first is an Anglican, the second a Catholic. I told him that I did not want to be visited by either. He stopped knitting the hideous, multicoloured scarf that I know he intends to give me for Christmas and told me that he thinks that I really ought to look into the spiritual comforts that either or possibly both of these clerics can offer.

Instead, I reflect on the career of another, different kind of holy man. A holy man who had a remarkable proclivity for burglary. I met him through the unconscious agency of Hautbois' mother.

Recall, Citizen, Dov's yellow fountain descending onto the Hautbois' faded drawing-room carpet in a perfect arc. As the pale droplets patter down, in a smaller room upstairs a handsome woman sits at work innocent of the affront that is being done to her husband, to her son and to her house.

Wallpaper of off-white stripes on a white background. Faded bird-pattern chintz curtains. Summer sunlight flooding in, bleaching the already faded furniture.

Hautbois mère sits handsomely in the sunshine in her workroom in a typist's chair at a simple pine table. She sits, her back straight, her small breasts displayed to their best advantage.

On the table objects also sit, patiently. Papers, pencils, pens, a small electric typewriter, a fading rosehead in a glass of water.

Hautbois mère sits like a statue in her workroom wearing a bright summer frock and an improbable straw hat.

She looks at her papers and from time to time tentatively taps at her obedient typewriter.

Although Hautbois mère is innocent of my boisterous watery insult she will, shortly, be informed of it. Informed, she will publicly express the expected horror. Unexpectedly, she will secretly approve of my act and wish, just as secretly, that she had the courage and the equipment to do the same thing herself.

Hautbois mère was not simply the handsome mother of Hautbois my school friend who denied me more than thrice. She was not simply the handsome wife of Hautbois père, father of my school friend who had denied me so frequently that I have lost count. To the wider world, Hautbois mère was Rita Bollingbroke, a writer of romantic novels. Tales for the most part, of distressed damsels pining in gloomy castles, of dispossessed younger sons of dispossessed older dukes, and, of course, of barbarian, Teutonic invaders.

As new-boys, we read one of her novels at school. Hautbois had smuggled it into our dormitory in his trunk with the intention of ingratiating himself with the other new-boys. We read it after lights-out, under the sheets by torchlight, hoping to discover daring descriptions of rape, incest, other sexual activities.

The novel dealt with the forcible abduction of a French princess by a Teutonic knight and the subsequent rescue of the damsel by the flower of thirteenth-century French chivalry.

The cover depicted a tower room at the top of a gloomy castle. The damsel, with a suitably fearful expression, sat beneath a casement window looking at the Teutonic knight who, shirt unbuttoned, belt loose, was, clearly, about to ravish her. She was also looking at the dispossessed younger son of the dispossessed older duke who had just burst into the room, sword in hand.

Who would win the race? Would the Teutonic knight rape her before her rescuer could prevent him? Would the dispossessed younger son abandon his oath of chivalry and rape her himself? When? Before or after the Teutonic knight? Would they both rape her at once? This and other permutations were considered and discussed. Our youthful minds boggled.

We opened the pages with mounting excitement. But we were disappointed. Each time the story reached a point of crisis where some violent sexual act seemed inevitable, seemed the only possible way to provide the necessary catharsis, each time we expected, on turning the page, to read of a masterful act that we fervently hoped would enlarge our extra-curricular education, the chapter would come to an abrupt end.

The following chapter always passed over in silence the events that we had been hoping would be depicted in the previous one.

Hautbois mère suffered similar disappointments to those that she inflicted on her readers. She discovered, in her middle age, that her husband was no longer able to lead her to the catharsis physical conjunction could and should provide. She was forced to categorise him as unsatisfactory. Not just sexually. The moment that she admitted to herself that their physical relationship provided no satisfaction she also realised how little she was able to derive from their friendship. She grew to hate his dry words, his submersion in formal argument, even at home, his increasing preference for formal manners over informal emotions. She realised that, far from being the aggressive courtroom orator of his public person, Hautbois père was, in fact, extremely timid. She realised that his timidity arose from a deep reluctance to take any risks with his self-esteem. Even with his wife.

This realisation, instead of providing her with a motive to free herself from her husband, prolonged her agony. She felt so sorry for him she found it impossible to contemplate leaving him.

So, you begin to see, Citizen, why handsome Hautbois mère secretly approved of Dov's insult to her husband, even though when it was put to her she offered the customary, oh my God, how awful, and the entirely expected frown of disapproval.

Finding her husband unsatisfactory, both physically and emotionally, Hautbois mère took to religion. By accident. She became mesmerised by the gaze of two very large, almond-shaped eyes that belonged to a young, Indian fatman who was not simply the possessor of enormous eyes, not even the unashamed owner of a very large girth, but the mystic and teacher known to his family, his friends and his disciples as Pearly.

* * *

Pearly's career as a holy man had begun in his seventeenth year. He had been impressed by a photograph of a distant cousin of his mother's that had been sent from India by another cousin.

He sat in his nightshirt in the kitchen of the family villa in north London. It was late morning. His mother was taking photographs out of an envelope and passing them to him one by one.

'All these cousins, Maar, who the hell are they?'

'Cousins.'

'Are they also in prison in Bombay with my father?'

'Of course not. They are cousins on my side of the family.'

Pearly ignored his mother's smug accents and studied the pictures of his many relatives with growing disinterest until his mother handed him a photograph of an Indian holy man.

Pearly stared at the photograph. A thin ascetic with wild eyes stared back. He had a red diamond painted onto the middle of his forehead, white streaks painted onto his cheeks. He had a long black moustache and long, straggly, black hair that ran to his shoulders. Naked except for a dirty white loin-cloth, he was sitting cross-legged, in the approved position, in front of a small, white-painted shrine.

'Shit, Maar, who is this?'

'That is our cousin Raj. He is a holy man.'

'Where is this holy man, Maar?'

'In Rajasthan.'

'Shit, has he got eyes.'

Pearly's mother stood up from the table and began absently to feed the tropical fish. Pearly studied the photograph.

'Hey, Maar, what's this relative do for a living?'

'For a living? He's in the religion business.'

'The religion business. I didn't think there was any money in that. How does he make it?'

'He just sits, Babu, and prays, and people give him money. He's richer even than Uncle Jaswant.'

'Shit. That's a fine way to get rich. Better than my idiot father.'

'Don't speak of your father like that or you'll get a thick ear.'

'Why did he have to go to Bombay and get arrested like that, Maar, if he wasn't an idiot?'

'There is morality.'

'There may be, Maar, even in Pa, but it is hard to see morality in a man who goes up the spout for twenty-two million pounds and brings a government down with him.'

'It was only a banana republic. Anyway, they said on the television that your father was one of the most honourable personal bankrupts in the world.' Mrs Lal wanted her son to respect his father.

'Why doesn't this holy man bail Pa out if he's so rich?'

'Your father wouldn't accept charity. He doesn't think it moral.'

'I shit on Pa's morality.'

Pearly stared at the photograph of the holy man.

'Is there any learning to the religion business, Maar?'

'Not that I know of.'

Sitting in the family kitchen watching his mother overfeeding the tropical fish, Pearly was seized with a vision. Not of God. Not of a multitude of uncured souls. Not even of souls cured by his teaching. He was seized with a vision of himself wearing similar paint to that of his cousin, of himself sitting similarly cross-legged on a large, silk cushion counting money from rich occidental disciples as it rolled endlessly in.

Pearly had discovered his vocation.

Then and there he determined to try his hand as a holy man, to see if he too could become a millionaire. Why not? He too could grow his hair. He too could sit in the lotus position. He too could stare at a camera with a wild look just like his cousin.

* * *

A few days later, Pearly made his first public appearance in a street-market near his home. Wearing suitable war-paint, a garland of marigolds and a white *dhoti*, he was carried through the summer heat on an improvised, flower-strewn litter. Two young Indian friends in front, two others behind, he swayed languorously past the stalls selling shiny vegetables, past the stalls selling improbably-pink, diaphanous underwear, past the stalls of kitchen appliances at unbeatable prices, the stalls of blaring hi-fi systems offering uncountable watts, the stalls offering second-hand army clothes.

The procession was accompanied by his sister and two of her female friends. The girls had garlands of flowers in their hair and empty bean-tins in their hands which they offered to all passers-by who were foolish enough to come into range. They were collecting money, they said, for the promotion of the words and works of His Beautiful Holiness the Supreme Spiritual Guide, Lal-ji.

'Peace,' they said as the coins dropped noisily into the collection tins. 'Hari-Krish,' they sang, as they chanted what they hoped startled passers-by would believe to be Hindu prayers, exactly as Pearly had instructed.

Sufficient startled passers-by were sufficiently deceived to make the outing a financial success. It was repeated the next day and the day after. Soon, His Beautiful Holiness' coffers began to swell.

As Pearly's business prospered and his clientele increased, so did his contempt for those who sought his advice and spiritual balm.

He began to dream of building his own empire. He saw a country house dedicated to the pursuit of spiritual enlightenment. And his own pleasures. He saw great rooms hung with gaudy silk paintings of Indian gods with three heads and twenty-three arms. He saw huge beds covered with bright silk cloths and strewn with colourful cushions. He saw crowds of admiring occidentals sitting cross-legged before him hanging on his every word. Above all, he saw his wealth increasing so much that he would be able to afford a private jet, a yacht, a flat in New York and another in Paris.

His vision of his future slowly began to harden into reality. After a few months he had accumulated enough capital from his sorties in the street markets to move out of the family villa and buy a three-bedroomed leasehold flat in West Hampstead with constant hot water, and central heating.

He had the flat decorated and furnished in a suitable style. Thick carpets, large cushions, small paintings of Indian saints, a shrine over the fireplace in the sitting room which he called his temple.

When he was satisfied that all was as it should be he opened his doors for spiritual business. Every day a growing number of troubled occidentals came to sit at his feet. And every day he saw how the funds in his deposit account at the National Westminster Bank in Golders Green were increasing, both by direct input and by the interest his money was earning for him.

Pearly was not simply a charlatan. He did have an unmistakable air of holiness. This does not mean that he was a holy man. Some men can seem holy simply because they manage to convince enough others that they are holy. Worship by disciples has an inevitable effect on the worshipped as well as its own rewards for the worshippers. Nonetheless, his Beautiful Holiness did provide some spiritual balm to some.

Day after day, Pearly sat in his large room in West Hampstead, looking east in the general direction of the Himalayas whence, so he said, his inspiration came. He sat cross-legged on an enormous cushion, like a gaudy, overfed parrot, imparting his vision of the world to his hungry listeners while his helpers served holy tea and lit holy incense.

'Peace and light.' He would begin. 'I am the peace that will bring the light that will illumine the darkness in your souls.'

His listeners sat uncomfortably, their legs crossed in the approved position.

'Your souls are like two lovers on a bench in the park. They have nowhere for their secret pleasures. They yearn. They experience longing. Let them come to me. I am their place.'

His listeners leaned forward to drink the milk of his wisdom.

'Yoga is the union of the darkness and the light. In Yoga the thunder falls silent. The long night becomes light. Yoga is union. I am Yoga. Meditate on me.'

His listeners sat back.

'Hear the words of His Beautiful Holiness,' his helpers chanted. 'Oh listen to his words,' they sung as they struck their holy bells.

And they did listen. The troubled seekers. Those Pearly called his disciples. Sitting in a circle around him. Those who could no longer derive any benefit from their traditional religion and came hoping that he might cure their souls. The cranks who were too afraid to make relationships. The lonely ones who came to make friends. The young men who had been rejected by their families, by their friends, who had too much sensitivity to take life on and who longed to join a family of like-minded like-sensitive sufferers. The young girls who had been disappointed.

'Oh, listen to his loving words,' the sisters chanted.

And they listened. But most of them didn't hear. Except what they wanted to hear.

* * *

His Beautiful Holiness' career advanced without incident until the police began to show an entirely temporal interest in his activities. His helpers had sometimes acted a little too enthusiastically in their attempts to extract cash from passing members of the unenlightened public. There had been complaints. If he continued to solicit for funds, the police informed him, they would have to act.

Pearly, like all great capitalists, rather than allow this intervention to set him back, turned it to his advantage. He claimed so loudly and so frequently that he was being victimised by racist police officers that a journalist heard his complaint and investigated it. A police officer was foolish enough, in a public house of his choice, to drink so much gin that he quite lost his grip on his discretion and described His Beautiful Holiness as a black-faced faker, under circumstances that he thought had been agreed to be off the record. The journalist, inspired by this remark, placed it and other injudicious remarks of his own imagining on the record.

The story of a holy young Indian who was being victimised by the police burst onto the nation's front pages one newsless Saturday morning and Pearly was famous.

Hautbois' handsome mère visited Pearly's *ashram* shortly after these events out of curiosity. She had an idea for a novel. She wanted to meet an Indian teacher.

She expected to discover a fraud as she walked up the stairs. She did. But Pearly's enormous, almond-shaped eyes, looking softly as they did upon all those who came before him, had a devastating effect on her. As she sat cross-legged in the approved position and strained to hear Pearly's softly spoken words, as she looked at his beautiful eyes, she found herself abandoning all her critical faculties.

Within minutes, a happy smile on her face, a dazed look in her eyes, she realised that she had no option but to follow, as best she could, the gravamen of Pearly's teachings, without comment.

Soon, Pearly was invited to stay at the Mill for a weekend.

* * *

The sound of water-hens on the mill-pool. A breeze, trying to make up its mind if it wanted to blow, was playing hide-and-seek with the leaves in the high places of the great plane tree that stood beside. Sunlight dappled all over the lawn.

Hautbois père sat at the white-painted garden table, apart, reading his newspaper, sipping noisily at an enormous Pimms. He was wearing his garden clothes with the unusual addition of a bright, paisley-patterned handkerchief around his neck. Putting out more flags, like a defeated general on the eve of surrender, in order to get better terms. Hautbois mère was sitting at the other end of the lawn ignoring her general, paying, instead, rapt attention to Pearly. Pearly sat on the hammock in a glistening white *dhoti*. His smile also was white. So were the whites of his eyes.

'I see a breakdown,' Hautbois mère was haranguing her Messiah in earnest tones, 'a breakdown in morality all around me. People have no respect for each other. For their work. For themselves. That's why they're all so miserable in the midst of such material success.'

She paused for breath. Pearly smiled, showing his dazzling teeth.

'Never before,' Hautbois mère went on after she had recovered from the teeth, 'has the human race achieved so much. Look at the great increases in sustainable population. Many countries are supporting undreamed-of populations. Yet the affluent countries are so miserable. As though they had reached their promised land and didn't like it. Look at the artists. If they could get away with it they'd hang their pictures face to the wall. Jazz musicians often play with their backs to the audience. The theatre is full of gloomy introspection.'

Hautbois mère drew breath. This was Pearly's first invitation to a country house. His first visit to what he thought were the zones of the gentility. He felt that he must make his mark early in the proceedings.

'Modern people,' Pearly seized his opportunity, 'do not like themselves. There is a war in their hearts, between themselves and their desires. They fight strongly. They are stubborn as oxen. But their desires pull them down by the legs. They should indulge themselves more.'

'But how can you separate desire and one who desires?'

This was no challenge for Pearly.

'You must learn to watch your desires as they arise. To watch them, to surrender to them, like a lady. Only in this way, can you escape attachment to them.'

In the silence that ensued Pearly smiled again, dazzling Hautbois mère's critical faculties as surely as the sun made her screw up her eyes.

'You're speaking of moral standards?'

'Lady Hautbois ... ' Hautbois mère laughed at this sudden elevation. 'Lady Hautbois, I am speaking of moral and immoral standards. All that is needed is to learn how to listen to the heart's voice. That is the seat of personal morality. People must learn how to abide by their own personal morality. Even if it tells them to rape and to kill.'

Pearly looked pleased with himself at the conclusion of this. Hautbois mère was puzzled.

'Yes, I think I know what you mean,' she said doubtfully, 'we need a new morality.'

'To listen to the heart,' Pearly broke in, 'that is the new morality.'

'Yes.' Hautbois mère's eyes were shining. 'I am an optimist. I believe in the essential goodness of people. Yes, let listening to the heart be the new morality. It will work. I'm sure that it will.'

Hautbois père was not listening to the heart but to the drivel, as he saw it, that his wife and the black fakir were exchanging. He turned the pages of his newspaper as noisily as he could, short of tearing them.

Pearly's sister, at that moment, approached him.

'Hallo, old man, why are you looking so goddamned glum?'

'Go away.'

She shrugged and wandered away, presently sat beneath the plane tree that stood loftily over this scene.

For its part the tree ignored the self-concern of those beneath it and just went on offering them its leafy shade, untroubled whether the offer was accepted or not.

Dov's introduction to burglary, was heralded, one dusty, summer evening, by a statement of the principles, such as they were, of Pearly's religious teaching.

The troubled seekers had been dismissed. Dov and Pearly were walking through Kensington towards Hyde Park.

'Desires arise because the man is fearful that they will. He asks himself, how shall I resist the temptation? And immediately the temptation appears in all its finery, like a beguiling prostitute. At first he hides his inner eye. At first he pretends that he has no desire for the thing that is tempting him. If, instead, he accepted that he had a desire and watched it float into and out of his consciousness he would not be tempted.

'But he resists. He struggles with himself and weakens his resistance. Usually the temptation wins. The only way to overcome your desires is to approach them. You cannot run away from them. Go towards them. Embrace them.'

Joggers jogged by. Loafers loafed.

'But tell me, Dov, is it not a great thing to relieve suffering? I am a modest Hindu practitioner offering simple balm to the troubled sons and daughters of the Occident. I tell you frankly, I have had no training. Only what I got for myself. It just comes naturally to me. Like music to a musician, words to a prophet.

'Between you and me, I don't believe that holy men are any different from men in other professions. We have a job to do. We do it. Just like a plumber or an electrician. Only we make more money. It isn't even necessary to believe in the soul. Any more than an electrician has to believe that an electric current is an exchange of electrons. A holy man can be a militant materialist.'

A skein of honking geese passed overhead, commuting from St James's Park to the Serpentine.

'Frankly, Dov, I do not believe in the soul. Why should I? I have never seen a soul. These people who come to me, these sufferers, they are all neurotics. It's not their souls that are sick but their heads.'

We approached the Cockpit. There were no cocks. Instead, a small squad of elegant, black roller-skaters drifted disconcertingly by.

'The great advantage of the religion business, Dov, there are no taxes and no trouble. The police daren't arrest a holy man, I can tell you.

'I had a spot of bother with the police. I squealed to a journalist. I told him the police were persecuting me. I told him that the police were racist. That they had made racist remarks. They put me in the papers. I was all over the papers. Now I can't be touched.

'Do you realise, Dov, the police won't touch me. Whatever I do. They daren't. I'm too famous.'

* * *

It was my first visit to London since childhood. I looked at the people. Everywhere they were busying themselves in the mindless round of life in a crowd. Getting food, getting sex, getting married, getting a family, getting old.

No doubt those who saw Dov assumed that he was just like them. That he had stepped onto the same steady social conveyor, that he too had joined the crowd.

He would have to show them that he was utterly unlike them.

Pearly and Dov stood in a tree-lined street of white stucco-fronted houses gazing at a tidy-looking, Georgian house in the centre of the terrace. A for-sale board was attached to the wrought-iron rails of the first floor balcony.

The board announced in large red letters that the property to which it was attached was for sale. It provided the name of the estate agent and the telephone number. If that had been all it would not have pressed itself so forcefully on my attention. But the estate agent who announced his name with such self-satisfaction in those large, aggressive, red letters was Archie Moore, the headboy who had beaten me so unreasonably and with such evident relish for dallying with the gardener's daughter.

I stared at the board. Archie Moore's name stared back. I began to feel unaccountably agitated. My heart, usually so well-regulated, began to pound uncontrollably. My belly, a complete stranger to butterflies, was suddenly full of them. The little hairs at the back of my neck, usually so well-behaved, started to itch.

Pearly noticed my excitement.

'Do you know the estate agent?'

'I knew him at school.'
'Do you dislike him?'
'Yes.'
'Very much?'
'Yes.'
'Has he wronged you?'
'Yes'.
'And you would like to have your revenge?'

I was silent. Until that moment I had forgotten Archie Moore. I had forgotten the gardener's randy daughter, my subsequent humiliation at Archie Moore's hands. I would rather have remained forgetful.

'Since you are my friend, I will avenge you. Wait here and keep your eyes open. If anyone approaches, whistle.'

Pearly hopped up the steps to the front door of the house with the for-sale board, fidgeted with the lock. Soon he was inside.

Dov waited.

After a few moments Pearly appeared on the first-floor balcony. He swiftly detached the for-sale board, disappeared inside again. He emerged in a few moments, the board under his arm.

'There, see, I have the board. Do you want it?'

I shook my head. Pearly tossed the board into the basement area.

'Come.'

He grabbed my arm and we ran off.

I felt elated as we sailed through the streets. My heart was beating rapidly but steadily. The butterflies had flown away from my belly. The little hairs at the back of my neck had calmed themselves. I had participated in a small but satisfying act of revenge. Further acts would follow I had no doubt.

As we slowed to an excited walk I began to enjoy another sensation. I felt pleased with myself for I had discovered how to demonstrate to the complacent citizens that I was not of them, that I was not and never would be a member of a crowd. I had discovered how to show the people of this city that when I opened my eyes and looked down at the world it was all mine. Dov had come to London.

We reached the park.

'Bravo, Dov. Bravo. We did it. We got away with it. Stupid bastards putting a lock like that on their front-door.'

Pearly bounced along.

'They thought they could keep me out with their flimsy thing. Now we can go into business together. Soon we will make a fortune. You with your eyes and ears and me with my fingers and my brain.'

He was dancing round me.

'Tonight we will go to a very expensive restaurant together and celebrate our success with a large dinner. But first we will take a leisurely drive.'

We had crossed the park and were wandering down Queensgate. Pearly stepped into the street, hailed a passing taxi.

'Take us to Hampstead. Slowly.'

We sat back in the taxi and stretched our legs. A notice thanked us for not smoking. The smell of a mild disinfectant.

Presently, Pearly looked slyly at me, putting his finger to his nose in a gesture of conspiracy, rummaged in his pockets and produced a wallet and a passport. He looked through the wallet. It contained a few hundred pounds in cash, credit cards, a shotgun certificate, a couple of personal letters.

'You see, my friend, the operation was profitable for us.'

The taxi wound on through London's evening streets.

EVENING AFTER EVENING that summer, when Pearly had sent the last of the troubled seekers away, we set out in search of houses with Archie Moore for-sale boards. We found small terraced houses with white stucco fronts to make them more imposing, red-brick houses with slate roofs, larger semi-detached houses with stone steps rising over basement areas, the occasional detached mansion.

Evening after evening, Pearly forced his way in, cut the for-sale board down and, whilst making his retreat, filled his pockets or any other convenient receptacle, with small items of value.

Then one September evening, leafy decay in the nostrils, the fatman made an unsolicited moral justification for the burglaries as we were strolling along a street in Holland Park.

'You should understand, Dov, that a teacher is also permitted to be a practical man. It is old-fashioned to think that a teacher must always be a man of instruction and contemplation. Just because I am a *guru*, there is no reason why I should be excluded from direct action.'

His thefts had never concerned me. All his offers to share his booty with me had been rejected.

'These householders are better off without their small change. I am a man who relieves other men of their spiritual burdens and, sometimes, of a tithe of their material baggage. Not enough to ruin them. That would be greedy. I am not a greedy man. I can watch my greed approaching and also watch it passing by.'

He smiled slyly.

I was disturbed. Pearly had never before made any attempt to justify the burglaries. I had always assumed that he had felt no need. As I had not. It occurred to me that Pearly's conscience might have begun to trouble him.

We had been walking through Bayswater for half an hour without finding a house with an Archie Moore for-sale board.

'I like the look of that house there. Why don't we try it?'

It had another estate agent's board on it.

'You're such a puritan, Dov. Very well. By your rules.'

We were just about to turn into Inverness Terrace and return to the park when, in a small, tree-lined street of white stucco-fronted houses we found what we had been looking for.

Dead leaves lay like dust in the gutters. The earth was tired of burgeoning. Dov too, that evening, felt a touch of the same weariness.

With a couple of bounces Pearly was up the steps. In a moment he had forced the lock and was inside.

Dov stood outside, staring at the for-sale board, seeing nothing.

Even when I heard the soft purr of the police car I couldn't wrench myself back to myself but stood staring vacantly at the board until I felt a rough hand seize my arm and another equally rough hand seize my shoulder.

* * *

The moment the police discovered that neither of us had any intention of giving them any trouble they relaxed and became surprisingly friendly.

'It won't go too hard with you if it's a first offence.'

'Probably get off with probation, wouldn't you say, John?'

'Very likely, if we give a good report.'

'Which we will. Provided you play the game.'

'It's the best way.'

'It's the only way, wouldn't you say, John?'

Dov began to feel a quite unexpected sensation. He realised to his surprise that there were certain comforts in arrest. All struggle was, temporarily, at an end. There were no more risks to be taken. All was now prescribed according to custom. He would be taken to the police station. He would be charged. He would spend a night in the cells. He would try to get bail. Probably succeed. Eventually, he would appear in court.

The constables were still chattering.

'The only way. Play the game. That's my advice, friend.'

Dov looked up at the for-sale board still hanging on the front of the house. It seemed to be shining with new pride. Dov looked back at the constables. They were pleased with themselves.

Naturally. For them, the arrest, was a great success. Their voices reflected their pleasure and their technique. The tone was deliberately beguiling. They were offering us the comforts of a crowd. They were telling us that if only we would join them in their vision of the world all would be well for us.

Dov looked back at the for-sale board and knew that they were lying. He knew that all would not be well for him, that the comforts that they were offering would not be comfortable at all.

Their chatter began to feel like an assault. Their honeyed words were intended, consciously or unconsciously, to exact revenge for what they saw as an attack on their values. Dov realised that the offer of friendship implicit in their tone was a deception.

A small crowd had collected. It was growing larger. Dov was beginning to feel breathless beneath the stare of the crowd and the continual chatter of the constables.

Where was the police van? Why wouldn't it come? Were these constables stringing him along to soften him up for the interrogation that he knew was inevitable? It occurred to him that they were purposely keeping him waiting on this exposed street precisely so that he would suffer from the accusing stare of the growing crowd.

I looked at the crowd. Citizens were staring at me with smug satisfaction. The police were smiling and strutting, basking in the evident approval of the onlookers.

I realised that I had suffered enough of this humiliation. It was time to strike out. The constable's hand was resting loosely on my arm. It was the work of a second to detach it. In two paces I was on the crowd. I surged forward breasting through men and women as a swimmer takes to the rough waves. Arms and legs began to fly. Theirs and mine. Faces passed by me in grim surprise. Time started to extend itself. Faces passed as though in slow motion. There was no sound.

I pressed on, pushing hateful strangers' bodies away from me. Jackets were flying open, people were stumbling against each other, one man fell heavily against a lamp-post.

Eventually, I saw a glimpse of the empty street beyond the crowd. I saw freedom approaching like sunlight appearing behind a slowly-drifting cloud. The struggle was coming to an end. In a moment I would be able to breathe again.

A vicious, clean-shaven, young man in a tidy suit floated into my vision. He was different from the others. They were retreating. He was advancing. Their faces were frozen in fear. His face was grimly determined. They were responding to my advance as I expected them to. The man was not. He had a vicious snarl on his lip.

As I tried desperately to lift myself up into the air the man's foot came out like a semaphore arm. I tripped and fell headlong into the road.

PEARLY AND DOV made an incongruous pair standing beside each other in the dock. I wore khaki military trousers and a similar shirt, sensible brown lace-up shoes, a crimson silk scarf around my neck. Pearly wore a gleaming white *dhoti* and a garland of flowers. His feet were bare.

The other actors in this farce wore the conventional clothes that belonged to their conventional roles. The stipendiary magistrate, a tall cadaverous man with spectacles, wore a dark suit. He sat beneath large gilded scales attached to the wall. The clerk of the court, a young, self-satisfied man, wore a similar suit. The prosecuting solicitor wore his fiercest aspect.

There was no defending solicitor. Neither Pearly nor I wanted one. Pearly, because he could not find an Indian who would take his case. I, because I had no intention of joining in this farce.

The charges were read, 'That you did take and carry away with intent to unlawfully deprive the owner thereof . . . that you did . . . that you did not . . . that you did.'

The clerk of the court asked Pearly how he would plead. He said that he was not guilty. Then he asked me the same question. He stared at me, no doubt hoping that I would be intimidated, but I could see the fear in his eyes.

'In the eyes of the court I am no doubt guilty but in my eyes I am innocent.'

This did not satisfy the clerk or the magistrate.

The magistrate explained in a kindly voice which I didn't trust at all, 'You must plead one way or the other. Guilty or not guilty?'

Both absolute, both exclusive of the truth.

I replied in a co-operative voice which the magistrate no doubt didn't trust either that I was unafraid of the truth and unafraid to state it clearly even if it takes more than guilty-or-not-guilty to express.

The magistrate tried again. I maintained my position. Eventually the clerk advised that a plea of not guilty had to be entered, presumably so that justice could be seen to be done.

At the conclusion of these exchanges Pearly's friends and relatives decided that the first blood had gone to Dov. They began to clap and cheer from the public gallery. The magistrate made a show of judicial anger. Stern warnings were issued. Silence was eventually restored.

An illiterate policeman entered the witness box and swore by almighty God that the evidence I shall give shall be the truth, the whole truth and nothing but the truth.

He consulted his notebook and told the court that 'at sixteen thirty hours I saw the accused ... *how did you know it was exactly sixteen thirty?* ... I had consulted my watch ... *very well* ... at sixteen thirty hours I saw the accused standing in Gideon Terrace acting in a suspicious manner ... *how did you deduce that the accused's manner was suspicious?* ... the accused was staring at a for-sale board with a weird expression on his face ... *weird?* ... as though he intended to take it down ... *why should that be weird? He might have been employed by the estate agent to do just that* ... he looked too weird. I've seen people, Sir, who take boards down and for that matter people who put boards up and the accused didn't look like them at all ... nor did the accused have a van to put the for-sale board in ... at least if he did I couldn't see it anywhere in the street ... *very well* ... in any case, as our patrol car drew up alongside the house the Indian gentleman came out of the house at a run and my suspicions were further aroused ... we had been on the look-out for a team who had been removing the for-sale boards of a certain estate agent in Notting Hill and at the same time committing various acts of petty-larceny ... I've been twelve years in the force and my instincts never let me down ... *instinct is not evidence* ... after his arrest one of the accused attempted to escape from custody ... *that, surely, is evidence of guilt ... why? perhaps he was afraid of arrest. I hope there is more to this case than we have so far been presented* ... yes Sir, there is ... we entered the house immediately after apprehending the accused ... *which one?* ... both of them ... we entered the house and discovered signs of forcible entry ... a locked door to the first-floor sitting-room had been forced ... the balcony window was open even though the owners, at a subsequent interview, confirmed that they had left the house locked and the internal door and the balcony window locked as well.'

The magistrate asked questions, noted down the evidence. Eventually the officer finished speaking. We were asked if we wanted to cross-examine him. We both resisted the temptation.

Another illiterate policeman came to the stand, took the oath and corroborated the first officer's evidence so exactly it was clear that they must have prepared their evidence in concert. The magistrate asked the second officer several questions and wrote his evidence down. Again we were asked if we wanted to cross-examine the witness. Again we refused.

Presently, the prosecuting solicitor told his version of the story all over again. Finally he told the court that the Crown's case had been presented and called for severe penalties.

The autumn sun shone into the dusty court-house and reminded me that there was more to the world than this pantomime. Whatever decision the magistrate took it would make no difference to me. Even if he sent me to prison.

Yes, Citizen. I discovered that morning that prison held no fear for me. I realised, as I stood in the dock, that the greatest sanction that the court could invoke, a prison sentence, was no kind of sanction for me. I realised that I was so utterly outside the world that these people inhabited whatever they did would not affect me at all.

The magistrate asked the clerk if either of the accused had a record of previous offences. The clerk replied that we did not. He reflected for a moment, then turned to Pearly and asked him, 'Is there anything you want to say to me?'

Pearly cleared his throat, opened his mouth, tried to speak. No sound emerged. He cleared his throat again, tried to speak but again he was silent. The magistrate asked him, 'Do you want a glass of water?' He shook his head. Silence fell in the court.

Suddenly a stream of words began to tumble out of Pearly's mouth. Strange words, words that clearly had meaning but were nonetheless incomprehensible. Words with lovely sounds. Passionate words. Beautiful words. Angry words. Fiery words. The magistrate looked mystified. So did the clerk.

Their mystification changed to anger as Pearly's supporters in the gallery began to laugh and shout and cheer. Pearly would shout a phrase. His supporters would shout a rhythmic refrain, like a chorus. Eventually, the magistrate realised that Pearly was speaking in Hindi or Urdu or some other oriental language. He held up his hand for silence. Pearly ignored him. So did his supporters.

Presently, the magistrate pulled himself together and, shouted, 'If you don't shut up I will have you taken to the cells.' Pearly stopped speaking. His supporters slowly fell silent.

When he had recovered his composure the magistrate asked Pearly, 'Do you want an interpreter?' Pearly said, 'I wouldn't trust any interpreter provided by the court.' The magistrate asked him if he was mocking the court. Pearly said, 'Certainly not.' The magistrate asked Pearly, 'Will you make your statement in English, the official language of the court?' Pearly said, 'Britain is supposed to be a multi-racial society so why can't I use my own language? This, your honour, is another example of the naked racism that brought me here in the first place. One law for whites, one for blacks.'

The magistrate was not impressed with this line of argument and told Pearly, 'There's no point in continuing with this charade, I've made up my mind on the evidence.'

Silence fell. The magistrate made further notes. Then he looked at Pearly and explained that he had decided 'You are guilty as charged. The evidence is overwhelming and clearly corroborated. Since it is a first offence, despite your obvious mockery of the court, despite your entirely unjustified accusations of racism cynically levelled against good, honourable police officers I am going to be lenient.'

He paused to gain maximum effect and then told Pearly, 'Burglary is a serious offence, I can't ignore the increase in the crime rate, as you are a teacher, of a kind, you should set an example. Taking everything into account I am going to send you to prison for eighteen months.'

This was greeted with a roar of disapproval from the gallery which took several minutes to die down.

Pearly waved bravely as he was taken down to the cells.

The magistrate made further notes. Presently, he turned to me and asked me if I wanted to say anything on my behalf, preferably in English, before he delivered his verdict. The court officials laughed politely. Pearly's supporters, who had transferred their allegiance to me, booed.

Dov stood in the court as the sun floated through the dusty windows and opened his eyes. He started to lift himself up out of himself. Higher and higher he flew until he was high above the court, higher until the magistrate, the clerk, the policemen, until all of them were tiny, insignificant dots arranged on wooden benches, beneath contempt.

Of course I wouldn't say anything. There was no point. Any words I offered wouldn't change any of these people's views at all. They simply wouldn't penetrate into their closed world. What I could see that they couldn't see, what I knew that they couldn't know, what I could do that they couldn't do separated me so absolutely from them, there was no point in trying to explain my vision, my knowledge, my capabilities. The words would be as meaningless to them as Pearly's had been.

Dov reflected on Pearly's lovely defiance. He was braver than I had expected. He had much more to lose than I. He was a capitalist engaged in a successful business. I had no business. Pearly wanted money. I wanted not to have money. Pearly wanted property. I wanted to be free.

Presently I heard the magistrate's voice, as though from far away, floating up to me.

'Guilty as charged . . . didn't actually steal but nonetheless aided and abetted another to steal . . . assisting the commission of a crime can be as serious as committing the offence itself depending on the nature of the aid being rendered . . . a series of offences as witness the removal of the for-sale boards . . . could it have been some kind of business vendetta? . . . the court has been unable to form a view since no evidence has been presented that the accused had any involvement in business . . . clear that the accused derived no material gain from these strange crimes . . . no previous offences . . . lenient on this occasion but not if the accused ever found himself in court again . . . a suspended sentence appropriate . . . one year, suspended for two years.'

THREE

T HE HOSPITAL AUTHORITIES, in vain hope, think that I am more likely to become a well-integrated personality capable, eventually, of living in society without damage to others or to myself if I am not denied all contact with the outside world. Accordingly, I am allowed certain visitors. Candida is the most regular.

Ah, Candida. I see her as she was in those first darling days, in the cornfields, her hair the colour of sunlight.

During my first weeks here, even though we hadn't seen each other for nearly two years, Candida came once a day. Every day. And if she couldn't get permission to visit me, she would wait outside until dusk, hovering around the gates like a migrating bird out of season. After a month or so, she settled down to coming once a week. Every Friday morning, at ten o'clock, precisely.

She brings me tobacco, matches, sometimes chocolates.

For her, I am a convenient object of charity, available for the foreseeable future as worthy of pity and affection. For me, she is a trial to be endured.

Her routine is the same every time she comes. She approaches Alexander, takes him by the arm, without a word sets off along the corridor. He accompanies her without protest although, strictly, he is in breach of his contract, particularly of the clauses relating to keeping a secure watch over those assigned to his care.

When Candida comes he allows these clauses to slip his mind. Why? Why does he take such risks with his career? Because, Citizen, he is flattered by Candida's way with him, her solicitous enquiries about his condition, her taking his arm, she so obviously being a member of a superior class.

As they walk up and down the corridor, they begin a hurried series of exchanges, *sotto voce*, both casting anxious glances at me through the glass pane in the door.

I see two heads through a square of glass. Appearing from the right.

Glancing. Disappearing to the left. Appearing from the left. Glancing. Disappearing to the right. Appearing from the right again. Two framed heads in my door. Coming and going.

Candida's expression is earnest, searching, a little haughty. Though I managed to knock much of the hereditary haughtiness out of her when I lived with her. Alexander's expression is servile.

She and Alexander think that their conversation is private because my door is sound-proof. Although I do not hear their words I know exactly what they are saying. Their lips make familiar shapes. Their expressions pass through familiar stages. The short fragments I gather as they pass and repass are no trouble to piece together. The entire story quickly emerges.

Candida asks Alexander if my health continues robust, if my habits have varied, if my diet continues to be nourishing, if my bowel movements are regular, if my mental state is improving. He replies in the affirmative to all except the last. As I have instructed him.

These exchanges are ritual. So is my refusal to notice her until I am ready.

Let the pantomime begin.

As Candida and Alexander walk up and down along the corridor, as they pass and repass my door, after the seventh or eighth pass, I modestly raise my eyes and permit myself to notice them. After another couple of passes I permit myself a smile. They both stop immediately and by this act give themselves away. By this simple act of stopping they show plainly that they have been waiting for me to signal to them that I am ready for Candida to come in.

I smile. Candida smiles her brightest smile in return. I wave. She waves an elegantly-gloved hand. I gesture for her to come in. Alexander unlocks the door, opens it with a flourish. Candida steps smartly into the room, walks straight to the chair beside my bed, sits. Alexander retires, closes and locks the door. Candida and I are alone together.

Silence.

Candida crosses her legs so that her stockings whisper and her skirt rides up over her knees hoping by this pathetic gesture to attract my attention to her undoubted sexual potential. I pretend not to have noticed. After a moment she pulls her skirt back down over her knees with a look of immense chastity. Then she fires a reproachful glance up towards the ceiling. Always the ceiling. Always it takes no notice. Of course. Why should it disturb itself with such petty posturing?

Presently, she turns, looks at me with that dreadful pity in her eyes that signals her intention to regale me, without pity, with tales of our son, hoping in some obscure way that this will succeed in luring me back to physical and mental conjunction with her.

She speaks of our son, his daily routine, departures from his routine. She assaults me with startling details of the childish illnesses he seems to be foolish enough to contract. The pox, the whoop, the colic, the mump, wherever there is an illness, the brute seems to contract it and she describes it.

After a few tedious minutes, after I have been taken through the symptoms, the treatment and so finally, brought to the cure, she pauses and looks at me with unbearable affection.

'You must be getting tired. I can see you are.'

You would expect, Citizen, that when Candida visits me, every Friday, weather clement or inclement, we take advantage of the time that we are allowed together to exchange news and views. You would expect that she speaks and I answer. That I speak and she answers.

In fact, she speaks but I do not say a word. The conversation is entirely one-sided. If you joined Alexander at the Judas-hole you would see a woman chattering away to a man who never opens his mouth, a man who appears, from his idiotic expression, to be too simple-minded to understand what the woman is saying.

I decided, when I left her, that I would not speak to Candida ever again. I sent myself to Coventry as far as she was concerned. By then, I had nothing to say to her, in any case. It had all been said. Often. Too often.

But don't permit yourself, Citizen, to imagine that my silence is sullen, aggressive, even unfriendly. I am beyond all that, certainly as far as Candida is concerned. And do not allow yourself to believe that Candida's tolerance of my silence, Friday after Friday, is patient or charitable. Things are not that simple. Even though I am always silent during Candida's visits we do have a conversation.

Candida speaks and imagines my replies. By this simple expedient, hearing words that belong to both sides of a conversation, she allows herself to imagine that we converse, that she speaks and I answer, that I say a few words and she replies.

Candida has her own way of looking at reality. Whenever things appear unwilling to conform with her perception of how they should be, she simply ignores events as they are and assumes that they are as she would like them to be.

'I can see you're tired.'

I remain silent. I am not tired, of course. Except of her futile assault on my solitude.

'Oh, come on. I know you so well.'

I once hit her for saying that. Years ago. To my surprise, I regretted it immediately. I see the echo of her pained recoil pass lightly across her face as she too remembers.

'I'll have to go soon.'

I can't wait.

'I've got to take little David to Harrods for a new sports jacket.'

I refuse to allow myself to think of my son.

'He looks so grown-up. Quite like his father.'

She offers me a ghastly, sad, smile and hopes that I will be affected. I am not. Presently, she stops speaking and looks away like a disappointed salesman.

Sweet silence. She insults it with more pathetic gestures designed to display her sexual advantages in the most brazen possible way, gestures that have no effect whatsoever on me.

When, at last, she realises that I am not taking any notice of her gestures, she puts the question, always the same question.

'Why don't you come and stay with us for a few days, for Christmas, for Easter, for Whitsun, for the summer holidays?' Depending on the season and her whim. 'It would be so good for little David. I'm sure the authorities would agree. I know they would. I've spoken to the Senior Medical Officer.'

I look up at the ceiling. We exchange sympathetic glances.

I refuse her invitation without word or gesture. Simply, I refuse.

Realising this, she begins her final speech. She chatters like a parrot. She issues other invitations. She makes provoking statements. She employs every means at her disposal to engage my attention and force me to speak until the dull thunder of her words makes my balls ache so much that I am forced to throw a tantrum in order to get rid of her.

I start to gasp. I shake my left leg. I roll my eyes like a white minstrel blacked-up. I begin to look as though I'm going to thrash about. Occasionally, I allow a little saliva to accumulate at the side of my mouth. If Alexander still doesn't come I begin to thrash about. Sometimes I even have to knock the bedside table over.

Then Alexander comes in, looking stern. I stop my exhibition immediately, make apologetic gestures to Alexander, smile my sweetest smile, demonstrate that my habitual calm is restored.

Candida stands, sighs, bids me farewell. Then she departs with Alexander at her side, wearing a well-rehearsed, wistful look designed not only to offer the balm of compassion to me but to draw Alexander's attention to her exceptionally charitable disposition.

I am forced to throw the tantrum. How else can I end her visit? Every time, I am forced. It's the only way to satisfy her.

Although it might appear to you, Citizen, that I am the loser in this final exchange, in fact, I win. I get my way. I get my solitude once more. Candida is the loser. She does not get her way. She does not get me.

Even though I am the winner, I'm always very careful not to show by the slightest sign that I know that I've won. I let her think that she's making all the rules, that her visit has penetrated my inner self and somehow disturbed me. I let her think that she is getting her puny revenge.

Yes, Citizen, it's revenge she wants. She has never been able to forgive me for abandoning her and the boy.

CANDIDA is a member of the landed class.

The landed class. Dominant species in the English countryside, born, generation after generation, to do their duty and rule.

At the top of the class sit the great landowners. Complaisant Dukes, bustling Barons, snappish Baronets, these great men all have great houses. Often too big to be lived in comfortably, nonetheless, they live in them.

The houses all have important gardens with wide lawns, well stocked herbaceous borders, lavender and rose walks. The gardens are opened to the public at least twice a year for charity, if not every weekend for the enrichment of the estate. Beside the houses are stables. Around the houses are tree-filled parks. At the end of the sweeping drives that wind through the parks are cottages for the estate workers. Surrounding the houses and gardens and parks are large farming estates.

These great families are the yardstick against which all other members and aspiring members of the landed class measure their own status.

At the next level down are the landed bourgeoisie. They have houses. They have gardens. They have stables. They frequently have parks. Usually they do not have estates to support them and so they derive their incomes from other pursuits. Above all, they do not have titles.

There are other subdivisions. To be a member of the landed class it is not any longer necessary to have a large landholding. In many cases members do not own any land at all. Some do not even live in the countryside. Nor is it necessary to be rich. Many who consider themselves members of the landed class have no land and no money. These ones live in lodgings in small villages or on the edge of great estates or as paying guests in other people's houses in London.

These un-landed members of the landed class are a necessary adjunct to the landed, for they are always available to join in their pleasures at the shortest notice, to make up a four at tennis, to stand in for an absent gun, to exercise a spare horse. They dress exactly as the great landowners do. Perhaps with a little more care. They speak with the same clipped accents. Perhaps a little too exaggeratedly. They have the same attitudes of mind. Perhaps more firmly held.

* * *

The landed class. How well its members play. How lovely their girls, wandering on long summer evenings across the newly-mown lawns. How skilfully they present their best features and disguise their less attractive parts as they saunter through the perfumes of an English summer evening.

How well Camilla looks in that white outfit. She wears no brassière. Her nipples stand up smartly beneath her cotton blouse. The high collar covers the red flush beneath her throat. How well Louise looks in that long skirt. It sets off her slender waist and hides her rather thicker ankles. How graciously Emma smiles at Henry's third telling of a not-very-funny story. And how charmingly, on this drowsy summer evening, Penelope pays attention to every one of young Dov's words. She appears to be interested in his stutters and mutterings. Could it be that she finds him attractive? Such things have been. But he thought that she was going to marry James.

Penelope casts a glance towards the house. Red bricks glow peacefully in the evening light. Doric columns stand guard over centuries of history. James is coming down the terrace steps with Anthony. Penelope shoots a glance across at him. He sees the glint of determination in her eye.

Her eyes are bright china blue. Very direct.

She pretends to be paying attention to Dov but, of course, she is not interested in him. She wants James to see that she is paying attention to Dov, that's all. I can see it all behind her eyes.

She pays more attention to me. More closely. James looks away with studied indifference and by this one act, by this pathetic gesture, shows that, far from being indifferent to Penelope's behaviour, he is conquered.

The only indifference, that evening, is in the glowing roses, blooming without effort, in the dark green of the yew hedge, in the majesty of the evening sky.

* * *

On other landed lawns, other games, other young girls, other young men.

But for the landed class, even though on all occasions members display their unshakeable self-confidence, offer their flashing teeth, their barking staccato sentences, life is not simply a walking on the lawns of an English summer, not simply an indulgence in a heightened sense of nostalgia, not exclusively a playing of complex games of emotional manoeuvre in scented rose-gardens at the end of long summer evenings.

It is a condition of the landed class that members have a defensive state of mind. They know that they have lost their automatic right to rule. They believe that it would be better for the country if they still had it. And if not, perhaps, for the country, certainly for them. For if they still ruled they would be better able to defend themselves. And they have much to defend, *mores* and property.

The defensive state of mind is born of fear. In the case of the landed class, an inordinate fear of the landless.

On long summer evenings, on long summer lawns, fear also steps out for an evening walk.

As the landed sit in their great houses looking out over their ancient landholdings they feel the inevitable approach of the landless. They feel these happy ones everywhere about them, these smiling ones without responsibility. Occasionally, they see them. Occasionally they see walkers with gaily-coloured rucksacks and odd shoes startling their flowery meadows and their ancient woodlands or stepping cunningly along public footpaths that the landowners hoped had been forgotten.

When they do not see them they see their detritus. Their plastic cups. Their shiny chocolate papers. Their empty paper bags.

Children from the village collect conkers beneath the chestnut trees in the North park without permission. Their parents wouldn't have dared. City dwellers appear out of the summer haze in their cars and consume plastic picnics beside the gate-houses to the blare of their portable radios. They wouldn't have dared twenty years ago.

It's no good sending them away. They become abusive. The more sly complain to the police that they have been harassed whilst exercising their legal rights. Sherry has to be dispensed to the local police sergeant. An invitation to shoot pigeons has to be issued. Such generosity doesn't by any means always work. Even the rural police no longer show the respect that they did.

IRRITATED BY THE daily incursions into their privacy, as they saw it, inspired by an increasing fear of the landless and a feeling of helplessness, inspired, perhaps, by Prime Minister Blunt, who presented himself to the public as a man of landed property, that summer the landed class seized upon a great idea.

The genesis of great ideas cannot ever be clearly identified. Such ideas are an expression of the frustration, the fears, the determination of a class of people, sometimes an entire nation.

No Tartar could possibly have been the sole inspiration of the great push westwards. Even the Great Khan himself was not the first of his tribe to dream of expansion. Nor could he have succeeded so widely without the great idea seizing sufficient of his people.

Raleigh could never have dreamed of his bold voyage to singe the King of Spain's beard if he hadn't lived among a people who had a great idea of voyages of discovery and acquisition.

Great ideas first appear in the air like a distant storm. They bring with them all the frustrations of thunder undischarged. When a storm threatens, people's heads begin to ache. In the same way, when a great idea threatens, people's minds begin to itch. In both cases, people become bad-tempered. They create unnecessary quarrels with members of their families and their friends. They feel alternately listless and overactive. Nothing satisfies.

While one group, in the library of an English country house on the knock of a summer night, stretched out their hands towards an idea that was in the air all around them, not yet articulated, other groups, in other rooms, in other counties, on the same night, were also feeling the frustration of a great idea not quite born, were also experiencing the same fear of the landless mob, were also groping towards the same expression of their determination to resist.

Much later, when the idea had taken root, when green shoots had appeared, when branches and leaves had grown from the trunk and a great tree stood defiantly grown, many persons claimed to be the originators of the idea.

And each was justified. Formidable ladies, determined men, in libraries and dining-rooms, in morning and drawing-rooms, all contributed to the great idea that led to a national political movement that grew and grew until it had offices, a secretary, a Chairman, a President, until it had several tens of thousands of wealthy subscribers and three hundred thousand less wealthy subscribers.

Although the idea was conceived in many locations, it was born in Lady Brompton's library.

* * *

Mahogany book-cases, countless rows of books neatly arranged in alphabetical order according to author. Gentle exhalation of learning. Exhalation also of cigar smoke, floating in flat strips across the room.

A decanter of brandy sat patiently on the ornate Regency table. Glasses, variously drained, on the occasional tables.

Lady Brompton sat at her desk, her back straight. Edward, her son, sat on a window seat. His back was also straight. Lord Brompton and Archie Moore MP were slumped in the deep leather-covered chairs.

Archie Moore was Lady Brompton's latest discovery. His estate agents' business had not prospered. Not least because property-owners in Bayswater, Kensington and Hampstead had soon realised that to offer their house for sale through Archie Moore and Co., was to issue an invitation to persons unknown to break and enter and remove precious stones, wallets, passports, small silver trinkets and anything else portable that took the intruder's fancy.

By the time we had been arrested word had got round so thoroughly Archie Moore had almost no clients. His bank-manager, so willing to lend at first, became unhelpful. The hire-purchase company that had financed his purchase of a shiny German car changed its mind about him and took it back. His telephones were frequently cut off.

Eventually, he was forced to call on the reluctant services of the Official Receiver.

Once he had accepted that he had failed in business he decided, like many others, that politics presented a more suitable career for his particular talents. He arranged for his maiden aunt who had always been excessively fond of him to introduce him to certain middle-aged ladies in Oxfordshire on whom he exerted his considerable charms.

In due course he was suitably rewarded with the nomination to their safe Conservative seat.

Candida wandered into the library, stopped, realised that an important discussion was taking place.

'Are you having a secret business conference?'

'It is confidential but I want you to be involved, darling.' Lady Brompton often relied on her daughter for support. 'We've been discussing political matters with Mr Archie Moore. I have an idea.'

Candida looked at her mother. She noted a certain light, not so much of inspiration as of determination, in her eyes. What on earth could it be? She looked at her father. He glowed with secret import. It must be something big.

'We are discussing the condition of the country. Your father and I have made up our minds to do something about it. It's going to involve all of us in a lot of extra work. I want you to help.'

'How?'

'We are under threat. Increasing threat. Something must be done.'

'Who is threatening us?'

'It goes very deep . . .' Archie Moore felt himself well qualified to answer.

But before he could develop his argument Lady Brompton interrupted him.

'The entire British nation is under threat. We have lost our way. We have lost our will. The people must be re-educated along patriotic lines. Only then will they learn to respect the social relationships that have evolved, over hundreds of years, for the benefit of all.'

'There are too many wreckers among us,' Lord Brompton added.

Perhaps because Lady Brompton had brought him a large fortune, perhaps because she was a stronger character than he, perhaps for both reasons, Lord Brompton obeyed his wife in all things even though both of them, in public, promoted the fiction that he was master of the estate and the woman that had so unexpectedly become his. Despite the imperturbable maintenance of this pantomime, despite the flashing smiles and the haughty glances, most people who knew the Bromptons at all well knew that Lord Brompton was not permitted by his wife to say much. Nor was he permitted, though he would have been quite happy, to remain entirely silent. Obliged to choose his words within such severe constraints, he rarely allowed anything but the most anodyne to escape his lips. In stark contrast to his spouse.

'Too many Jews,' Lady Brompton got under way, 'in too many important positions. Too many blacks all over the place. The Jews and the blacks are stirring things up. We are under increasing threat.'

Archie Moore winced. Not because he didn't agree with Lady Brompton. His political instincts told him that to be openly racist was dangerous. He realised that Lady Brompton had noticed. He coughed loudly.

'There's no point in throat-clearing. There's absolutely no reason to keep it to oneself. Certainly not here in my library. I know it's not fashionable to hold such views but fashion is often a bad guide, especially in politics.'

'I do think, Lady Brompton, however much some people might agree with you, that it would be most unwise to allow the public to think that the movement is to be in any way racist.'

'Movement?' Candida raised her eyebrows.

'We are going to begin a political movement. It is, at the moment, to be kept secret.' Lord Brompton knew that he was on safe ground here. The need for secrecy had been agreed by all.

'I'm not racist. I simply want a national home for the English. And with God's help, I'm going to get us one.' Lady Brompton's bosom filled out with pride like a great sail taking the wind.

'We need real men and women in this country. Men like you, Mr Archie Moore.' She knew how to flatter when required. 'Not the pathetic, limp-wristed apologies we have in authority today.'

'Hear, hear.' Another safe contribution from his Lordship.

'But Mummy,' Candida said, 'you'll have to keep your more eccentric prejudices to yourself, otherwise any political movement you want to start will never get off the ground.'

'My prejudices, as you call them, are not eccentric. They are simply the expression of the hopes and fears of countless ordinary English people.'

'What is the movement to be called?'

'Great England.' Edward had been silent, sitting quietly, watching these ideas float around him. 'Great England,' he repeated, firmly.

Edward had no need to be in the library that night. Indeed, his presence there would have surprised the rest of his family if they had allowed themselves to think about it. It surprised him. He could have been in his room listening to the music of the night as it floated in through his always-open window. He could have been outside walking in the friendly moonlight. Something that night had drawn him to his mother. He felt that she needed him. He felt that he, uniquely, would be able to help her.

Edward had been sitting in the library wondering why he had this obscure feeling. He had seen his mother advance along this path before. He had seen his father's wary complicity. He had seen important outsiders like Archie Moore. In the past all these excitements had passed over him. But this time Edward knew something that neither his mother nor his father nor Candida nor Archie Moore knew. He knew that this time, his mother's enthusiasm would become reality, he knew that the idea that his mother was grasping for, in the same way that she had grasped so many times before, this time would bear great fruit.

As Edward was sitting in the library listening to the mounting enthusiasm he saw crowds of people looking up towards his mother and Archie Moore.

'Great England.'

'No, that's no good, darling. It's too obvious.'

'Great England.' Edward repeated the words with extraordinary calmness. He knew that they would stick. He knew that they would be the two words that would represent everything that his mother was groping for, that she could not yet see, that he could see clearly.

'What do you think?' Candida asked Archie Moore.

'It's . . . I don't know.' He could not let this opportunity to agree with Lady Brompton pass even though Edward's two words were beginning to affect him.

'Whatever we call it, Mr Archie Moore is going to represent our views in Parliament. We will be seeing a great deal of him. We trust him absolutely.'

'You are too kind, Lady Brompton.' Archie Moore smirked and fidgeted in his chair.

'I mean it.' Lady Brompton was a woman of sudden enthusiasm. 'I mean it. Good. Mr Archie Moore. Very good.'

Lady Brompton began to move slowly back and forth in front of the fireplace like a well-laden ship swinging at anchor.

* * *

Great England. A great idea had entered the world clothed in those two words.

Great England. Soon in great houses all over the country the words began to appear. They issued out of libraries and dining-rooms, out of morning-rooms and billiard-rooms, joined up, parted, met each other again everywhere in the air of that summer until, like the refrain of an enormous chorus, they were on every landed lip.

Great England. From the beginning, the two words became independent, of Edward Brompton, of his family and their friends, of those who joined the movement and of all the countless television and radio announcers, the pundits and the politicians who found, as summer turned to summer, that it was increasingly necessary to use them.

Great England. Each time the words were repeated they took on greater weight and significance and so enhanced their right to exist as independent actors on the stage of human affairs. As they were heard, more and more often, they had to be repeated. Both by the landed and the landless.

Great England. Thought. Whispered. Spoken. Shouted. The two words were to crystallise, for a generation of the *haves*, the greatest hopes that they had for themselves and their children. And for a generation of the *havenots*, the selfishness, the greed, the complacency, as they saw it, of the *haves*.

FIGURES IN BRIGHT clothes on the sand. Some stand still, staring at the sea in wonder or at each other's scantily clad forms wondering. Others are in motion throwing balls, chasing dogs, chasing each other, chasing ideas. Some are speaking, some shouting, some laughing. Some, yes, let some be silent.

From among the figures on the beach two form into Candida and Dov walking along the strand. A picturesque tableau with promise of comforts undefined but nonetheless palpable.

A promising tableau that I sometimes allow myself to enjoy in my weaker moments.

Candida and Dov walking along the damp beach beneath a bright, grey, east-coast sky.

Candida is wearing a blue two-piece bathing-suit. It is scanty and reveals more than it conceals.

Sand-martins wheel and shriek above our heads.

Even here, in my hospital bed, I can hear their screams. Even here, when the sea pauses for breath, in the startling hole of unexpected and brief silence, I can hear the click of their beaks as they seize helpless insects.

Two figures walking in earnest conversation. The undulations of the beach are reflected in their gait. Although the strand appears broadly flat, it is, in fact, full of small depressions, sudden, unexpected ridges, other uneven features created by the departing tide.

One figure, the young woman, copes with the terrain lithely. The other figure, the young man, is less successful. He finds himself bumping into his companion.

These bumps could be entirely accidental. Bump. Shoulders touch momentarily. Bump. Dov's hand brushes her flank. Bump. His left hip touches her right side. Bump. The gentle waves of the grey North Sea bump onto the shore.

* * *

Lady Brompton insisted, once every summer, on going to the seaside for a picnic. The rest of her family accompanied her with varying degrees of reluctance. That year Dov, too, was invited.

Whilst Edward and the chauffeur set up the picnic table, arranged the food and drinks with due reverence for the occasion, Lady Brompton sat in an enclave that she had staked out, bordered to the south and north by great, striped, canvas windshields held in the sand by wooden poles, an enclave open only to the sand-cliffs behind and the sea in front.

The ground-plan of this temporary demesne was conceived with one object. To enable Lady Brompton, her family and friends, to gaze at the sea and, at the same time, prevent the *vulgus*, as far as possible, from gazing too easily onto Lady Brompton.

Lady Brompton sat majestically beneath the cunning shade of her enormous cotton hat, in a gaudy metal-and-plastic picnic chair. She was wearing a large, flowery cotton dress, a pair of unexpected plimsolls. From time to time, she glanced at the sea with an aggressive expression, as though challenging Poseidon to emerge from the waters and explain himself.

She was giving Archie Moore her instructions with regard to Great England. Hautbois and Lord Brompton were listening, the one for reasons of personal ambition, the other out of obedience.

'What we need, Mr Archie Moore, is support in the House. You will be responsible for organising that.'

'Leave it to me.' Archie Moore MP exuded confidence, as MPs are supposed to do. 'I'll organise some of the new members. Some of them are good libertarians. They'll support us.'

'We don't want too many freedom-lovers. We want men who see things clearly, men who can see that the country's going to the dogs. We want men who'll do what has to be done.'

'Libertarians aren't really interested in freedom today. They're old-fashioned Whigs. They generally hold the same views as you do, Lady Brompton.' Hautbois felt it was time for him to intervene.

'They find the libertarian banner convenient. It gives them a kind of definition,' Archie Moore added. 'They believe that people should only be as free as is good for them.'

'But who decides how much freedom is good for them?' Hautbois was not expecting an answer.

'Some people,' Lady Brompton said, 'have a gift for leadership. Some people are prepared to take responsibility. But nowadays they've been exiled by the consuming classes. Exiled to their estates.

'They're ready to come back and take up the reins again. They simply need to be called. We must make sure they are. That is the purpose of Great England. Our movement will create the climate that will make it possible for our natural leaders to emerge and take up their duties once more.'

Lady Brompton looked at Archie Moore and confirmed her first impression that he was not suitable to be a leader. Archie Moore looked at Lady Brompton and decided that she was realising what he had always known, that he was a natural leader destined for greatness.

As these two looked at each other in perfect misunderstanding the chauffeur opened a bottle of champagne. Pop. The cheerful sound signified that Lady Brompton's picnic had formally begun.

Despite Lady Brompton's precautions some of the other people who were on the beach that day were beginning to collect at the mouth of her enclave. They were so struck by the scene that they stopped, turned their backs on the sea and stared in gaping astonishment.

The gaudy, plastic picnic chairs they had seen. Many of them possessed exactly such chairs themselves. The canvas windbreaks were not uncommon. Though fewer possessed them, they had certainly seen them on beaches before. The clothes of these extraordinary personages, the old school blazers, the white cricket trousers, the old-fashioned swimming suits, Lady Brompton's huge hat, all of these they had seen before, even if only in picture-magazines or on the television. What they had not seen was a well-organised and well-served picnic, well laid out on a large folding table, with fine white linen and good china, well served by a properly trained servant.

They stood and gawped. For most it was astonishing. For some it was provocative. Not just what they saw. They were also struck by what they heard. Though they were not especially politically conscious, certainly not then and there, they soon understood that these people were speaking of political matters that might affect them.

Good-humoured cries of 'Fascist', 'Snob' and 'Silly old cow' began to drift over the sand.

Eventually Lady Brompton permitted herself to notice that she was becoming the centre of unwelcome attention.

'Go away.'

The crowd grinned.

'Do go away, will you.'

The crowd tittered.

Lady Brompton turned to Archie Moore in exasperation.

'Tell them to go away, Mr Moore.'

'But, Lady Brompton, this is a public beach.'

'Never mind that. Use your authority.'

The nonplussed Archie Moore was unable to decide how to act. On this occasion he was saved by the good humour of the crowd. With a collective shrug they began to move away, to turn their attention once more to the sea and to the sun, which just then began to shine.

'They just don't know respect any more.' Lady Brompton turned to Hautbois. 'What do you think of Great England?'

'It's a splendid idea, Lady Brompton.'

Hautbois had, by this time, developed into a fervent supporter of the landed interest. He didn't have any land but wanted to. He felt, in an obscure way, that, if he supported those who did, some of it might eventually come to him.

'I shall see that Michael speaks to the Prime Minister.' Hautbois was grateful for this opportunity to demonstrate that he was on first-name terms with his employer, the Minister of Agriculture.

Lady Brompton frowned. The first stages of a new political movement required great discretion and finesse.

'No, for goodness' sake don't. Mr Archie Moore is in charge of all that. Promise me you won't say a word. Not even to your Minister.'

Lady Brompton didn't think for a moment that Hautbois was likely to be more loyal to her than to the Minister who employed him. Why else would she have invited him for the weekend? Why else would she speak about the movement in his hearing? Of course she didn't want Hautbois to keep her ideas to himself. Silence was the last thing a movement needed. She wanted him to report to his Minister. But she did not want Archie Moore to think that she had access to any other politician. If he felt that he was not the exclusive parliamentary representative of the movement he might refuse to be a representative at all.

He was an odd one, Hautbois. Gauche. Tactless. Too ready to show off. Lady Brompton examined him in silence. His clothes were just a little too neat, a little too new and tidy. He was surprisingly insecure for one so reasonably bred. Come to think of it, hadn't he been sacked from school for cheating at maths? His mother, poor dear, had had to move heaven and earth to get him into Harrow for his sixth-form year. And to pay for it.

Lady Brompton realised that she would have to be careful what she said to this too-eager young man.

'How is your mother?'

'Mother's fine. I think. I haven't seen her for a few days.'

'Oh, do give her my love.'

'Of course.'

'Such a friend.'

The sun flew its leisurely summer way along the sky. Lunch progressed to the satisfaction of all present. The time came for coffee.

The chauffeur was walking from guest to guest with a large vacuum flask when Lady Brompton looked up and realised that she and her party were once more the centre of unwelcome attention. A crowd was again collecting to witness this novel form of entertainment.

'Oh God, will they never leave us in peace?'

Lady Brompton glowered.

'Do go away.'

Lady Brompton's request was greeted with mirth.

Archie Moore looked up. Prayed that he would not be asked once more to move them on. His god was unhearing.

'Mr Archie Moore. I really must ask you to use your position. Move them on.'

'But Lady Brompton.'

'Mr Archie Moore, you aspire to be a leader of men. Now is your chance to demonstrate your powers.'

Archie Moore saw that he had no escape. He looked at Dov, shrugged his shoulders. Perhaps he was expecting a sympathetic smile. He was disappointed.

'What can I do?'

'Lady Brompton wants you to use your authority.' Dov smiled. 'Use it.'

Archie Moore got to his feet and walked indecisively towards the gathering crowd.

I watched with pleasure as he struggled with Lady Brompton's command. Then, heady with pleasure, I lost my head.

* * *

I was aware that Candida had plans for me. I was also quite clear that any plans that she might have for me would conflict with whatever plans I had for myself. I knew perfectly well that any relationship with Candida would mean a surrender of my freedom.

Nonetheless, as Archie Moore moved uncertainly forward I asked Candida if she would like to go for a walk along the beach. She accepted the invitation with flattering alacrity. We walked away from the others.

The gentle afternoon breeze touched our cheeks. The summer light flickered off the moving waters and played at the edge of our eyes. The beguiling voice of the sea murmured in our ears.

We walked away from Lady Brompton, from Lord Brompton, from Hautbois, from Archie Moore, further and further until we became two figures walking along the strand beneath the east-coast summer sky, bumping into each other from time to time in friendly bodily enquiry.

EDWARD WATCHED AS Candida and Dov wandered off along the beach. He was smiling. Not at Archie Moore's discomfiture. Not at his mother's eccentricity. Not because the sun was shining. He was smiling because he could see that Candida and Dov were falling in love and he was pleased.

Despite the view of those who knew him, Edward Brompton was a wise man. He had a wisdom of a kind not usually recognised by society. He had only to look at someone and he would understand how that person felt. No matter who it was or what the circumstances, simply by looking at other people he could somehow put himself so completely into their shoes that he felt all their feelings, all their fears, all their joys, all as acutely as they did. Not only could he do this, he could hardly prevent himself from doing it.

Edward's parents, from the earliest days, were afraid of the brilliant insights this facility brought. He had been a precocious boy. By the time he was five he could hold a conversation with any and all of the adults he met. The light of the intelligence that shone from his eyes blinded his parents. The startling perceptions that he expressed frightened them. To protect themselves, Edward's parents decided that he was mentally backward. They treated him accordingly.

Edward soon realised that his perceptiveness was an embarrassment to his parents. A dutiful boy, he decided to oblige them by conforming exactly to their vision of him. He began to play the idiot and soon fell into the habit of it.

Dov, like all others, was deceived by Edward's pretence. Unlike most others, Edward decided to take me into his confidence.

I was walking on the lawn one afternoon waiting for Candida to finish some work for her mother. I was looking up into the sky watching the swallows wheeling and dipping in their relentless search for insects. As I watched, unexpectedly, they all started to dive towards the house.

I followed their line of flight until my eyes rested on Edward walking smoothly down the terrace-steps. He stopped. Looked up. The swallows swooped towards him, as though greeting him, then broke their formation and swirled away in every different direction.

I stared at Edward. He was smiling at the swallows. I felt in an obscure way, that he had wanted me to see their astonishing greeting.

'How's it going with Great England?'
'All right, I think.'
'My words.' He looked at me with a penetrating glance.
'I know.'
'Bringing clarity to cloudiness.'
'Yes?'
'Words doing their job. Pointing a way through the fog.'
'Yes.'
'Releasing the necessary energies for a great national movement.'
'Absolutely.'
'I knew you would understand.' His grin showed his pleasure.
'Walk?'
'Why not.'

We set off across the lawn towards the park. In a few moments we arrived at a small, wrought-iron gate. Edward passed through, strode off towards a distant, tree-covered hill. I followed.

Pigeons, their wings clattering in summer flight, rose and fell overhead as we walked along a narrow path created by the frequent walks of sheep and cattle.

We came to a stream lined with alder and willow, crossed by a small, brick bridge, began to climb the grassy slopes towards the summit of the hill. The path wound on before us.

'The cattle know the way.' Edward's words disassociated themselves from him, hung for a moment in the soft summer air. His step was unusually determined. I began to feel a pleasant sense of dreaminess as though I were entering that delightful state between waking and sleeping.

Solitary pines ran up the hill, standing guard over ancient rabbit warrens. As Edward passed them, they seemed to salute him. We passed beneath huge elms and oaks. They too seemed to be waving their branches at Edward in some obscure, private greeting.

Unaccountably, my steps felt lighter and lighter as we climbed the hill. The sun shone down.

Presently, we arrived at the edge of an ancient wood of oak and elm. In front of us stretched an apparently impenetrable thicket of bramble. We skirted around it until we came to a narrow, almost invisible cutting, hardly wide enough for a man to pass through. Edward plunged in. I followed. We wound our way down and down, seeing nothing but brambles each side and the sky above until, quite suddenly, we came into a broad, shallow, circular hollow, several hundred feet across.

At the centre of the circle, an ancient standing stone pointed upwards towards vast periods of past and future time.

I turned slowly, catching glimpses of distant hill-tops at regular intervals. It was clear that the stone lay at the precise centre of a complex circular system of hills. As I turned I was seized by the astonishing thought that the stone had been here first and had somehow, in some early and different period of time, arranged for the hills to be thrown up all around it.

Edward was watching me closely, watching my wonder and pleasure.

'I brought you here to show you my stone.'

Edward stood quite still, perfectly self-contained, like a hermit grinning from a hilltop at the wild earth all around him. I saw that he had no insatiable desire to outmanoeuvre, no burning desire to conquer, no implacable rage to overcome, no ambition to pursue, no lust to destroy. He had no need to give, no need to take, no want to love or want to be loved.

'I carry the stone around in my head. It comes between me and other people's troubles.'

In that place, on that afternoon, his words did not sound strange.

'You must promise me to keep this secret. No-one knows about me and this stone. It's dangerous for me. The others wouldn't understand. My parents, Candida, they wouldn't understand. They think that I'm mad anyway.'

'Why don't you get out, Edward? Why don't you just abandon the whole lousy thing and run?'

'Yes, I know what you mean but I don't need to. Not yet, anyway.'

'I would. I'd say goodbye to your whole family and wander off. You'd be better off by yourself.'

'I'm all right.'

'They'll get you in the end. They'll have to.'

'I don't mind.'

Edward stood as still as his stone, smiling.

Suddenly, I was overcome with a great love for Edward, a love that has always, since that day, been constant.

CANDIDA ARRIVED AT my house accompanied by her determined gait a few days later.

The knocker fell with a thud. I opened the door, wearing an expression of suitable surprise even though she must have realised, at once, that, if not expecting her, I had certainly been hoping that she would come.

'I walked over.'

'Come in. No need to knock.'

'Thank you.'

I stood in the doorway staring at her, at the light on her hair, at the friendly smile on her lips.

'I've always wanted to see your house.'

'Come in.'

'Thank you.'

She smiled at me. I smiled at her. Silence fell. I stood at the top of my front steps. Candida stood below me.

A breath of her perfume mingled with the scent of her skin, floated to my nostrils. At once, I was overcome by a series of images, both lovely and terrifying. Despite myself, as I stood staring at her, I realised that I was about to cease to be my own master. Worse. I realised that I didn't mind. My customary self had been replaced by an irresponsible, dreamy self, as though I had been caught unawares by the mysterious chemistry of a hallucinogenic drug.

Disturbed images began to float into my mind. I saw myself walking along the path in the Rookery Wood with Candida beside me. I saw myself putting out my hand. I saw our hands holding. I saw the top branches of the high oaks drifting along above us sparkling with shards of sunlight. I watched myself and Candida as we sat down beneath the huge oak by the inner gate. I watched myself with excitement and fear, again and again, slowly lowering my head down onto her breast, falling slowly down into the deep oblivion of her female warmth.

I stood in the doorway, staring speechlessly at Candida, unable to move and make way for her to come in. However hard my more sensible self told me to dismiss these images from my mind I simply could not.

The summer breezes slipped softly past. The leaves of the trees whispered to each other like lovers.

Candida stood on the step below me, puzzled. At length, she broke the spell.

'How are you?'

Her voice felt like a gentle rope. It drew me from my dreams. I recovered myself and drew back a few paces. She took advantage of my retreat, stepped smartly into the hall. We stood facing each other again.

'How are you?'

By these steps, mine and hers, I was snatched from physical paralysis only to stumble into a worse predicament. Although her friendly howare-you, so warmly expressed, so lovingly asked, as I imagined, had released my body, the paralysis had merely passed from my body to my mind. My mind became a pleasant blank. The simple enquiry that had been asked of me on so many other occasions, on that occasion, seemed to me to be utterly pointless.

'How are you?'

Candida stood in the hall, facing Dov, wondering why he was behaving so oddly, why he was standing there, staring at her in that dreamy way? She thought of retreating but decided that it would be cowardly. Besides, he looked so perplexed, so childlike she wanted to comfort him.

How are you? A simple question. But under the full weight of her confident gaze I had no idea how to answer it even though I knew that I had to if matters were to progress.

She was obviously determined that I should. She stood in silence waiting for my reply.

'It's such a hopeless question,' I spluttered eventually, entirely in defence, 'under all the circumstances.'

'What do you mean?' she asked with a smile that was not entirely warm.

'I don't know.'

'You must know what you mean.'

'You're not enquiring about my health. Are you? After all, you can see that I'm fit.'

'What a funny man you are.'

'I'm sorry. I'm really not trying to be difficult. I'm glad you came. I've been hoping that you would. It's just that I don't know how to answer the question. The more I think about how I am the more I can't answer. I do want to answer. To please you.'

Eventually I began to recover some of my poise.

'If you'll be patient with me I'll try to join the dance and reply as expected.'

'I'm in no hurry,' she said, somewhat grimly.

I lifted my eyes from her breasts where they had been fixed, up through the azimuth of her face to her eyes. Behind her the black and white flagstones of the hall ran away from us in two closing parallel lines. Infinity was beckoning.

'My physical health is robust,' I said, at last, 'as is my mental health. But that's not what you mean, is it?'

'It's not a bad start.'

We were wandering towards the drawing-room. She looked boldly around her.

'But only a start,' I was trying to be agreeable. 'I know. That's the trouble with trying to answer your question comprehensively. Only a start. What you really want to know is my condition, isn't it?'

She said nothing. She had decided that she had made a mistake coming to Dov's house. Still, it was interesting to see the house. It had always been a mystery. No-one she knew had ever been inside.

'My condition,' I said. 'That's what you want to know.'

'You have such a funny way of talking.'

We had reached the drawing-room. Candida was examining the furniture and the pictures. I watched her surprised approval with amusement.

'It's funny I've never been here before. Our parents know each other. Knew each other.'

'My father was something of a hermit and my mother – well, she was a complete hermit.'

'Do you miss your parents? I bet you do.'

'Not much.'

'Oh.'

'I didn't see much of them.'

'Your mother kept herself very much shut away, didn't she?'

'Thank God.'

She completed her inspection of the room and its appointments. We crossed to the high windows, looked out onto the lawns. Presently, she turned, smiled, waited for me to make the next move.

'Would you like to sit down? You must be tired walking all the way over here.'

'I like being tired. It helps me to relax.'

She looked at me. I felt weak and excited.

'I just came over. I should have waited for you to ask me, but I thought you might not. It's very rude. I'm sorry.'

The wise drone of bees at work in the roses floated in through the open windows.

'I've often wondered what it's like, living alone. Do you like it?' She turned again, looked out of the window. 'God, England is lovely when the weather's fine. This summer, especially.'

He hadn't even offered her tea or a drink. In fact, he had made her feel thoroughly uncomfortable. Why? She was sure that he was interested in her. He had shown it plainly on the beach. Perhaps he had no experience of talking to women. She looked at him. He was staring at her in a discomforting way. There was a strange stillness about him that made her want to comfort him.

'What do you do here, all by yourself?'

'Oh, I don't know, things. You know.'

'Do you farm?'

'A bit. Most of it's let.'

Why did she keep wanting to comfort him?

'Did you enjoy the picnic? Mother's so eccentric.'

'It made me laugh.'

'I don't blame you.'

'Not so much at your mother, at the extraordinary world.'

'Excellent world.'

She began to move lightly around the room.

'You must think it's a bit odd, me coming here like this, uninvited.'

'You look at home.'

'It's a very friendly house, isn't it. Do you go out much. I haven't seen you at the local dinner parties.'

'I don't like the food.'

She laughed, turned to the window, looked at the peonies in the border outside as they gently nodded their fat, pink heads. She had made up her mind.

'Those are peonies.'

'Yes, I know,' she said.

Ordinary, commonplace phrases can have a disproportionate effect if they are spoken at the same time as other feelings are being felt.

'Yes, I know,' she said, looking at me, meaning that she had recovered her poise after the first few destabilising exchanges and intended to execute her plan.

'Yes, I know,' she said, meaning, on that lovely English afternoon, that she had decided that Dov was to be hers.

Her stance expressed her absolute confidence that all that she wanted would be granted. Not just by right of youth, by right of sex, by right of birth, but by right of habit of being obeyed.

'Yes, I know,' she said, and I surrendered.

LONDON SLEEPS. I lie awake and permit the silence to become Dov and Dov to become the silence. This is not a process that would appeal to Alexander, so I have not told him about it. If I did, it would simply frighten him. As did my description of the death of my father and the subsequent loss of my estate.

My father was always remote, even when kissing me goodnight.

'Dov ... Dov.'

My mother calling. The fading evening sun on the Scots pines. I running, hot, sweaty, happy to be on the move.

'Dov ... Dov.'

My mother's intrusive summons.

Enough of my mother. She is disposed of.

What of my father? I don't remember him calling me. Ever. I do remember his coming to say goodnight to me.

I remember the summer evenings of my childhood, the feel of the cool, linen sheets, the cool linen pillowcases of my bed.

I hear my father's ponderous step on the deep red carpet. His figure looms in friendly pose in the doorway. In a moment he steps to my bed and bends down over me. The feel of his rougher cheek on mine. The smell of the cigar he has just finished.

My father always finished his cigar before coming up to my room to say goodnight to me.

Sometimes, it has to be admitted, Dov would have liked his father to have stayed with him a little longer, to have perhaps visited him less out of duty and more out of natural pleasure, to have perhaps kissed him again.

I was conned by Wendy, by Austin, by the entire household into believing that this goodnight ceremony would be rewarding. Each one, whenever I went to bed, after saying goodnight to me, would always end by promising that my father would be up to say goodnight to me shortly.

This promise was spoken in such a way as to invest my father's nightly visit with deep significance, as though it was an extraordinary concession, a benign act from which I would derive great reward. But my father's goodnight visits always ended without any satisfaction. Even though my father went through the motions with a kiss on my cheek, occasionally with a pat on my head or my shoulder, somehow I always expected more than I received. I expected to feel a great affection for my father and I expected to discover that my father felt a great affection for me.

Sometimes I want him to have been a good father, in my moments of weakness, lying here in my immaculately white hospital bed, between daily changed sheets, sometimes, in the darkness of my most midnight solitude, I determine to pretend to myself and especially to others that he was a good father. Once I caught myself beginning to explain to Alexander what a good father he really was, how gentle, how kindly, how wise, how talented.

I caught myself and told Alexander the truth. That he was a terrible father. That he was incapable of being a good father and so he could not be blamed, except, possibly, for bearing children but that I could not blame him for that because it would provide me with an excuse for my behaviour.

This confession had an unfortunate and unforeseen consequence. Alexander, startled by my unaccustomed readiness to speak, startled even more by my readiness to speak of my father and my feelings about him in such a straightforward way, informed the authorities that I was making unexpected progress. The Senior Medical Officer appeared the next day full of excitement. It took a considerable expenditure of effort and of guile to disabuse them both of any idea that I was making progress.

* * *

As a child, Dov had assumed that the place and circumstances of his birth would more or less correspond to the place and circumstances of his life and, for that matter, of his death. He had assumed, as he ran helter-skelter through the hay-fields, his nostrils full of the smell of newly-mown grass, his eyes delighting in the scarlet blaze of poppies, heads dancing, or as he stepped softly through the snow, quieter than a hare's footfall, he had assumed that the fields of his father would inevitably become his fields, that the park and landscape that his father had inherited and had taken full responsibility for, not taking more than he gave, would become his park and his landscape, his responsibility and his not to take more than he was ready to give. Dov had assumed that the nobly-proportioned house that had been bought by his gold-getting great-great-grandfather, the house of high windows and comfortable smells, of polished brass and King Peter's long red carpets, the house of glowing red bricks after rain, of sunshafts tumbling into the morning-room and the drawing-room while Maudie dusted and cleaned, the house with the blue silken bedroom where his mother kept her counsel, Dov had assumed that all, including the servants themselves, would continue.

My childish assumptions were fulfilled until my father died. Then my assumptions were taken away from me.

Yes, Citizen, the authorities took my estate away. Others say that I dissipated it. That I could have retained it if I had been more prudent. That's their way of looking at it.

* * *

My father gave up his life without much of a struggle. He had never resisted anything. Resistance was not in his nature. He died suddenly, in his sleep, not long before the dawning of a Sabbath that he had no reason to believe that he would not see.

Death comes peacefully to those who are just and to those who do not resist. He died peacefully.

At the funeral, I barely noticed the strange-looking man who was called Executor and the other, even less agreeable-looking man, who was called Mortgagee, friends, apparently, of my father, though I had never met them before and found it difficult to imagine how my father could possibly have ever formed a friendship with either. Entirely proper grief excused me from paying any attention to their appearance, their attitudes or their behaviour.

Many thought that day that it would have been better for me if I had had a good look at these two. Many thought but none said. Even if they had spoken I would not have listened. Even if I had listened I would not have acted. Even if I had made an attempt to act I would not have been able to prevent the loss of my estate. Even if I had been able to prevent the loss of my estate I would not have wanted to. Seen from here. Now, much later.

After the burial these men returned to the house with the other mourners and enjoyed the refreshments liberally provided by the servants. Even when Mortgagee and Executor had seemed to be behaving in a proprietorial way, as they did, that very afternoon, before my father's flesh was properly consumed by the worms of the earth, even then I had assumed, simply, that their impudent behaviour could be invoiced to their ignorance.

But as the days passed I found myself increasingly unable to understand either the *locus* or the needs of Executor or of Mortgagee. Their wishes, even the words they used, at each meeting, became more and more offensive to me.

They started their sentences with respect when they meant to be disrespectful and they started them with no respect at all when they were trying to be agreeable. I soon lost interest in their words and marvelled instead at their duplicity. I wondered why they found it necessary to undertake such deceits, which, it was clear, they considered opaque, but which were, in fact, entirely transparent.

Day after day, they came unannounced, uninvited. Day after day, they called at the house, marching into the drawing-room, sitting on the friendly sofa as though it were their own, ringing the bell for Wendy to bring tea as though she were their housekeeper. Day after day, the two of them, sipping from my fine, porcelain cups, muttering and chattering amongst themselves, asking me impertinent questions about my possessions.

* * *

Dov steps quietly into the drawing-room.

Executor and Mortgagee sit talking in lowered voices. My rough trousers and open shirt in happy contrast to their seedy suits and ties. I stand, wait. Their conversation subsides slowly, unhurriedly. Eventually, they get to their feet, smile, sit again.

Either these are men without manners or they are men who calculate their manners exactly. Presumably for their own satisfaction. Such nice distinctions cannot possibly be of any use to others.

I sit, stare past them out of the long windows, across the lawn to the wood on the top of Coronation Hill.

'There is mention of a gold pocket-watch ... '

The voice of Executor floats across the sofa, over the drum table.

My father had a fine hunter. It had two fingernail slides, one on either side. If one was activated it struck the hours. If the other, the hours, then the quarters, finally the minutes would ring.

I cross to the walnut bureau, take the watch out of a drawer.

'I have it here.'

I activated the slide on the west side of the face.

Ding, ding, ding, di-ding, di-ding, ting, ting, ting, ting. Three, thirty-four.

'Good, as long as I know ... '

Executor's voice falls heavily onto the carpet.

* * *

My father surrendered the estate to Mortgagee without realising. The charitable explanation. My father surrendered the estate to Mortgagee without realising until too late and through weakness. The most likely explanation. There could be others. It was not a single act. There were many loans. Each secured on the estate, over a period of years.

Oh, my father.

By the time the Earth had mourned my father's death by a single turning, the matter of my inheritance had come to a head.

I was quite capable of understanding figures. I was more than capable of grasping the implications of my actions and my inactions, financial and in other ways material, had I wished, if I could have wished, if I could have wished to know what was in store for me.

But I did not. Then or now. I have never been neurotic about my future because I have always been and remain absolutely without fear. Why should I fear the future? At the end the struggle will be over.

Accordingly, whenever my advisers warned me of the consequences of my actions and inactions, as they did frequently by letter, by telephone and face to face, I told them, with a smile, that all would undoubtedly be well.

What I did not tell them was that it could not but be well for me whatever the outcome. Nor did I tell them that the events that they felt should by all means be avoided held no fear for me, that I watched their inevitable approach with fascination and growing acceptance. I knew that the loss of my estate would increase my personal freedom.

And I did not tell them what I knew better than they: that from the moment of my father's death, the estate was lost. To me, certainly.

I could see all that I wanted to see behind my advisers' eyes. I saw that they never told me the whole truth. I saw that for them the whole truth was not available. I decided that there was no point in listening to their half-truths.

After a short time, my advisers did not respond to this attitude in a sympathetic way. Even though they never gave me any advice that was not first in their own interest and secondly in my interest, so far as the latter did not conflict with the former, my advisers are not to blame. I never asked the right questions, nor did I expect the right answers. In fact, I never asked any questions at all. The unrequited answers they offered me passed me by.

* * *

Dov returned from his summer fields one hot afternoon, back to the black and white flagstone floor of his splendid hall to find Mortgagee and Executor standing there, yet again. Yet again they were uninvited.

Executor was standing beside the fireplace, leaning on the mantel. Mortgagee was sitting on one of the fine mahogany hall-chairs.

Dov stood in the hall of his house, looking at them. At their shabby suits. At their garish ties that tried to distract his attention from the dishonesty in their faces.

He realised that these two disreputable figures were becoming unbearably offensive to the noble proportions of his hall, offensive to the open atmosphere of his drawing-room, offensive to all the harmonies of the house.

They entered the house as though it were their own. They allowed their feet to tread the floors as though they belonged, not to Dov, but to them. They allowed their calculating eyes to rove everywhere without respect, over the pictures, over the furniture, over the china, over the antique clocks.

Dov came into the hall. Mortgagee and Executor watched him, relaxed at first, their unfriendly smiles fixed to their lips. Presently, they grew alarmed. Too late. Dov had found his uncomplicated, unyielding, irresistible stare and fixed both of them to their places.

Then, watching himself, as though from high above, he saw himself as slowly in slow motion as you please to imagine, Citizen, so slowly that each motion was divided into connected slivers of stationary action, saw himself drift over to these two scavengers and without effort take Executor by the collar of his well-cut suit and Mortgagee by the collar of his less well-cut suit, one in each capable hand.

Dov saw himself lift these two parasites by the collars of their suits, without a word lift them across the hall and throw them both out of the front door, out, up and over the stone steps.

From the apogee of their flight they fell several feet to the gravel below without so much as an attempt to fly.

The gravel was startled as it was struck by the two bodies. As were the double oak doors when Dov slammed them shut a moment later.

I T IS TIME, Citizen, to introduce you to Cohen.
When Cohen reached manhood he determined to find a wife to provide him with the customary physical comforts and especially to do his washing. He hoped to enter into marriage without incurring the immense burden of the other mental and spiritual obligations that usually attach to such relationships. All he wanted was a simple business arrangement, not emotion, certainly not love. You do the cooking, he would have said, the washing, look after my other needs. I support you. A simple deal.

That's what he would have said had the opportunity arisen. It didn't.

Instead, a Miss White walked into his life one Thursday as he was waiting for his washing in the local launderette. She fell hopelessly in love with Cohen the moment that she caught sight of his sturdy figure placed squarely in front of the spin-dryer.

He was staring at his shirts whirling round and round in the bowels of the machine. He seemed so engrossed that she soon realised that she would have to adandon the usual niceties and make the first approach. A most determined girl, Miss White began then and there to lay seige to his reason with indications and promises, physical and emotional, so generous and so various that had only ten per cent of them been redeemed he would have been a blissfully happy man.

Her cunning assault continued day after day in venues as various as they were cheap. Cohen was mesmerised by the flattery of it all.

While Cohen had the loftier vision and the high spirits of the *Sephardim*, his inamorata had the earthy determination of the *Ashgenazim*. It took Miss White less than two months to persuade the poor man to surrender the last bastion of his better judgement. This interval would have been much shorter if she had decided to marry a gentile. It was only by calling on the deepest reserves of his racial instincts that Cohen was able to prolong the agony for so long.

I was chosen to witness the formal beginning of this conjunction.

It was clear to me on that crisp spring day, exhaled breath condensing in the frosty air, that Miss White had brought Cohen to complete obedience. He appended his signature to the Chelsea Registrar's record-book, if not with relish, certainly without hesitation.

That signature was the greatest testament to Miss White's abilities as a negotiator. It was also the beginning of the waning of Cohen's hopes. Once contracted, his lady had not made much effort either to redeem her promises or to carry out any of the duties that are usually associated with the female part of the marriage bargain. After the honeymoon in Ibiza, Mrs Cohen rapidly developed a vision of the kind of life that she considered suitable to her newly acquired station and determined to put Cohen to work on her behalf.

Cohen wondered why he had been so blind and took steps to see that his income was largely paid in cash so that he could keep the greater part for himself.

At the end of the third month of their marriage Mrs Cohen asked him to buy her a car. Her legs, she said, not her best feature, she did not say, were giving her cause for concern. Cohen refused. In retaliation, she withdrew normal service and said that it would not be resumed, neither washing nor cooking nor physical conjunction, until the specified vehicle together with suitable documents proving her ownership to it was handed to her.

The following day, a Friday, Cohen withheld the housekeeping money, locked himself in the marital bedroom and decided to sit it out.

After two days and many hours of shouted entreaties Mrs Cohen admitted defeat and retired to her mother in Peckham.

The disentanglement had been complex.

Bruised by the bonds of marriage, lacerated by the expense of divorce, his small house full of his dirty linen, Cohen decided to offer his laundry out to contract on a weekly basis.

One pair of Egyptian cotton sheets, white. Two pillowcases, similar. Five shirts, cream. Five pairs of underpants, white. Five cotton vests, off white. Five pairs of socks, black wool. Three white handkerchiefs.

There were no takers. Worse, there was not a tremor of reaction in the markets. Sterling remained firm.

He would have to beg his mother to do his washing once more.

* * *

Cohen responded to my telephone call as I had hoped that he would.

'If your Wendy will do my washing,' he said, 'I'll join you in the Bunker. Our last stand will be remembered for its glory, for its extraordinary splendour.'

'Who by?'

'Executor and Mortgagee. We'll show them what you're made of.'

'They'll soon discover that I'm not made of very much.'

'So much the better for them. We'll teach them to abjure the material world for the spiritual. We'll lift them up from the slime of their sordid materialism to a higher vision. Know what?'

'What?'

'We're going to go for an all-balls world.'

Cohen moved in the following day with his dirty washing.

As I had expected, I found Cohen a welcome distraction. I laughed at the hard-edged words that sputtered out of his almost closed mouth. When I could make them out.

* * *

Cohen was able to divert me but he was not able to divert Mortgagee. Mortgagee did not delay. He applied to a doctor to cure his body and then limped to the Court of Chancery to obtain a Summons which he gave to an enquiry agent called Flowerdew with instructions to serve it forthwith.

Not much dewfall on Flowerdew as he stepped along the length of the drive through the lovely summer park. The jerky, uncomfortable rhythm of Flowerdew's walk was quite out of step with the slow, deep measure of the countryside. His shiny grey suit was out of touch with that glory of English peace.

Cohen saw him through the hall window.

'I don't like the look of him. Dogged. Could be a creditor. Looks like he always gets his man. You got debts I don't know about?'

'No. I don't think so.'

'Oh God, I can't bear it. I've just found a comfortable berth at last. Good food. Good company. My laundry attended to. It's all going to go, just as I'm settling in. I thought we had a year or two at least. How can you do such a thing to me?'

Wendy opened the door to Flowerdew and showed him into the drawing-room. He sat without being asked.

Cohen and Dov, both standing, watched him in silence.

Flowerdew's glasses were steamed up from the unaccustomed exertion. When they had cleared his shifty eyes appraised the furniture and pictures. Eventually he spoke.

'Two thousand quid, if you're lucky. Maybe two and a quarter.'

I asked him his business. As if I didn't know. Somehow, that day I was a stickler for formality.

'It's a most unfortunate business, Sir. But I'm sure there'll be a way out for a sensible gentleman like you, Sir. There usually is where gentlemen of your stamp are concerned. If you don't mind me saying so.'

I didn't mind him saying so, at all.

'Good of you to take it so well. I've had some difficult gentlemen in my time, Sir. I have. I've even been shot at by a gentleman from out of a fine old house like this one, once.'

Cohen laughed.

'It wasn't funny, Sir. I got a wife and a family to keep. I'm a breadwinner, Sir. I got to keep going for their sakes. Not so much for myself. For them.'

'Cohen had a wife.'

'I did.'

'Good-looker, was she?'

'She was a flower.'

'Can't say that about my Margaret. But she sees to the house and kids well enough.' He cast one last calculating glance around the room. 'Maybe two and a half on an exceptional day.'

'What?'

'Value in here.'

'Oh.'

'Well, I suppose we'd better get to business. My advice to you, Sir, is to get yourself a good solicitor. It's not for me to say, but if you have a solicitor already then he's no good. Otherwise he wouldn't have let you get into this position.'

'They're all the same.'

'Oh, no, Sir, that's where you're wrong, if you don't mind me contradicting. That's where you're quite wrong. I've been a process server for thirty-four years and I seen them all. Most are no good. Some are very good. When they're very good they work miracles. Even when the client is in the wrong. Like you, Sir.

'You got to get a good solicitor. In fact, you need a miracle-worker. Otherwise, Sir, the whole thing will be gone.'

Flowerdew looked miserable at the prospect.

'Ever seen one of these?'

He produced a legal document from his inside pocket.

'It's what we call an Originating Summons, taken out in the Chancery Division of the High Court. It's a very serious document. A document that changes lives. It's a document of great power. This document, this simple piece of paper can reduce this fine house to rubble.'

He handed the summons to me as though it were an unexploded bomb. I put it on the side table.

'If you don't answer it I shall have to return with a Notice of Appointment.'

Anticlimax. The bomb was defused. There were other legal steps to be taken.

'Whichever way, unless you get a good solicitor and take steps now, you'll lose the lot.'

He looked at me, wanting confirmation that I would follow this advice. He was disappointed.

'I don't know what it is about gentlemen like you, Sir, begging your pardon. You seem 'ell bent on self-destruction.' He began to excite himself. 'I wouldn't if I had a lovely old place like this. House, grounds, vegetable garden, park, acres, I'd give my eye teeth for it. I'd go out of my way to keep it, I would.' He shook his head. 'I'd move heaven and earth, I would.' He reached into his inside pocket again. Took out another paper. 'I seen your type before. Gentlemen, like you, 'ell bent on self-destruction.'

The prospect of my losing my estate offended his vision of how things should be.

'Just sign this, please.'

Flowerdew handed me a form. I signed it without reading it. Handed it back. Flowerdew took it, put it back into his inside pocket, sighed with satisfaction. He had, after all, just earned his daily bread.

'Some gentlemen is so difficult. Not like you, Sir. Most accommodating, if you don't mind my saying so.'

He took out a steel pocket-watch. Wound it noisily.

'Well I'd better be getting along. It's quite a walk to the village. The next bus is at six, I believe.'

I saw him out of the drawing-room, out into the hall with the red carpet that had been friend to my childish bare feet for so many summers. Flowerdew's feet fell awkwardly. However hard he tried to be respectful, and he did try, his unfriendly shoes crushed the carpet and left their mark in the nap, like footsteps on a damp lawn.

He turned at the door, took out his wallet, produced a card.

'If you ever need a bed I'll see you right. I can see you ain't going to do a thing to help yourself. Thanks for the tea. You can keep the card, you may need it.'

Flowerdew departed. I put the card in my pocket, returned to the drawing-room.

Cohen was pacing about, head down. He kept shooting glances at me. Eventually he exploded.

'He's obviously right. Your solicitor's no good. You'll have to get a different one. I know a tough little yid in Finchley. Very clever. If it's sortable, he'll sort it.' He paused briefly for breath. 'And he's right about another thing. What in God's name is the matter with you? I don't know, in the end you're much more *goy* than Jew. No self-respecting Jew would have got himself into this mess. Ever. You've got a nice place here. You're well organised. You're comfortable. Somehow, despite all that, you're determined to throw it all away.

'That nark could see it immediately. Until then I thought you might have the bottle to fight for it. Your ancestors did.'

'Listen, Cohen. I don't want the estate. Not enough to be prepared to fight for it. I'll be better off without it.'

'Why, in God's name?'

'I'm too comfortable here.'

'Madness, complete madness. It must be the *goy* in you.'

He shook his head and paced and shook his head again.

Day after day, Lady Brompton grasped the telephone in her elegantly-ringed fingers. Day after day, reluctantly, stubbornly, it responded. Sometimes she had to make several attempts but she was a determined woman and always obtained her connections in the end. Connected, she explained, urged, demanded. Soon, she had obtained commitments from enough important, landed families in the county to feel reasonably confident that the inaugural meeting of Great England would be a success.

All those who were invited were sworn to secrecy so that Lady Brompton could be sure that they would spread the word. She knew that only if she demanded confidentiality would her friends and aquaintances telephone their friends and acquaintances and tell them excitedly that they had been invited to join Lady Brompton's new political movement, what's it to be called? Great England, I think, in such terms and with such enthusiasm that those who had not yet been invited would start to send discreet signals that they too would be delighted to help in any way that they could, that they too believed it was time something was done for the landed interest, high time, that they too could think of none better than Lady Brompton to become the first President of Great England.

As the evening skies were filled with the glow of stubble fires, no-one in the county could talk of anything but Great England.

Lady Brompton decided that the inauguration of the movement should be held at the end of the summer on the weekend of the harvest festival, a celebration of particular importance to the landed.

The Victorian ballroom was prepared. Unused since Edward's twenty-first birthday party some two years before, this fine room was reawakened. The parquet floor was polished until it shone like glass. The grand cornice was dusted, as were the flowery plasterwork architraves and the mantel. The mahogany doors were washed with vinegar and then polished. Their effusive, Victorian brass door furniture was rubbed until it glowed like gold. The hollands were taken off the curtains and the sofas. Trestle tables and folding chairs were brought down from the attic. The tables were arranged in the shape of the letter E, for England, and covered with white linen cloths. The finest family china was brought out of the cellar. Cheap glasses were hired. There's no point, Lady Brompton told her Lord, letting the guests bite the rims off the crystal. Huge china vases were found, dusted and placed at appropriate intervals along the tables. Summer flowers and ears of corn were carefully arranged in them.

The *place-à-table* gave Lady Brompton a great deal of trouble. She spent many hours wondering what combination would cause the least offence. Offence there was bound to be. The skill was to direct it at those whom Lady Brompton wished to offend and to demonstrate to those whom she wished to please how much trouble she had taken to see that their neighbours at her great table were as agreeable as possible.

The Honourable Mrs Johnstone could not be put next to Major Galloper. He had made a pass at her at the hunt ball and been firmly rejected. He was after a widow's portion, in her case large, in any case. The Dowager Lady Birdgrove could not possibly be asked to sit within a mile of Cecilia Houndwood. They had quarrelled so ferociously last season and had not spoken to each other since. Cecilia was a cantankerous old maid. It would be best not to put old Broomford next to young Fredericks. Broomford was such an old gas-bag and Fredericks so hot-tempered that any argument was likely to be inflammable. When Fredericks had had a glass or two he could be violent. Still, he had one of the largest estates in the country. His presence was essential.

The table plan was drawn and redrawn. Eventually a solution was found.

* * *

Lady Brompton woke to the great day determined that all should be a success. She telephoned all her closest friends and went over their instructions again and again, particularly in relation to her appointment as President, which she intended would be by carefully-planned, spontaneous general acclamation.

She changed her dress three times before noon. Even Lady Brompton could, on occasion, exhibit nervousness.

The arrival of a reporter from the local paper, despite the absolute secrecy that was supposed to be attached to the proceedings, was not entirely unexpected. Indeed, there were those who thought that Lady

Brompton had telephoned to the Bail Gazette and offered an anonymous tip-off concerning the events that were to take place that day.

Mr Brendan, the butler, showed the reporter into Lady Brompton's study. He was given a large glass of sherry and a short preview of Lady Brompton's speech. She made sure that he noted down the important phrases correctly. She helped him, without being asked, to spell the longer words.

'You realise that I am giving you this exclusive interview because of our personal friendship. Eff, Ar, Aie, Eee, Enn, Dee, Ess, Aich, Aie, Pee.'

Friendship?

The young reporter looked at Lady Brompton with happy surprise. Vistas of important connections opened before him. Briefly. As soon as he reflected, the vistas vanished. He had never met Lady Brompton before.

She dropped obscure hints concerning the quality and importance of those that she had invited. She explained that the harvest festival was an important celebration for the landed. She urged him to consider the plight of those who had the stewardship of the nation's most precious resource.

'Land,' she added, in case he hadn't understood. 'Ell, Aye, Enn, Dee.'

She explained that the nation was crying out for leadership, that the ruling class had been prevented by Socialists, some, alas, in the Conservative Party, from doing its duty. She admitted that the government was not entirely to blame, that it was up to our traditional rulers to take up the reins again.

Ar, Eee, Aie, Enn, Ess. Reins.

As the September sun shone into her study through the thinning mists and danced in spots on the walls, Lady Brompton urged, pointed out, drew parallels, spelled words until the young man's head was stuffed to the full with golden impressions of the lofty ideals of Great England, the determination of Lady Brompton, the wealth of herself and of her friends.

* * *

The first guests began to appear just after twelve-thirty. They came in the habitual uniform of the landed. The men in grey flannel suits and suede shoes. Their striped ties proclaiming the better aspects of their education or military service, if any. The condition of their shoes proclaiming their wealth or their self-respect. The women appeared in flimsy, summer dresses and large hats. Straw, cotton, plain, bearing flowers, bearing fruit, each hat spoke for the condition and outlook of its wearer. The simple hats belonged to the other-worldly women. The expensive hats belonged to those who liked to show their wealth. The fruitful hats belonged to the frustrated ones who still wanted to bear fruit.

They all assembled on the splendid lawns with their glasses in their hands, their cigarettes in their other hands, their white teeth shining, their glances and smiles exchanging.

Lady Brompton, on the arm of her Lord, wandered beneath the shade of the great cedars. She was agreeable to some. She gave orders to others. She encouraged a few.

The sun also shone on Archie Moore as he wandered in Lady Brompton's shadow. He spoke of the House, of the Leader, of the Majority, of those frightful yobs on the other side. Everywhere he went he was careful to cultivate the most agreeable impression. And to note and memorise the names of the guests who struck him as especially important.

At one o'clock precisely Lady Brompton suggested that they might like to wander into the ballroom and be seated and by a quarter past, this complex task had been accomplished with the minimum of opposition.

The great ballroom filled with the rattle of public conversation mixed with the merry clatter of knives and forks and the sparkling tinkle of glasses. Outbreaks of laughter and the occasional snort mingled with the snapping of teeth, the scraping of plates, the chewing and swallowing of English country food.

Eventually, when the consumption had ceased, when the debris had been cleared away, well-rehearsed cries for Lady Brompton began to be heard from certain carefully-selected guests.

With becoming modesty she accepted the role of first speaker.

Lady Brompton stood. The ballroom slowly fell silent.

'I don't intend to mince my words. This is my house and we are, all of us, friends. Not only are we all friends, more important, we are all landowners. Not one among us is without an estate of some kind. Some have great estates. Some have modest holdings. But we all face the same threat.'

'Hear, hear.' The first of Lady Brompton's carefully-selected assistants performed his duty. Her audience began to relax.

'It is the landed who have made this country great. We have fought and won war after war. Against the French. Against the Spanish.

Against foreigners of all kinds. We have fought two wars in this century.'

The sheep in the park outside said, Baa, Baa. But no-one took any notice of them.

'Some of us are not sure that we should have been fighting the Germans last time. Some of us feel that Adolf Hitler may well go down in history as a man who made a noble attempt to save, not only the white man, you all know what I mean, but humankind. I know that not all of you will agree with me on this point. It's a free country. I'm entitled to speak my mind.'

Her hearers, with the exception of Archie Moore, had no obvious objection to her flirtation with Hitler's ghost.

'Not only must we protect ourselves against enemies abroad, we must defeat enemies at home, the enemy in our bosom.'

Her great bosom heaved, swarming with enemies.

'We've got to protect ourselves against the sons of Israel and the blacks.'
'Absolutely.'

This was an unexpected bonus. The speaker had not been put up to this intervention. He received a gracious smile. Archie Moore looked uncomfortable.

'There are several Jews in the government. Soon we will see black faces smiling at us from the towers of Whitehall. Blacks in high government positions, unimaginable until a few years ago, quite imaginable now. It's simply got to stop.'

This was greeted with a murmur of general agreement.

'I'm not a racialist. It's not a question of racialism. But they consume. The Jews and the blacks. They know how to eat and they know how to breed. If you see a new Rolls-Royce on the road, ten to one it's being driven by a Jew or a black. Rolls-Royce. Our lovely English car. Proud symbol of all that is best in England. The Jews and the rich blacks have priced it almost out of our reach.'

The Rolls-Royce owners present were hurriedly examining their ancestry and the colour of their skins for any aberrations.

'They consume, the blacks and the Jews. They consume our wealth and they give us nothing in return. Except more blacks and more Jews. It might have been acceptable, once, but not now. Not now they have begun to riot, to commit arson, to rape.'

The room was silent.

'Two weeks ago, in our capital city, a white girl was raped sixteen times by assorted blacks.'

She paused to allow the full horror of the crime to sink in. It did.

'These sort of people should be repatriated. Compulsorily.'

Archie Moore had not been expecting this. He looked increasingly miserable. At this stage in his career he had not realised that some of Lady Brompton's views bore an exact similarity to the less articulated views of the majority of voters.

'The Jews can return to Israel. It's not as if we haven't given them a home to go to.'

There were no objections to this blatant travesty of history.

'If our rulers hadn't been so cowardly in the fifties we wouldn't have the problem of blacks today. The blacks can go back to Africa and the Caribbean Islands where they come from.'

This last was greeted with murmurs of assent.

'Great England,' she turned to Edward, smiled generously, 'Great England will be a movement dedicated to giving England back to the English. That is our first great task. It's our country. There is absolutely no reason why we shouldn't enjoy it.'

Cheers. Archie Moore smiled wanly trying to make the best of it.

'I now turn to the matter of our estates. Successive governments have taken to squandering our wealth on handouts to people who simply don't deserve them and in many cases don't really want them. Many poor families wish that they hadn't been moved out of their terraced houses and thrust up into the sky in those ghastly tower blocks that Socialist planners built in the sixties.'

Archie Moore nodded with relief.

'Worse, in order to pay for these ever-growing handouts, the government taxes *us*. Capital taxes. Wealth taxes. Transfer taxes. There is even talk of rating farm land. This has got to stop. Our second great task.'

Lady Brompton paused as arranged. In the ensuing silence the second of Lady Brompton's assistants, the widow Slattery, lost her nerve and was unable to articulate the simple words she had promised, intended to signify her agreement. She received a penetrating stare of disapproval. Slattery cowered in silence.

'The third great task of Great England will be to ensure that there are no more depredations on our estates by way of laws that give strangers rights over our land. All the existing restrictions must be swept away. We must have an absolute right to our privacy, guaranteed by law.'

Archie Moore agreed with this. He had no difficulty with the second or third great task.

'The fourth great task of Great England will be to ensure, as far as we can, that our sons and daughters marry suitably. We are white.' Her listeners murmured their assent to this proposition. Archie Moore winced again. 'We are Anglo-Saxon.' Her listeners assented again, louder. 'We are Christian. We want to stay that way.'

This was greeted with cheers and clapping. Lady Brompton held up her hand for silence.

'In the last decade governments of both parties, I am sorry to say, have encouraged a breakdown in the natural barriers that exist between black and white, between gentile and Jew, most important, between rich and poor. These natural barriers, called class barriers by Socialists, have evolved over hundreds of years.

'Our people have got to be re-educated. Not just to be patriots once more. They must be persuaded that the social distinctions that have evolved over countless years are benign and are in their interest.

'Our people must be persuaded that it is essential that taxes on the landed are reduced and that we are left alone to do our duty. To breed the strong, healthy young men and women the country needs if it is to be governed properly. We want no more limp-wristed perverts in charge. We want no more of those inter-class marriages that have become so fashionable.

'Those are our four great tasks. We intend, through this our movement, to see that they are completed as soon as possible. Mr Archie Moore,' she bowed towards him, 'has kindly agreed to be our Parliamentary representative. We are most fortunate to have his wise counsel and his energy and devotion.'

This time the applause continued for several moments. Happy faces looked up at Lady Brompton in wonder. She had articulated their worst fears. More, much more, she had shown them a ray of hope.

Great England was on its way.

So was Archie Moore, although he did not, at that time, realise how important a part Great England was going to play in his career.

ARCHIE MOORE HAD not been in Parliament for more than a year when he decided that he needed a full-time research assistant. He advertised in The Times for an educated young man to act as his political secretary and researcher, replies treated in the strictest confidence. After interviewing a selection of spotty students, most of them American, he found a young Englishman, without spots, who had just come down from Oxford with a reasonable degree in politics, philosophy and economics.

For these reasons alone Archie Moore would have singled Staines out from the other applicants. But he had an even greater qualification. It was clear to Archie Moore that Staines had great political ambitions but did not have the presence of body or of mind to fulfil them.

The long political partnership between Archie Moore and Staines was born.

When Staines had obtained his plastic identity card which allowed him to pass into and out of most, but not all of the Palace of Westminster, when another, very small desk had been placed in Archie Moore's small office, when Staines had sat down and had had time to reflect, he proposed that they try to evolve a distinctive, appealing political philosophy of their own. A philosophy that would come to be associated with Archie Moore's name.

'Who knows, it might even come to be called Archie Mooreism.'

'What do you mean come to be called? We'll call it that ourselves from the beginning.'

'You can't do that. It'll be seen as too pretentious. We'll have to find a more impersonal name. At least to start with.'

Archie Moore agreed reluctantly.

The June days passed. The long summer recess beckoned. The creation of a distinctive and appealing political philosophy proved a more complex task than Staines had, at first, envisaged.

As a result of his research Staines discovered that the electorate was surprisingly fickle. Past election results revealed that a majority of electors had, for example, voted for the party that represented the union movement at one election and then, at the next, voted for the party that stood against the union movement. Similarly, they had voted for the party that could, broadly, be said to have represented the *haves* at one election and then, at the next, presumably overcome by some incomprehensible sense of collective guilt, they had transferred their votes to the party that represented the *havenots*.

June slipped into July. Archie Moore and Staines pondered the caprice of the electorate.

'You can't avoid identifying yourself with one or other side of the great political questions of the day.'

'Why not?'

'We're creating a political philosophy.'

'We'll explain why politicians should be above such petty divisions. We'll speak of statesmanship. We'll give them all that one-nation balls that Disraeli gave them. He's a man to study. Read him.'

'I have.' Staines allowed a modestly triumphant smile to break out.

'Well, read him again. And again until you stop making stupid statements.'

Staines' smile was extinguished. The cream-painted walls of their tiny office at Westminster were shining with condensation.

'Disraeli never bothered his head with principles. He spoke of them, yes. And changed them whenever it suited him.'

Archie Moore loosened his tie. Even though it was summer the central heating was being run generously by elected representatives determined to secure in temperature what they could not have in working-space.

'We need to evolve a philosophy of no philosophy.'

'Sounds a bit Japanese but I suppose you're right.' Staines was disappointed. He saw himself as the author of an entirely new political philosophy, a philosophy that would grip the world.

'I know, we'll call it the Philosophy of the Middle Way. It doesn't mean anything, so nobody will object.'

Staines was not impressed.

'It'll have to mean something. You can't just wander into the public gaze and spout meaningless platitudes. The practice of politics requires you to stand on your legs and speak in meaningful phrases, inside and outside the House.'

'We don't need real political ideas. Just exhortations. People don't understand the issues anyway. They're too complicated for most, including most MPs. Don't always understand them myself.'

Staines interpreted this unexpected disclaimer as a peace-offering.

'You're much brighter than most of your colleagues.'

'Course I fucking am.'

'That's why I work for you.'

Staines accepted Archie Moore's rudeness because he thought it demonstrated the kind of vitality and will to win that should be found in a nascent political leader. Besides, Archie Moore allowed Staines to answer back when he could no longer tolerate the insults.

The first solid inspiration for the Philosophy of the Middle Way came to Archie Moore some days later. He and Staines were driving to Westminster. They were sitting in traffic in Buckingham Gate.

'Pen and paper. I've got an idea.'

Staines produced his cheque-book and a *biro*.

'Ready?'

'Ready.'

'Write: First principle: All extremes are to be avoided. Got that?'

'Got it.'

Cars hooted behind them.

'The lights are green.'

'Fuck the lights.'

Archie Moore accelerated away.

'Well, what do you think of the first principle?'

Staines hurriedly put on his seat-belt.

'Yes, we are certainly not extremists. In fact, we are moderates.'

'Second principle: Extremes are the product of ideologies. Therefore ideologies are also to be avoided.'

'Look out. That lorry . . .'

'Sod that lorry!' Staines closed his eyes. His right foot depressed an imaginary brake. The car and lorry somehow passed each other without touching.

Archie Moore smiled, pleased with himself, as much for avoiding the lorry as for evolving the second principle.

'The English don't like ideology.' Staines spoke from what he hoped would be seen as the depths of his education. He also hoped that the slight tremor in his voice would not be noticed. Archie Moore ignored him.

'Third principle: The best way to get from a point A to a point B may be by a straight line on paper but in politics no line is straight.'

Archie Moore looked at Staines in triumph.

'Fucking smart, don't you think?'

They drove on, narrowly avoiding an unsuspecting pedestrian who had stepped into the street foolishly imagining that Archie Moore had stopped to let him cross.

From that day the political philosophy took shape. Eventually, Archie Moore and Staines evolved a series of formulae that were published in a pamphlet called The Politics of the Middle Way. The pamphlet offered what appeared to be a coherent political statement. On closer examination, it was, in fact, no more than a set of uncontroversial exhortations clothed in spohisticated political language.

Those Conservatives who studied the pamphlet breathed a sigh of relief. There was no discernible ideology. Ideologies were anathema to good Conservatives. As were idealogues. Archie Moore soon became known inside and outside the House as just the kind of sensible, practical man who would go far in the Conservative Party.

A WOMAN'S smile has an infinite range of expression. It can suggest innocence. It can suggest complicity. It can suggest conspiracy. It can suggest charity. It can suggest chastity. It can suggest all these and many more singly and in any combination.

Women are not each limited to a particular smile. They can change their expression to suit their circumstances. A woman who, with her smile, grips the manly strings of pity and stretches them to breaking point can, in a very few moments, offer another, very different aspect and part her lips with such lascivious pleasure that all memory of pity is washed away in a great uprising wave of lust.

Modern women, Citizen, will no doubt tell you that men are just as capable of this kind of deception.

On most occasions a woman's smile is in counterpoint to her feelings. A smoke screen.

So with Candida.

Candida's smile expressed warmth and promise of more warmth. It overtook her spontaneously. And it overtook me, regularly, utterly, so utterly that I found myself inside the warm embrace of that glad smile all down the long days and nights of that summer of our love affair. Everywhere, in cornfields beneath towering skies, in meadows of buttercups and scarlet poppies, in dark secret woodland rides, on carpets of last year's leaves.

Candida's smile illuminated all of our exchanges. Whatever I said, she smiled. Whatever I thought, it brought a smile to her lips.

We were in love. We understood each other perfectly. Her every thought was clear to me. My every dream known to her. We sailed along the long days in a daze of inexpressible happiness. Neither asked any questions of the other. There was no need. All the answers were there as soon as the question came to mind. Hour after hour. Day after day. Night after summer night.

Until one September afternoon.

The sky had changed its hue. Deeper, cooler blue. The clouds too, had changed their tone. Gone, the soft, misty grey of summer heat. Come, a cooler white, promising winter rain and winds.

Candida and I were walking in the outer park looking for mushrooms. I spotted a group of small white buttons hiding in the grass. I bent down and pulled them carefully from the earth. Their damp musk floated to my nostrils. I felt their sticky moistness on my fingers.

I was about to stand and put the mushrooms into her basket when I was suddenly, unexpectedly, overcome with a terrible fear.

I realised that I was afraid to look into Candida's face.

Moments. I looked up. She was standing over me smiling in a new and horrifying way. Gone was the delightful conspiracy. Gone was the twinkling mischief. Gone was the unashamed lasciviousness. Gone was the unique friendship that only lovers know.

In their place, a new and awful maturity. A knowingness. A terrible satisfaction.

I had never seen this look before but I recognised it, instantly.

'Have you guessed?'

I had.

'Are you pleased?'

There was no question of pleasure. Instead, reflecting, I felt a sense of relief. I had done my duty. The insistent voice of my unconceived child that had begun to call to me as soon as Candida and I had become lovers had stopped calling and focused its attention instead on the blind division of its cells in the warmth and wet of its mother's womb, on willing the execution of more and more detailed instructions as, molecule by molecule, step by step, ineluctably its form grew and developed.

'I hope it's a girl.'

It would be a boy. I had absolutely no doubt.

'I am without hope.'

'What do you mean?'

'It's going to be a boy.'

'Don't say that.'

A touch of desperation in her voice. And a dullness in her understanding. An unexpected lumpiness in her thoughts. A new weight in her step.

And mine. We had both been brought down to the surly earth and had become its servants once more.

* * *

It will come as no surprise to you, Citizen, that Lady Brompton insisted on interviewing me on the subject of Candida's pregnancy. She summoned me to the library.

The rows of books lay quietly on their shelves. Mr Brendan, the butler, brought tea and biscuits on a silver tray. He placed it on one of the tables, withdrew with a kindly smirk. He knew what I was in for.

Lady Brompton moved majestically from the fireplace to the table.

'Milk?'

'Please.'

'Sugar?'

'Thank you.'

'How many?'

'Two. Thank you.'

'Help yourself to a biscuit.'

'Thank you.'

'You haven't done very well, have you?'

There was no point in replying.

'I understand that you have no home to offer Candida. Apparently you've lost your estate.'

I stared at Lady Brompton.

'You realise that I regard you as quite unfit to be married to my daughter.'

'I quite agree, Lady Brompton.'

This threw her.

'What do you mean, you agree? I hope you're not going to jilt her. I really don't know what we're going to do with you.'

'You don't have to do anything with me. I'm going to do things with myself.'

'Don't you dare do anything without my permission. Nothing at all. Not a single step is to be taken without prior consultation. Do you hear? My daughter is irrevocably involved with you. You're a member of the family now. You simply can't act without consultation. It would be too irresponsible, even for you.'

She sipped her tea, put her cup and saucer on a side table, paced to the fireplace, stood with her back to the mantel.

'I accept that you have some excuse, since neither of your parents are alive and so cannot exert a steadying influence over you. But a man has to face his responsibilities in the end. I suppose you have no home to offer Candida?'

'No.'

Lady Brompton thought for a moment.

'Candida wants you to live on the estate. Lord Brompton has suggested the Dower House.'

I realised with an inner smile that her Lord had been deployed in this way so that if the suggestion was refused Lady Brompton would escape the insult of seeing her charity rejected.

'No thanks. It's very kind of Lord Brompton but I would rather not. We'll go to London.'

'I won't hear of such a thing. Candida won't either. You can't go to London. It's unhealthy, particularly for young children. You'll have to stay in the country. It's time you started to do what you're told by those who know better.' Her tone changed subtly. 'And who have your best interests at heart.'

I was astonished. A great feeling of comfort swept over me, despite myself. This great dreadnought wanted to protect me, for the sake of her daughter, for the sake of the unborn child, possibly even for my sake. It would never for a moment enter her head that I might prefer to fight my own battles.

'You can make yourself useful on the estate.'

There was a sense of deep, secure peace in the library.

'There will be no rent. I understand you have no money.'

'I have furniture. Some of it valuable.'

'You can't sell that. It's all that's left of your inheritance. You must pass it on to your heirs. It's not for sale.'

I crossed to the library window, teacup in hand. I could see the roofs of the Dower House through the trees on the other side of the park. A fine, small, Georgian house. Old, glowing bricks. Steep, tiled roofs. A well-kept flower garden. Space for a vegetable garden. All set in one of the most beautiful private parks in England.

Perhaps it was the pools of sunlight dancing over the dark places. Perhaps it was the smell of the old books. Perhaps the estate really was secure against a changing world.

'We could try it for a while.'

'Good, well it's all settled, then. You can move in next week. I will arrange for the estate staff to pick up your furniture. Where is it at present?'

I turned from the window, looked at Lady Brompton. She stared back, a look of kindly, innocent enquiry in her eye. She knew perfectly well that my furniture was in her stables. She had arranged to have it put there at Candida's request.

'Candida tells me that it's in my stables.'

She stood in the sunlight. Large. Stately. Determined. She was wearing a plain, dark blue, cotton suit. A long string of fine pearls. Sensible blue shoes with flat heels.

We stood face to face in her library in silence. Suddenly I realised that she was smiling. A surprising smile. Twinkling. Full of complicity and humour.

'In my stables, by God.' Lady Brompton's smile widened. I began, despite my best efforts, to smile. 'He's left his furniture in my stables and he knows that possession is nine tenths of the law.' Lady Brompton's smile became a laugh. Unable to control myself, I also started to laugh.

Both of us stood in the library, staring helplessly at each other, laughing and laughing, until salty tears streamed down our cheeks.

COHEN WAS NO more impressed with my news than Lady Brompton had been. We sat at a small, round table in the Via Vecchia, an indifferent Italian restaurant in Westbourne Grove where he ate regularly. The walls were rough-cast and had once been painted white. Long years of dust had transformed the white to grey. The floor was covered with dirty rush-matting, as were the seats of the chairs. Either side of the street-door, two large, fly-blown plants stood in great earthenware jars.

Indifferent sparkling wine was served with home-made pasta by a Signor Pantucci, who was also responsible for the sensual direction. His Signora was responsible for the rapacious accounting procedures.

We sat amid the clatter of other people's conversations, the smack of cutlery on china, the occasional mournful hiss of the coffee machine.

Sparkling wine was brought, unasked. Cohen swallowed his with relish, picked up a menu. Pantucci appeared to take our order. He stood beside our table, a contemptuous leer on his face, his pen poised over a small order-pad. His head was thrown back like a conductor waiting for his orchestra to achieve that high degree of silence that is apparently necessary before a performance can begin. It was clear that this was a ritual both men enjoyed.

'Yes?' he enquired ostentatiously. He was anxious to commence the overture. And he wanted the whole restaurant to know it. 'Yes?'

'What in God's name is Penne Matriciana?'

'For both gentlemen, sir?' Pantucci began to write.

'Stop writing at once.' Cohen spoke with desperation. 'Don't rush me. I asked what is it?'

Each time Cohen made an enquiry or called for a translation, Pantucci began to write and each time he began to write he was stopped by a strangled command from Cohen, followed, each time, with a plea for more time. And more explanation. Each plea was itself greeted by a noisy tearing-off of the paper slip from the order-pad and an expression on Pantucci's face which went as far as he dared along the path to contempt.

'The pasta is rolled into large noodles and made with a pleasing sauce of *pomodoro,* bacon and basil. No good for you, Cohen.'

'Why not?'

'You're a Jew, a God killer. You can't eat bacon.'

'Jesus was a Jew. You Romans killed him.'

Cohen ventured another enquiry and another. Eventually he was bullied into a decision. Pantucci retreated with a satisfied expression. The first round had, that day, gone to him.

'It all tastes the same, in any case. Lots of different words. The same bloody spaghetti. Who does he think he is, Proust, writing a menu like that?'

Cohen took a gulp of his sparkling wine.

'God knows why we're drinking this stuff. You've got nothing to celebrate. They'll never let you get away, those two women.'

He took another gulp of sparkling wine. This time the effervescence shot up his nose. He snorted, coughed, spluttered.

'She must be mad. A good reason for calling the whole thing off. Only a committed masochist would contemplate settling down with you. She must be off her head.'

The pasta arrived. Although the two offerings were decidedly different on paper, on the table they looked remarkably similar. Cohen attacked his food as though it were trying to escape.

'It is my duty,' he gasped through a huge mouthful, 'as your best and probably only friend, to warn you that this conjunction will leave you scarred if you're lucky, broken if you're not.' He was spitting small pieces of pasta everywhere. 'You'll never be the same again. Look at me, limping towards an uncertain future, crippled by alimony, weighed down with dirty linen.'

At other tables couples celebrating relationships in varying stages of decay. They should have served as a warning to me. One has only to look at couples sitting in restaurants, couples arguing, couples sitting in silence staring around them, couples destroying each other, actively or passively, to be put off coupling for ever.

Mesmerised by the future, I could not see the present. I looked around me and saw nothing. My mind was dominated by an indistinct but comforting amalgam of Candida, my unborn son, the Dower House, my furniture, the apparent security provided by the Bromptons' estate.

Cohen began one of his favourite dissertations.

'I can't understand why anybody has anything to do with women. You take them out for dinner. They know why. You take them home for a drink. They know why. They don't have to accept. They can say, "No, I don't want to have dinner with you. No, I don't want to have a drink in your house, you randy bastard." They can stay at home if they want. They don't have to eat their fucking heads off at other people's expense. But they do.

'They eat and eat and just as you're recovering from the shock of the size of the bill you're staring at a full glass of expensive brandy on your coffee-table and contemplating the further quantities of liquor that are certainly going to be required before there is any hope of getting their knickers off.

'You get them home and they pretend that they think you want to hear them talk. Yack. Yack. Davina is so restless. Yack. Yack. Jane is going to leave Henry. After six years. Can you imagine? Yack. Yack. What do you think of marriage as an institution? Yack. Yack. Will you take me home in the morning?

'Who cares about the morning? What about the evening. Sometimes I get so bored of their puerile conversations I get desperate and jump on them before they're sufficiently befuddled with drink to succumb. There have been some very nasty scenes.'

Rain began to fall outside. I looked through the plate-glass window, longed for the countryside, for the silent perfume of damp earth after rain.

'It takes a hard woman to fall for you, Cohen.'

'What do you mean?'

'Not exactly Captain Romantic, are you?'

'You're not the greatest prospect yourself. No house. No money. No prospects of either.'

He finished his glass, swept the crumbs and other debris of his meal from the table-cloth onto the floor.

'Women are only good for taking the *angst* away, most of it created by them in the first place. If you can't get one for free, you just have to pay. I've passed my whole life spending unbelievable fortunes on whores. All the time I'm searching for my ideal woman. Want to know what my ideal woman is?'

I nodded.

'A deaf mute.' Cohen pulled his chair closer to the table, began to enthuse. 'Imagine. Tall. Blonde. Good legs. Small breasts. A friendly figure. You know. Lascivious thighs. So far so good. You know. Many women look like that. But if I could find one who was deaf and dumb as well. Imagine. Incapable of speech. Yackproof. Deaf. I could say what I liked. She wouldn't hear a word. Above all, she'd be filled with gratitude.'

He leant back.

'And another thing. Her mother makes Hitler look like a beginner.

You can't marry into that family. They're not just anti-semitic, racist, fascist. They're backing the wrong horse. They're onto a loser. It's old hat, all that landed classes stuff. Nobody gives a toss about the landed fucking classes any more.'

He emptied his glass.

'Most landowners are busy selling their land to pay their gambling debts, or for their divorces, or for their financial incompetence. And if they're not selling, they're trying to make friends with the achieving classes. The lawns of England are littered with working-class boys who happen to be quite good at something. Riding motor-bikes, drivelling into a microphone, throwing paint at canvas. It doesn't matter what they do. If they're successful and working-class the landed snatch them up. A party doesn't go if there aren't a few tame rock stars wandering around putting the family silver into their pockets.'

Cohen sat, head slightly lowered, like a short, angry bull about to charge.

'God, I can't stand the landed fucking classes. They've lost their balls. Instead of acting like an aristocracy should, showing people how to succeed, how to behave, how to live, setting all kinds of examples, they copy the first five-minute-wonder they can find. He, of course, is only a wonder because he appeals to the lowest elements in the nation's taste.

'Lady Brompton is just as bad as the rest. There may not be any rock stars on her lawns. But she's copying a nasty, common, little Nazi the German people were foolish enough to make their dictator. I should escape while you can.'

'I didn't impregnate Lady Brompton.'

'Candida's just the same.'

Pantucci appeared again, smirking. Neither of us wanted Zabaglione.

FURNITURE POLISH, when skilfully applied, can do much more than transform the appearance of chairs and tables, side-boards and bureaux. It can transfer ownership, just as effectively as a Bill of Sale.

My furniture had been rendered unrecognisable by Candida's attentions. Each piece glowed with unaccustomed light and cleanliness. An elm windsor chair that had stood underneath the window in my bedroom had forsaken its modest friendliness and now blazed with aggressive shine. The oak cricket table from the inner hall that had provided me with seclusion and shelter when as a small boy I had wanted to hide looked quite unwelcoming now. It had lost its dark, protective colour. It was so brightly polished it looked transparent. No-one would have been able to hide for a moment inside its web of carved legs. The sofa from the morning room had been recovered. I had sat on that sofa in silence every day when, after breakfast, my father had taken himself from the dining-room to the morning-room to read the daily papers. The sofa had faded and faded in the sunlight, summer after summer, until it had become almost indistinguishable from the faded carpet. Now, it was so bright in its fashionable new chintz that I hardly dared sit on it.

Candida kept what you, Citizen, with your inescapably bourgeois way of looking at things, would consider to be a fine, orderly house. The windows sparkled. The carpets were dustless. The floorboards, where they could be seen, were scrubbed and polished. There were always well arranged vases of flowers in all the principal rooms. The kitchen was spotless.

Candida fed and wined me well. Too well. I started to put on weight. Both of us swelling, in different places. And when my longing for solitude became unbearable she encouraged me to cast my troubles away from me in the usual way, three times a week, as physiologists writing in the Sunday colour magazines suggested would be most likely to contribute to health and long life.

To escape this perfection of domestic bliss, I began to take long walks out in the friendly winter dark and refreshing cold, out, over the park, over the frosted grass, careless of unsuitable shoes, careless of wet feet, glad to be free in the enormity of the clear winter nights. Sometimes I walked alone. Sometimes the icy moon walked with me.

When I returned Candida was always waiting for me with a smile. And a glass of warm claret with cloves and cinnamon.

I had said that I especially liked mulled wine, unthinking, one evening. Now, every time that I went out at night I found it ready for me on my return. Even though I would rather have drunk whisky it was too late to change the routine. I could see from Candida's worried look that any disturbance in my habits would simply lead to an upset. I drank the claret.

Our conversations declined until the only topics that arose were practical or argumentative. As with:

She: The roof needs attention, there's damp coming into one of the attic bedrooms.

I: I'll look at it tomorrow.

She: The herbaceous ought to be cut back now.

I: I'll get round to it shortly.

She: That's what you said last week.

I: I know.

She: It was so marvellous in the summer. It would be a pity to let it go back.

I: Would it?

She: I do want baby to have a beautiful garden to play in.

I: I know.

She: It's so very important, don't you think?

I: I don't think about it.

Silence. For a moment.

She: We're so lucky, aren't we?

I: I suppose so.

She: I don't want to make a thing of it, but, don't you think you ought to be a tiny bit grateful? Not to me. Not even to my parents. To life. You know. For being so generous to us. For making us so happy.

I: No.

She: Why not?

I: It can't help it.

She: What?

I: Life.

She: What do you mean?

I: Life can't help it. What's happening to us. There's no question of gratitude to life.

She: But, darling, (I wince at this use of the first person possessive) you have to admit that you've fallen on your feet.

I: Fallen is the operative word. I need a drink.

She: There's some claret left. Shall I get it for you?

I: No. I'll do it.

She: I'm not that fat, am I?

I: I didn't say that.

She: I'm still quite capable, you know. Don't you think?

I: (Not paying attention.) What?

She: I'm still quite capable, don't you think? You know, in all respects, if you understand me.

I: I don't.

She: Don't what? Understand or think I'm capable?

I: Understand, of course.

She: (Moving close to me) Of course you do understand.

I: Oh you mean fucking?

She: I don't like that word.

I: But you like the deed.

She: Yes.

I: You used to like the word.

She: Yes.

I: What happened?

She: I don't know. Since I've been pregnant my likes have changed. And my dislikes. Things taste different. In the eyes and ears as well as in the mouth.

I: You're a prisoner of your chemistry.

She: Don't say that.

I: Why not?

She: Don't let's talk about it.

I: (Standing and beginning to pace) I want to.

She: It frightens me.

I: Question. Does the chemical change bring about the change in personality?

She: I haven't changed that much, have I?

I: Or does it simply accompany it? Is it the decision to get pregnant, conscious or unconscious, that changes a woman, or is it the impregnation that leads to subtle changes in the blood chemistry that lead to unsubtle changes in behaviour?

She: Do you think I've changed that much? I know I'm fatter. But then that's to be expected. Isn't it?'

I: Is it?
She: I wish you wouldn't talk like this. It frightens me.
I: Why?
She: I don't ... I don't know.
She bursts into tears. I drink my claret. Unhappy moments.
I: For goodness' sake, stop crying.
She: I'm sorry.
I: It's not a crying matter.
She: I know. I'm sorry. I'm much more weepy than I used to be. It's the baby.
I: No son of mine will be weepy.
She smiles. Moves closer to me.
She: You are pleased, aren't you?
This, Citizen, is where weakness comes in. I allow myself to tell a series of what you would call white-lies. All lies are, of course, black.
I: Of course.
She: I don't want to be a burden on you.
I: I know.
Note her mendacity, Citizen. Of course she wants to be a burden on me. And note my cowardice in the face of her huge hurt.
She: That's why I haven't put any pressure on you to marry me.
I: I know.
She: Despite my parents.
I: I know. Very brave of you.
She: Tell me you're pleased about the baby.
I: Of course I am.
She: It might be a girl.
I: It won't.
Silence. More unhappy moments.
I: I think I'll go for a walk.
She: Now? But it's so late.
I: I like walking in the night. You know I do.
She: Why don't you stay in with me, tonight? We could watch television.
I: Let me go.
She: You'll do what you want, anyway. You always do.
I: Would you want it otherwise?
She: It would be better than nice if you were to stay here with me by the fire this evening. Just once. To please me.
I: But it should please you if I'm doing what I want.
She: It does. Of course. Go. I quite understand.

It doesn't please her. Of course. And, of course, she doesn't understand.

I depart with relief out of the fog of this emotional pressure into the clarity of an icy night.

LADY BROMPTON DISCOVERED that the practice of politics was not without cost. On those weekdays from September to February when, frost permitting, she had habitually been transported together with her horses from Norfolk to Leicestershire to boom at horsemen who dared to ride in front of her and hounds that dared to ignore the scent, now she stayed in her great house and shouted into the telephone at politicians who dared to contemplate acts, legislative and executive, that she considered to be against the landed interest. With the same voice that carried so well across meadow and moor, often using the same volume. And in much the same uniform. For she insisted on exercising one of her horses herself early every morning and she was almost always prevented from changing out of her riding clothes on her return by the demands of the telephone which invariably began to ring before she had finished her breakfast.

As it became clear that Great England was going to succeed, beyond even her wildest expectations, Lady Brompton found that success brought a glow to her cheeks and a sparkle to her eyes. This had an immediate effect on her spouse.

And on Edward. As Great England progressed Edward noticed that something in his father's life was changing. He knew that it was connected with his mother. He knew that it was to do with the relationship between his mother and his father. But, at first, he had no idea what it was.

Some weeks after Edward, Candida noticed the changes in her father. She brought the matter up with her mother at the first opportunity.

Mother and daughter sat together in mother's regency-striped dressing-room on an early summer evening, an early daylight moon flying high above.

'Daddy's looking a bit down at heel, these days. Is there something wrong?'

'Down at heel?'
'A bit knackered. You know.'
Lady Brompton hadn't noticed.
'Do you think?'
'I do. Is he all right?'
'Absolutely.'

There was something in the way her mother affirmed Lord Brompton's allrightness, with such relish, that alerted Candida. Alerted, she was determined to pursue the matter as far as she could.

'Absolutely?'
'Your father is very well.'
'Are you sure?'
'Yes, I am quite sure. Why do you ask?'
'There seems to be something different between you two.'
'Does there.'

Lady Brompton was on her guard. She tried a feint.

'Oh my dear child, you're not worried . . . no you can't be . . . you're not worried about things between your father and I, surely?'

Candida permitted herself to be taken along this diversion. It might, after all, yield some further discovery.

'Is everything well between you, you know, are you two getting on all right?'

'We're not getting divorced. If that's what you mean.' Lady Brompton parried.

Candida was much too clever to be deceived.

'No, I'm sure you're not. It never entered my head.' She tried a thrust. 'There's no point. You're both beyond affairs and things like that.'

It got through her mother's guard.

'What do you mean? I'm not too old to have an affair.'
'With your husband?'

Lady Brompton started. She realised, with some motherly pride, that her perceptive daughter had understood. There was no point in dissembling any further.

'Yes,' she said in a flirtatious voice, 'with my husband. Who could be a better partner for an affair.'

'Indeed.'

Candida smiled at her mother, more out of triumph than affection. The sunlight dappled the ceiling and walls with warm spots of glow. Mother and daughter stared at each other for a few moments. Outside, the long evening quietly lengthened.

* * *

Candida wasted no time in conveying her newly-discovered secret to Edward. Not because she was indiscreet. Like most women, she was capable of great discretion. Not because she felt that Edward needed to be informed. Indeed, her feelings for her brother were limited to formal affection as prescribed by the social demands of her family. She defended him in public when he needed defending, for her own sake and, in private, also for her own sake, felt mild, friendly contempt for him.

Candida found all thoughts of her parents' physical conjunction startling and disgusting. She wanted to share this latest intelligence on the matter with another. To spread it a little thinner so that it wouldn't hang quite so heavily over her.

Candida found Edward alone in the library waiting for dinner. He had changed and was standing very still, back to the fireplace.

Candida swept in.

'Have you noticed how exhausted Father's been looking lately?'

Edward's habitual calm had been disturbed the moment Candida had come into the room. This was not usually the case. The friendly stone that he carried in his head had long been pressed into service to protect him from his sister's boisterousness, from the mild contempt he knew that she felt for him.

This evening her entrance had penetrated all his defences. He realised, as soon as she opened the door and their eyes met, that she intended to speak to him and he saw immediately that what she would say would disturb him. He also knew that he could do nothing to prevent it. There was an inevitability about Candida's entrance, a determination in her approach to him that he knew he was powerless to resist.

'He's all right.' Edward vainly tried to dismiss the subject.

'I'll say.'

Edward winced at the vulgarity, not of her words but of her tone.

'Do you know what? They're enjoying some kind of an Indian summer. Extraordinary at their age.'

Edward did not know what an Indian summer was. Candida's words came at him with sharp edges and blunt surfaces. They cut and hurt him.

'Extraordinary, why?'

Edward listened dully to himself asking a question that he knew would lead to more hurtful words.

'Come on, Edward. Don't be stupid. They're both facing their sixties. They've both lived peacefully in their own worlds, in their own ways, in their own bedrooms for as long as both of us can remember.

Suddenly they're doing it like rabbits. It's extraordinary.'

The vulgarity helped Candida to feel better. The immediate effect it had on Edward helped her even more. She saw at once that he was troubled. She watched her own trouble transferring some of itself to him.

'Well don't look so startled, for goodness' sake.'

But Edward was profoundly startled. Candida's words had undone the work of years. They had tossed his stone right out of his head. A terrible, graphic vision wandered into the space it left behind.

'You won't tell anybody about our conversation, will you?'

Edward looked at her helplessly. He had not heard her last words. All his senses were focused on the terrible vision of his parents, white, naked, doing unspeakable things to each other.

A new feeling was rising in him. Anger. Anger against his parents. And against Candida. He looked at Candida. She had caused his distress. She had caused the pain that he felt somewhere in the region of his belly. She had caused the debilitating chaos that had invaded his mind.

'Say you won't, Edward.'

The blood was rushing to his head. He was feeling hot. He knew that if he didn't escape he would do something terrible. With a supreme effort he turned slowly on his heel, stepped slowly out of the room, out into the passage, out, through the garden door, into the cool evening air.

Dew on the ground glowing faintly white. He strode across the lawn, towards the park. The high-flying moon was white. The trees towered darkly overhead. He began to run towards the oakwood at the top of the grassy hill. He ran and ran until finally, out of breath, trembling, he came to the bramble-bushes that surrounded the clearing where his stone lay.

He found the break in the bushes. Plunged in and down the slope. He rushed down, regardless of the thorns, regardless of his clothes, regardless of the blood that soon appeared on his hands and his legs.

At last, he emerged into the clearing. The stone stood in its place, huge, silent, friendly in the moonlight. He threw himself on it. He threw his arms around it. He pressed his cheek against it. He inhaled great lungfuls of its friendly smell.

An estate farmworker discovered him beside the stone the following morning. He was sleeping peacefully.

* * *

Although Edward wrestled mightily with his stone and eventually got it back into his head, he did not succeed in recapturing the grace of his former mental state.

Edward was naturally thin and pale with wispy, sandy-coloured hair. He began to look even paler. And thinner. His hair began to be even wispier.

It is unlikely that Lady Brompton would have noticed any change in Edward's pallor or in his hair of themselves but she soon noticed that he was losing weight as she would have done had one of her horses begun to lose condition.

She consulted Archie Moore as they sat on the terrace after breakfast.

'Something's wrong with Edward.'

'Oh?'

'He rushed out a few days ago, without a word.'

'Probably his age.'

'Possibly.'

'He'll get over it.'

'I don't know. He slept out in his dinner-jacket. Something about a stone.'

'A stone?'

'Yes.'

'Odd.'

'He's losing condition.'

'What do you think it is?'

'I don't know.'

'Body or mind?'

'Could be either.'

'Why not send him to a psychiatrist. They can work wonders these days?'

Edward was sent to a psychiatrist in Harley Street. The psychiatrist soon discovered Edward's peaceful stone. He located it in Edward's frontal lobes and offered to demolish it by a course of electric shock treatment.

Lady Brompton, once she had been informed of the psychiatrist's discovery, decided that a stone in the head must be an impediment to normal life. She accepted the psychiatrist's offer to demolish it, on behalf of her son, who, even though he had reached the age of responsibility, had, by then, been adjudged by two other psychiatrists to be incapable of deciding anything for himself.

LADY BROMPTON'S DECISION that Edward should have electric shock treatment, a decision accepted by all members of her family, with or without misgivings it matters not, convinced me that I must escape. Not just Candida's suffocating embrace. Not just the breathlessness of living off another's charity. Although the Bromptons represented the standards by which sanity was set for most people, their treatment of Edward made me realise that the Bromptons were irretrievably mad. All of them. Except, of course, Edward.

When Candida told me of her mother's decision, I said nothing.

'You might show a bit of interest. I know he's stupid but he is my brother.'

We were eating dinner.

'The treatment may make him better.'

'It's not very nice for me.'

'You're not being treated.'

'To have a mad brother.'

'Oh, I see what you mean.'

She looked at me over a forkful of shepherd's pie. Candida's suspicions should have been aroused at this. I would not normally have let her get away with such selfishness.

'We're lucky to have each other.' She smiled in a possessive way and allowed her attention to return to her food.

I wondered if I should try to rescue Edward. His parents would be furious if I was caught. So would Candida. We probably wouldn't get far but it might, at the very least shock his family into reconsidering. It would be cowardly not to try. By the time we had finished dinner I had made up my mind.

I went upstairs to our bedroom on the pretext of getting another pullover, got the other pullover and took two hundred pounds from the purse that Candida kept in her underwear drawer in case of emergencies. It was an emergency as far as Edward was concerned although I knew that Candida wouldn't see it like that.

Presently, I told Candida that I was going out for my customary walk. After the usual attempt to persuade me to change my mind, that night, just for once, and my usual refusal, I stepped out into the cool spring night, headed across the park.

The great house lay brooding in the darkness. A light shone from Lady Brompton's bedroom on the south front. Another from Lord Brompton's bedroom beside it. Edward's room was on the east side above the ballroom. It was also lit. I skirted carefully round the yew hedge on the front lawn to the ballroom terrace.

An owl called.

Edward's room had two windows. I went to the corner where the ballroom was joined to the house. A large drainpipe ran up to the distant roofs. I climbed it without difficulty and, halfway up, managed to step off onto the flat roof.

Edward's curtains were not quite closed. A crack of light shone out into the night. I put my eye to the crack and looked in. Edward was in bed, alone.

I tapped on the window. He looked round, smiled, waved, climbed out of bed, came over to the window. In a moment he had opened the bottom half of the sash and I was in his room.

I put my finger to my lips. He nodded. I looked at the door. He shook his head. There was a key beneath the handle. I crossed silently to the door, turned the key.

Edward stood in striped, flannel pyjamas, smiling at me. I realised again how much I loved him.

'I thought I'd pay you a visit,' I whispered.

'How kind.'

We stared at each other in silence for a few moments.

'You're not mad, Edward.'

'I know.'

'I have never for a moment, thought you were.'

'I know. Neither have I.'

He smiled.

'You've got to get away. I've got some money here.' I produced the money from my back pocket, waved it at him. 'Let's take off. Let's just walk away. Let's go on the road. It's a good time of year. Summer's coming. It's easy on the road in the summer. We can go north. We can go to the Borders. Nobody'll find us there. It's wild country. It'll be great on the road. Sleeping out. Living rough. Just us.'

He looked at me in a kindly way, as though I didn't understand. There was a touch of condescension in his eyes.

'I can't.'

'You can't?'
'I couldn't. Especially with you.'
'Why not, for God's sake?'
'Surely, you of all people understand?'
I did not understand.
'It would upset them all too much.'
'They're going to upset you.'
'They mean well.'
'No they don't, not really. They don't have any idea about you, Edward, they don't understand you at all.'
'But then, why should they? Why should they understand me?'
I stared at him in horror.
'You're your mother's son, your sister's brother.'
'It's too difficult for them.'
'I understand you. I'm not your mother or your father or your sister. I also understand that the treatment that they intend for you will do you no good.'
'Oh yes it will. It'll do me the good of making them feel better about me. They are my family, after all.'
I felt cold.
'It's really decent of you to come here like this. But I'm going through with the treatment.'
'Do you know what it is?'
'Yes.'
I realised that there was nothing I could do. I put the money back into my pocket, turned towards the window.
'You don't have to go yet.'
'I do. I can't stay, Edward.'
'I understand.'
I put out my hand, touched him gently on the shoulder.
'Stupid bastard.'
'I understand.'
I was desperate to leave. And desperate to stay.
'I must go.'
'Yes.'
'I'd love to stay and chat.'
'You'd better go, I'm not supposed to see anybody.'
I crossed to the window, climbed up onto the old cast-iron radiator. As I was about to step out onto the roof I turned. Edward was still smiling but tears had begun to roll silently down his cheeks.
'I've always loved you, Edward.'
'I know.'

FOUR

PALE GRAVEL PASSED smoothly beneath my feet. I walked along the deep east-coast lanes, north in my face. Lime trees, ash trees, dark oaks, walked silently beside me.

I was free. Not just to inspire the full delight of early summer. Not just to breathe in the gentle strength of the country silence. I was free from the parents that bore me, from the education that had tried to make me conform, from the woman that had kept me warm, from the child that otherwise would have flattered and confused me with intimations of immortality, from all the ties of the society of which you, Citizen, are an integral and acquiescent part.

White butterflies fluttered unpredictably by. The air was beginning to be warm and full of the pleasure of long days. An enormous, uncontrollable grin began to overtake my face.

For uncounted days I walked up the east coast, through fields of poppies and hare-bells, beside meadows of cowslips and buttercups. By day, the sun walked with me. At night, I slept under hedgerows.

Eventually, the unmistakable pallor of the northern skies appeared and I came to the moors. Above me, the mountains lay silent. Their shapes like the limbs of a sleeping woman. I began to climb along a path made by the occasional walks of sheep and deer. The bell-heather was in full flower. Bright purple, brighter by far than the most imperial robe and more noble in its simplicity, its purity, its clarity of purpose. Occasional breezes picked up the dust of the peat hags and threw it into tiny tornados. From time to time mountain hares inspected me, standing on their hind-legs, twitching their whiskers in an effort to pick up my scent. Startled grouse clucked their young into flight, rolling and sailing away on the wind.

I followed the course of a river, up and up, until it narrowed into a stream. Finally, I came to a loch that appeared to be the river's source. The water was as smooth and silent as glass. Beside the loch, a scraggy

Rowan tree had somehow managed to make a poor living. Evening was approaching.

I sat down and contemplated a small beach of silver pebbles that I fancied had never known the presence of man. A huge, palpable peace lay everywhere around me. Presently, I began to hear the first, faint whisper of the lovely black silence of eternity beckoning me towards the unreachable source of all creation. I sighed at last.

* * *

I walked in the heather and bracken for several days. Then, late one morning, I saw a small gathering of caravans and tents in the distance below me. A country fair. The tents glistened in the sunlight. Flags fluttered. The narrow lanes were full of horse-boxes and cars sliding along like tiny, glistening beetles.

As I looked down, I was overcome with a nervous excitement that I had not felt since I had left Candida. I had managed to avoid all but the briefest human contact on the road. Whenever strangers had waved at me, mistaking me for a friend or an acquaintance, I had lowered my head and walked on. When shopkeepers had begun to ask me questions, I had smiled and remained silent.

My first reaction to the fair was to hurry higher up into the hills. But after an hour or so, I felt more and more tempted to go down. I stopped and sat down on a stony hillside to reflect.

Did I really want to be amongst people? Would they stare at me and make trouble for me? Would the police make trouble for me? I was not a very pretty sight. My hair was matted. My beard had grown. My trousers were torn. My shoes were down at heel. But I wouldn't be the only scruffy one. Farmers and cowherds were not likely to be very tidy. There would be quite a few people whose clothes were just as bad as mine. Who knows, there might be others who were living as I and who, as I, were attracted to the fair? Besides, the police would have no time to interfere with me. They would be busy directing traffic, looking for pick-pockets, snatching a quick cigarette.

I decided to abandon my solitude for a few hours and go down into the valley.

The fair was arranged around a central ring in which the bulls and the cows, the rams and the ewes, the billies and the nannies, the boars and the sows were to be paraded before the judges. On one side of the ring a large tent had been erected to provide a restaurant and a bar. On the other sides were smaller tents and caravans for the companies who had sponsored the fair and who hoped to sell their products to the fairgoers. There were shiny new tractors, red, blue, green, yellow. Huge combine harvesters that looked far too big for the small fields of the area. Great ploughs and cultivators that looked as though they could have tilled half of the world. There were stalls selling horse equipment, stalls selling pet food, stalls selling office equipment, stalls selling lawn-mowers.

At first, as I wandered in the crowd, I felt nervous. The noise was great. People were shouting. Tractors and other machines were roaring. Bulls bellowed. The sounds were much louder than I had imagined that they would be. Every glance that was directed at me was more aggressive than I had expected, every stare more comprehensive. But I soon realised that this sensitivity was the creation of my solitude and that no-one was making any more noise than usual nor taking any more notice of me than of any one else.

I stood at the ringside and watched the farmers showing their cattle. I saw bulls that were so clean they must have been shampooed. I saw sheep with such tidy fleeces they must have been combed. I saw charming pigs with friendly twinkling eyes and well-scrubbed skins.

The judges stepped carefully among the exhibits in their suede shoes, their country suits, their bowler-hats. The farmers, in long brown coats, paraded their charges with such pride they could have been showing-off their children. Eventually, the judges came to their conclusions. The notables presented the prize cups to the winning owners. The rosettes were pinned to the winning animals. Smiles were offered to the losers.

I wandered away to the south of the ring where young women were exercising their horses before entering for the equestrian events. Small girls on small, fat ponies. Larger girls on larger horses. They were all immaculately turned out according to the custom of the area. They wore tight, buff breeches, dark green or black riding coats, boots to their knees. Their hair was plaited and beribboned just like the manes and tails of their horses.

Their anxious mothers wandered beside them giving advice. 'Mind you keep him well up as you go into the five-barred gate.' 'Don't turn too tight.' 'Keep your back straight, the judges look at the riders as well as the horses.' And encouragement. 'You look smashing, darling. Don't worry about a thing.' 'Of course, he will, he could jump a haystack if he was ridden at it.'

Everywhere I went I sensed the happiness of these country people. Their world was a friendly and predictable place. Their lives were governed by the routines imposed on them by their animals and crops. In the morning the sun rose. In the evening it set. They fed their animals by day and slept at night. In the spring they planted. In the summer they harvested. In the autumn they ploughed. They had no intention of letting their lives be disturbed.

As the afternoon slipped towards evening I began to feel a distant sense of unease. At first, I assumed that the crowds were beginning to oppress me. Then I realised that a small voice had begun to call me. A small, beseeching, voice. At first I tried to resist it but it would not be ignored. I realised that my son had emerged into this troubled world and wanted his father.

I was caught entirely off-guard. I had considered, in the fullness of my own solitude, that my son would be as solitary as his father. That he would have as little need or desire for his father as his father thought he had for him. I had always assumed that I could bring nothing to him but confusion and trouble.

But my son was calling for me. There was no doubt. And there was no doubt that I could not answer his call. To answer his call would be to destroy myself.

Even so, as the hours passed in this happy crowd, as I watched mothers and fathers with children in prams, in arms, in cars, as I saw their tender looks, their secret smiles, their gentle touches, my eyes longed for a sight of my son. My hands longed for a touch of his skin. Even my ears, usually so passive, seemed to stretch out for a sound of his sleeping breath. I felt increasingly desperate to know what he was feeling, how he viewed the world that I had caused him to be born into, what sensations his skin was registering, what shape he was growing into, what his own unique presence was making of the war of existence.

As I wandered among the crowds I began to dream of my son being on the road with me, strapped high up on my back, sleeping to the rhythm of my walk. I dreamed of taking my son in my arms in the evening and rocking him gently to sleep. I dreamed of us waking together, stretching out our arms and touching the morning face of God, picking up our things and stealing quietly away through the mist.

Not just to be with him. I dreamed of teaching him country things. To see the track in the grass where a fox had passed. To recognise the strange roar of a fallow buck in the autumn. To hear the faint, white whisper of wild ducks' wings in the winter.

And I dreamed of teaching him about the world of men. How to be a solitary like his father, if that was his wish, or how to be a member of a crowd and derive the greatest benefit from it, if that was his wish.

The fairgoers began to pack up their charges and make for home. Bulls were persuaded into cattle trucks. Horses were walked into horseboxes. Judges were taking off their bowler-hats and climbing into their estate-cars. Farmers and farm-workers were drinking and arguing in the bar. Girlfriends and wives were smoking and smiling. Salesmen were looking satisfied.

The manifest happiness of these people began to offend me. Their satisfied smiles made me angry. It was this crowd as much as any crowd that was keeping my son from me. The rules that they lived by were the rules that kept us apart, however ancient and widely respected.

I realised that I wanted to make a demonstration. I wanted to stand on a box and explain to them that I held them personally responsible, each one of them, for the pain that I was feeling. I wanted to shout accusations at them until they put their hands over their ears. I wanted to take them by their throats, each one of them, and explain that they were committing a terrible crime against me and my son, a crime that I would certainly avenge.

I made no demonstration. Instead, I stole away back up onto the moors to rediscover my solitude.

INMATES OF THIS hospital are paid a small weekly allowance so that they can arrange for their keepers to purchase tobacco, soap, other essentials. It is supposed to engender a sense of bourgeois responsibility. I never spend mine. Candida brings me all the little things that I need. Since I do not have any cause to spend the money, I find that it accumulates. Not simply. I lend it out to the more improvident members of the staff at a modest rate of interest. Not because I have regard to the parable of the talents or to sound commercial practice. By lending it to the staff I am encouraging them to break the rules. In this way, egged on by their needs and my willingness to fulfil them, the staff are taking the first, small steps towards rebellion.

This doubly fruitful activity began some years ago when I discovered, from an interrogation of Alexander's eye at the Judas-hole one morning, that all was not well with him. I waved for him to come in. After a few questions I realised that he was short of money. I offered to lend him some of mine. After making the usual protestations and loudly citing rules forbidding hospital officers to borrow from inmates, he accepted ten pounds, until the end of the month, at two per cent per month, an equivalent rate of twenty-four per cent per annum.

He repaid me on due date. I put the principal and the interest in my cupboard beside my bed. Then, some months later, Alexander asked me if I would like to lend to another orderly, Hugo. I agreed, on terms. Soon, others were borrowing and, with Alexander as my agent, I had laid the foundations for a sound business which continues to flourish to this day.

Last week, inadvertently, the hospital authorities, in the person of the Senior Medical Officer, discovered this enterprise. Instead of sacking Alexander and the others he praised my initiative and said, 'You should have gone into business. It would have saved us all a lot of trouble.'

The authorities often respond to rebellion by legitimating it.

* * *

I did go into business, of a kind, with Cohen.

I arrived at Cohen's small mews house above the Lad Brook on a warm October afternoon and explained that I was homeless.

He received this intelligence with great good-humour, offered me a sofa to sleep on and, as an earnest of his hospitable intentions, made me a mug of tea.

'So you've taken my advice at last and run out on those two women? They would have been the end of you if you'd stayed with them. Hitler and Goering, Stalin and Beria, not one of the great oppressor-two-acts in history have got a thing on Lady Brompton and her daughter.'

'You're still a misogynist, I see.'

'Me? Certainly not. I'm the last of the great fucking romantics.'

He took a gulp of his hot tea, winced as it burnt his mouth.

'A mother and daughter team is always the most deadly. The mother daunts while the daughter flirts. The mother makes the plans, the daughter executes them. Experience applied to the creation of strategy, youth and charm to its execution. Deadly.'

I found Cohen's misogyny disturbing. It was so unrelenting it made me feel the first glimmerings of sympathy for women in general and Candida in particular. The very last feeling that I wanted to entertain. I decided to divert him.

'How about a game of chess?'

Cohen liked to play chess. He regarded it as an excuse to demonstrate the more aggressive aspects of his personality. I did not. I found it too revealing. Despite this, I decided to indulge him. I knew that it was the only way to get him to stop his endless tirades against women.

Cohen attributed his imaginary skill as a chess-player to his racial characteristics. 'Only Jews and Russians can play chess. I'm a Russian Jew. That's why I play such good chess.'

Day after day, we sat amid his dirty washing, listening to very loud rock music and playing chess. Very quick games in succession, games that I won more often than I lost, without any great difficulty. I was acquainted with Cohen's habits of mind.

We sat, day after day, playing faster and faster. The more Cohen lost, the more frustrated he became and the more he insisted on playing again. The more he insisted on playing again, the more he insisted on playing quickly. The quicker he played, the more certainly he lost.

Until I allowed myself to make a foolish mistake. If he noticed it, he would seize on it and attack with such reckless delight it was all I could do to make sure he won.

'I could have been National Champion if I had studied earlier, under twenty-ones, maybe. I could have been in contention. Come on move, for fuck's sake. Don't take so long.'

I moved. And I won. And Cohen insisted on another game. Day after day, until one day he suggested that we go into business together and, for a time, we ceased our chess-playing.

* * *

Rainy London outside. Inside, the gas fire provided inadequate heat. We sat in our overcoats. Cohen had just won a game.

'You realise it was my knight-ploy got you. Right, that's it. Enough. I want to talk to you about the business we're going to begin.'

I stepped over to the gas-ring, picked up the kettle, took it to the tap, filled it with water. He stood up, paced with his customary limp. That day on his left leg. It could as easily have been his right. He had a mysterious ailment that from time to time struck one or other of his legs. Fortunately, it never attacked both legs at the same time.

'You're a clever fucker. At least you think you are. But you're not so clever as Cohen. I've worked it all out. All the figures, monthly budgets, pro-forma profit and loss, balance sheet.'

Cohen was getting so excited he looked as though he was going to burst out of his overcoat.

'We can't fail. You know why? We both have brains. Mine's entirely Jewish, yours is sullied by your gentile blood. No matter, we'll make the best of it. I'm going to make you financial controller. What do you think of that?'

'What is the business going to do?'

'Don't go so fast. First, I need a commitment from you, a wholehearted, uninhibited commitment. You can't go into business with someone else, even your best friend, unless they're utterly committed. Just say, yes.'

'Yes.' I was touched by his describing me as his best friend.

'Again. More committed.'

'Yes.'

He looked at me, apparently satisfied.

'What is the great quest of my life?'

'Chess Champion of the World.' I had no difficulty in answering.

'That's where you're quite wrong. You think you know me. You don't. Not as well as you think. Try again.'

The kettle was boiling.

'You hope to find a deaf-mute female.'

'That's more like it. A deaf-mute female who will be grateful to me.

That's what I want above all things, what I'd give anything for. I've come up with a gem, an idea that will not only lead me to my ideal woman but will make both of us rich.'

I handed him a mug of tea. He took a noisy gulp.

'Know what, we're going to start a model agency. The Elite Agency. I thought of the name last night. What do you think of it? It's a great name, isn't it?'

'Elite?'

'Show a bit of fucking enthusiasm. Elite. Can't you see the discreet, brass name-plate on the door? Elite. Can't you see the copper-plate letter-head? Elite. I've just told you how I'm going to make you richer than your wildest dreams and you don't turn a hair.'

'What is the Elite Agency going to do?'

'We're going to send silly tarts to photographic sessions and take a commission. I've got a couple of friends who are photographers.'

'How will this help you in your quest?'

'God, you're thick today. Eventually, when we get well known, when there are hundreds of girls on our books and thousands of pounds in our bank account, when we both have chauffeur-driven limos, one sultry afternoon, a woman will walk into our plush offices in Mayfair, the woman, the one I've been longing for all my life. She will come into my room and ask me to take her onto my books.'

'How will she ask you if she's a deaf-mute?'

'Don't be so fucking pedantic.'

He took another gulp of his tea.

'Sign language, of course. I'll have learned deaf-and-dumb sign language, by then. Listen. Look. Imagine.'

He started to stride about.

'Me behind a big, reproduction-antique desk, here,' he pointed to a spot on the floor, 'wall-to-wall carpet everywhere,' he indicated a great sweep of carpet exceeding the modest dimensions of his room, 'patterned, heavy curtains there.' He waved to indicate two enormous windows, looking, no doubt onto St James's Park. 'Me sitting with my feet up.'

He paused, looked at me to make sure I was paying attention. 'A beautiful woman walks in, smiles modestly. I take the cigar out of my mouth, speak to her. She smiles with charming incomprehension.

'I realise that she has come, that the woman I've been longing for has come, at last. I lift my hands and with a few swift gestures introduce myself. She is surprised that I can use sign language. She introduces herself, also in sign language. Our hands speak. Soon, my hands say 'I love you'. With a couple of deft strokes of her delicate hands, she sends a suitable but modest signal in reply. A few more hand signals from me, a few more replies from her and you,' he started to grin, 'you'll be on your knees, begging me to translate because you'll be desperate to know every detail of what's going on.'

I laughed.

'Don't laugh, I'm serious. It'll work. The Elite Agency. We're on our way, boy.'

As the Elite Agency rose in Cohen's dreams, the sun slipped quietly below the London roofs, abandoning the city to winter cold and damp.

THE BUSINESS BEGAN badly. Cohen insisted that we had to have capital. Neither Cohen nor I had any capital. Accordingly, it had to be borrowed. I suggested that if Cohen really felt capital essential, he should ask his mother to find it in return for shares in the enterprise. He refused, on the ground that he wanted to be independent of his family.

For two weeks we made no progress. Then Cohen found a money lender in Paddington who was foolish enough to lend him two thousand pounds in cash. The first foolishness. The money lender found in Cohen a man who was foolish enough to borrow at a rate of interest equal to five per cent a month. The second foolishness. Both should have known better.

Cohen came into the flat in high spirits that evening.

'I've got it.'

He took four shiny, plastic envelopes from his overcoat pockets, dropped them onto the kitchen table.

'You're the financial controller, count it.'

I counted one hundred dirty, twenty-pound notes.

'Two thousand.'

'Exactly?'

'Exactly.'

'Good, now we're moving.'

'What do you need all this for?'

'We can't get into business without front. It'll buy some for us. We need proper clothes. You'll have to wear a suit. And we'll have to take clients out to lunch, to a proper place. The Hilton, probably. We can't expect our clients to put up with Pantucci. We'll have to pay ourselves proper salaries. People won't respect us unless we do.'

'What about the girls? Where are you going to get them from?'

'Leave that to me. I'm managing director. You're financial controller.'

The flat was transformed. An Irish painter came and slapped magnolia paint everywhere. Next a dealer in carpet remnants arrived with a charcoal-coloured cord-carpet. Then, two men struggled up the narrow stairs cursing and sweating with three enormous packages which they eventually managed to manoeuvre into the room. They took off the protective plastic sheets and erected a reproduction antique desk large enough for four men. Cohen gave them a fiver. They departed. Finally, two shiny, red telephones arrived, were placed on the desk and connected.

Cohen and Dov were also transformed. Cohen purchased two new suits. His was black. Mine was grey. And two new pairs of shoes. His were black without laces. Mine were black with laces.

Cohen organised our days on a rigorous schedule. We would get up at about eight, perform our ablutions, dress in our new suits and shoes. At about half-past eight we were ready to confront the working day. My first task was to put the kettle on. My second, to go out and get the newspapers.

By the time I returned with the newspapers, Cohen had made the tea and laid the cereals out on the kitchen table. We both sat eating and reading. Cohen had usually loosened his tie by then.

'Sterling's weak again. The market's taken a tumble.'

'Will it affect our business?'

'Of course it will. All businesses are sensitive to market changes.'

'In what way?'

'If all the indicators are plunging, people won't spend so much on advertising. If they spend less on advertising they hire less models. Don't worry about the strategy, you just concentrate on the bookkeeping.'

After breakfast Cohen insisted on playing one or two games of chess to sharpen his appetite for business, as he put it. Finally by eleven o'clock, he was ready to go out.

'I've got to go and talk to my clients. Look after the 'phone. Remember, you must note the time of each call and the number of each caller, as well as his name. Put it in the book.'

He had bought an accounting book for the accounts, a book for telephone messages and a box of blue biro-pens. One of these was issued to me together with the two books so that I could keep the accounts and write down the telephone messages.

But Cohen controlled all the finance by the simple expedient of keeping the money in his pocket and no-one ever telephoned, except strangers who had got wrong numbers.

* * *

Every evening Cohen would return and ask me if there had been any telephone messages. There had not. The Elite Agency had no custom because it had no clients. And it had no clients because Cohen didn't know and didn't want to know any girls.

Every evening, on his return, I would ask him how he was getting on with the girls. Every evening he refused to reply. Eventually, I confronted him.

'You can't get your business going without girls.'
'I'm not daft.'
'I guess you're down to five hundred pounds and the interest is due next week.'
'I know. You don't have to tell me.'
'You must get some girls.'
'Where?'
'Pick them up.'
'How?'
'Accost them.'
'Accost them? Accost them?'
He looked wildly at me. Then he smiled.
'Accost them. Why not? You're not as much of a *schlamiel* as you look. Accost them. OK, let's go. I've got the *chutzpah*. We'll go to a high-class pub and see if we can pick up a couple of *shikses*. We'll go to the bar in the Hilton.'
'When?'
'Soon.'
'Tomorrow?'
'Not tomorrow. Maybe the next day.'
'Right.'

The days passed. The telephone was silent. We began to play chess in the afternoons. Winter turned to spring.

I decided to confront Cohen once more, to make a last effort to persuade him to stir himself and find the girls that were so necessary if his enterprise was to flourish.

'Look, Cohen, you're down to your last two hundred pounds. You must act.'
'I know.'
He was pensive, moody, unhappy.
'What's the problem? You've got the nerve. Just go out and get them.'
'There's nothing for it, we'll go to a posh restaurant and pick up a couple of tarts. They'll be our first clients.'
'When?'

'Tonight.'

'Right.'

A few hours later, in our suits and smart shoes, as well turned out as we could be, we were sitting at an enormous table in the dark and very expensive basement of a large and very expensive international hotel in the centre of London. Opposite us the entire wall was illuminated by a huge photograph of a tropical beach. Two complicated cocktails stood before us. Imaginatively-dressed waiters and waitresses hovered around above us.

Cohen was clearly uncomfortable.

'It's a bit fucking dark in here for pulling tarts. They might not see my signals.'

'You'll manage.'

'I hope so. If we don't pull this one off it'll be not so good for Cohen. My money-lender friend could rapidly become an enemy. Those two don't look so bad.'

A couple of young females walked in and sat at a table. They looked entirely suitable to me. Cohen appeared to have lost interest.

'How about them?'

'Too tarty. Our first clients must look respectable, otherwise we'll get the wrong sort of reputation. People will think we're pimps.'

'They look fine to me. One of them is quite pretty.'

'Leave the decisions to me. Let's have another drink.'

More complicated cocktails arrived. The two girls evidently knew the place and the waiters well. They exchanged words with several of them. Then they started to stare at us and to smile and make signs.

'They want to talk to you, Cohen. Why don't you invite them to our table?'

'I told you they're the wrong type.'

'They might be amusing company for a few minutes, until the right types walk in.'

'But if we've got those slags at our table and the right sort do walk in they won't have anything to do with us.'

We ordered two complicated salads. By the time they arrived, the two girls had gone to another table and were giggling and pouting and making arrangements with two Japanese businessmen.

More cocktails arrived. Cohen and I were beginning to get tipsy, too tipsy to undertake the delicate negotiations that were required if the Elite Agency was to recruit clients. We sat in silence for ten minutes or so.

'Cohen, you must act.'

'Who do these fucking people think they are, poncing about like this? They ought to be ashamed of themselves.'

Cohen was about to explode. I knew there was nothing I could do to stop him.

'God, I can't stand all this *glitz*. And it's a rip-off. Look at those two. Nice way to treat the Nips. A coupe of slant-eyed television salesmen get off an aeroplane, bow deeply and before they know where they are they're in this joint having their wallets lightened by a couple of tarts who are probably dykes in any case. It's no way to treat an ancient and honourable race!'

Cohen stood up, swayed, sat again.

'Who cares anyway?'

* * *

The following morning, heavy of head and heart, I got up to answer the door-bell. Cohen was still asleep.

The bell was ringing a little too loudly. In normal circumstances I would have noticed and prepared myself. That morning, I was suffering from abnormal alcohol poisoning. I noticed nothing except the ringing of the bell and my fervent desire for the ringing to stop.

I realised that we were in trouble the moment my hand touched and began to turn the door handle.

The door flew open against me. Two men rushed in. One grabbed me. I didn't resist. He pinned my arms behind my back.

'You Cohen?'

Before I could reply the other man punched me in the stomach.

'Answer me.'

But I could not reply, even if I had wanted to. I had no wind. My mind's eye was spinning wildly.

'There's another one, in that bed.'

The first man threw me down on the floor. As I writhed on the carpet, my knees pulled up, struggling to get my breath, I heard the two men step over to Cohen's bed. I heard Cohen shouting. I heard scuffling and then moaning.

It was all over in a few moments.

'He wants it all back by Monday next. Otherwise you know what will happen.'

The voice moved across the room as it spoke. There was a brief pause. Then the door was slammed shut.

ALEXANDER SAYS THAT HE is under pressure to achieve a result with me. As if, in my case, a result could be achieved.

Doubtless, the Senior Medical Officer has told him that my progress is unsatisfactory. There is no other way to explain the change in Alexander's attitude to me. Although he still worships me, he has started to try to get me to see things his way.

No doubt Alexander excuses himself this deplorable behaviour by telling himself that he is acting in my interest. Nothing could be further from the truth. I have no intention of seeing things his way, the same tired old conventional way of seeing reality that he shares with all other members of crowds.

Fortunately, reality doesn't care how I see it. Any more than it cares for Alexander or anyone else's way of looking at it. And it is this thought, Citizen, that sustains me, even in my darkest moments. Yes, there are dark moments. Moments of uncontrollable fear and trembling. Moments of naked terror when my hair is loosened and my bowels turn to water.

At such times I try to think of the nature of God and contemplate His benign indifference. It is a contemplation that sustains me. Indeed, it is a thought that has always provided me with the greatest inspiration because it affirms my personal freedom.

Despite uncountable words written and spoken, unnumbered individual beliefs, mountain ranges of wishful thinking, there is no evidence that God is concerned for small human disappointments, for tiny human advances and pathetic human retreats. There is absolutely no evidence that He is nodding or frowning at any one. Only the most extreme mystics think that God has winked at them. And they are mad.

Imagine how restricting it would be if the universe was governed by a deity that took a close personal interest in every individual's affairs. The thought fills me with dread. I'm not a fool. Even the Senior

Medical Officer knows that I am not. If such a deity existed I would forever be looking over my shoulder, waiting for a nod of approval or a frown of disapproval, hoping, perhaps, for a wink of affection.

Ugh. I shudder to think of such imprisonment.

* * *

God is not watching over me but Alexander is and in his eyes my life has been a great going down. Failure at school. Failure in my first career as an accessory to a burglar. The loss of my estate. Especially the loss of my estate. It grieves Alexander more than anything else that has happened to me, even my having to leave Candida and the brat.

Alexander believes that my life has been a great going down. I believe, on the contrary, that it has been a great going up. An irreconcilable gulf.

But how could it be otherwise? Members of a crowd are only ready to consider a free spirit a success after he has surrendered his individuality to them. Only when his most heroic actions, his extraordinary taking of risks has been restrained by them, defined by them and brought within their understanding, only then will members of a crowd let him speak.

That is why a free spirit is always mocked. It is the only way members of the crowd can come to terms with his wild eyes, with his burning gaze, with the strangely compelling murmuring that he sometimes makes, the sudden outbursts of wild, praising hymns that occasionally shoot out of his mouth.

Free spirits, those who survive, especially those who discover and hold to their individuality, are seen by members of a crowd as tramps, buffoons, outcasts, dwellers on the edge of society. In their appearance, the unconscious reflection of their vision. Even if they dress conventionally there will be some unconsidered and unavoidable clue in their choice of tie, in the state of their shoes, in the colour of their shirt, perhaps, simply in the hang of their head. In their speech, the conscious reflection of their vision. In their words, each emerging from a series of burning memories of place, of light of a place, of time, of most delicate shades of feeling carefully gathered. In their choice of friends. In their choice of bedfellow. In the way that they begin and end their friendships. And especially in the way that they begin and end their love-affairs.

Free spirits are reported, distorted, decorated with ridicule, in private and in public. On the instructions of members of a crowd, a gaudy, grinning fool's mask is slowly fitted over the personality of a free spirit, carefully layer by layer like a winding sheet, every day for as long as he lives, even after he dies it grows over his personality and the memory of his personality, disguising him, softening the fearsome edges of his soul, concealing from public view the uncountable cuts and abrasions that his soul has sustained in its unending search for the undiscovered country of his ideal.

The mask is constructed by all those with whom the free spirit comes into contact, all those who cannot dare to understand the courage of his thoughts, who cannot but make shallow interpretations of his words, who, even if they do understand and can interpret fully, are simply not prepared to permit such demands to be made of them and so close their hearts.

Members of a crowd cannot accept that the actions of such a one, apparently utterly incomprehensible, are undertaken from the greatest love of ordinary humanity, from the greatest relish for life, from the greatest lust for experience and devilry of all kinds.

Most men, even most free-spirits, pass their lives without ever having become an individual. It is too great a task for them. As it was for Adam. It was too great a task for him to stand naked and unashamed before God. Even he hid among the bushes in the garden called Eden once he had eaten of the fruit of the tree of knowledge.

* * *

Cohen abandoned his house to me and went into hiding in his mother's council flat in Kennington.

Every morning, as soon as it was light, I got up, stretched, turned my face to God, asked for His absolution, then strolled through Whitehall to Covent Garden where a friendly restaurateur I had known years before, Jennings, allowed me to wash in his staff washroom and then gave me breakfast of the scraps of last night's service.

Jennings had been to a good school but had not made much of it. He had been to an indifferent university and had not made any more of that. He had started his business career as a wine merchant in Mayfair where he had learned how to speak of 'bouquet', 'nose' and 'perfume' with the affectation required by that profession. Since then, although he had increased his affectations, he had slowly moved down, one step in front of his growing overdraft and had become, temporarily, the owner of a bistro in Covent Garden.

Possibly because he saw in Dov a terrible warning for himself, possibly because he was lonely, as all affected men are, he treated me with great kindness.

This arrangement continued happily for several months until one sunny, spring morning. I was sitting at the back of the restaurant.

Jennings would not allow me to sit too near the front in case his customers saw me and were put off entering. I was sitting, warming my hands at a mug of coffee, staring unfocused at the large plate-glass window that gave onto the street, when a pair of huge almond-shaped eyes floated into my field of vision and stared at me.

At first I pretended not to recognise Pearly. Entirely from self-interest. It occurred to me that Jennings, prepared as he was to feed me, might not be so ready to feed my friends.

I stared blankly at the window. The eyes stared back. It became clear that Pearly had no intention of retreating. And I was beginning to be curious. I hadn't seen Pearly since he had been imprisoned and I, as his accomplice, had been given a suspended sentence.

Eventually, I waved a greeting. Pearly moved to the street-door, pushed it open aggressively, stepped in. In a moment he stood before me, smiling.

'Shit, Dov, how are you?'

The eyes were the same eyes that I had known, large, beautiful, perfectly shaped. But the figure had changed, as had the step. The fatman had shrunk and the bounce had gone. Gone, too, was the *dhoti*. He wore jeans, a simple shirt, a military-style jacket.

'You've fallen on your feet, I can see.'

'Hallo, Pearly, how are you?'

'As you see.'

An awkward silence fell between us. Jennings was staring at Pearly without enthusiasm.

'Well, aren't you going to buy me a coffee?'

I looked at Jennings. He looked back.

'I can't provide breakfast for every down and out in London. Destitutes from a decent school are one thing, perfect strangers from the colonies are another. This isn't a doss-house.'

Jennings wiped his hands on his apron.

'I haven't seen Dov for years. I'll pay for my coffee. And for his.' Pearly's formal politeness was icy.

'We don't serve coloureds here.'

Pearly stood staring at Jennings, a blank, warning stare.

'Whoever their friends are.'

'I asked you nicely.'

'I don't care if you ask me nastily. Out!'

Jennings stood, started to advance on Pearly. 'Come on, out!'

Pearly stood his ground. Jennings halted. Sweat began to appear on his brow.

'It seems that we're not welcome here. Let's go.'

With surprising speed and great anger Pearly turned a table over, then another, kicked chairs, picked up another and threw it at the coffee machine.

'Come on,' he commanded.

We were out of the door and running down the street in a moment. All the old excitement and pleasure of being with Pearly flooding back.

* * *

'Well,' he said when we had slowed to a walk, 'we're back together. I always knew we would be.'

'You've just destroyed my only means of support.'

'Don't worry about that. I'll keep you.'

We walked and talked and made faces at passers-by just as we had before our arrest. We looked in shop windows, asked each other careful questions, gave each other delicate answers, felt good being in each other's company, just as we had before.

Presently we found ourselves in Parliament Street. Autumn leaves grated along the gullies blown about by passing buses and taxis. Smart men with determined looks and sensible clothes hurried into and out of large doors.

'I made some good friends, inside. They gave me books to read. Now I'm in the political business.'

'What sort of political business?'

'I and my friends are going to strike blows for ordinary people.'

'What blows?'

'Don't be in such a hurry, Dov. You will see. We will speak of these things in the correct order.'

Pearly took a packet of cigarettes from his shirt-pocket. I stared at him in surprise.

'A habit I picked up inside. Passes the time. The people I met inside changed my life. I've joined a political group and dedicated myself to the struggle. We are the vanguard of the insurrectionary fight-back. You should join us. It's the only way, Dov, for outcasts like you and me.'

We found ourselves in Whitehall. Huge, impersonal buildings stared coldly down at us.

'Look about you. This is Whitehall, the heart of the State. This is where the flag flies. This is where the lies are manufactured and fed to unsuspecting citizens. This is where the legal family is maintained, where votes are calculated, where laws are devised that take freedom away. Where mistakes are made and covered up. Where our money is taken from us and spent on feeding these fat cats and paying them to screw us.'

We stopped in front of the Foreign Office. A large, rococo building standing with entire satisfaction around its own courtyard. At the entrance two sentry-boxes. A brightly-clad officer of the Queen's Guard sat complacently on a black horse outside each box. Dressed for the tourists, each wore a silver breastplate and a silver helmet, held a shiny dress-sword in front of him.

'Do you realise, Dov, in that building are the shits that degraded my country. The colonialists. They haven't got the power now but they still have the colonial inclinations. Not just in the Foreign Office. In all of the Offices of State they treat ordinary people as though they were colonials.'

We wandered on past Field Marshal George, Duke of Cambridge, standing in the middle of the road, past the Privy Council Office, past the Cabinet Office, came to the mouth of Downing Street.

'This is the headquarters of Capitalist privilege in Britain. It doesn't matter which political party is in power. Even those who begin intending not to enter into the establishment conspiracy quickly surrender to the State. The State always wins. It's grown stronger than any political party. It bends them all to its will.'

Pearly was calmer than he used to be. And much more angry.

'Democracy has become a farce. Vote once every five years for one of two possible party leaders. Every one a member of the ruling class, a member of the establishment conspiracy to keep us down. No choice. No freedom. What difference does it make to ordinary people if the government's Labour or Conservative? A few more handouts for one group or another. Nothing significant changes. The State grows bigger and more remote. They've taken the value out of the vote.'

Two large black Daimlers appeared from Parliament Square escorted by four police motorcycles, two in front, two behind. The policeman who stood at the mouth of Downing Street opened the barrier, saluted. The car and escorts hurried in and disappeared. The policeman closed the barrier.

A FEW DAYS LATER Pearly took me to a meeting of his political friends. We arrived outside a small, terraced house in a rundown street in the East End. The windows were covered with corrugated iron sheets. The door had no handle. It was raining.

Pearly slapped his hand on the door twice. In a moment it was opened. We stepped into a gloomy, barely furnished room. There were cracks in the walls. The floor was bare. A single, bright bulb hung from a wire stuck to the ceiling with black insulating tape. A small, transistor radio hung from a nail on the wall between the windows. On a low table in the middle of the room lay piles of bound newspapers.

Young men and women, sitting on broken down chairs and boxes, stared at me in aggressive silence.

'This is Dov. He's OK.'

'You didn't say you were bringing anyone.'

'Dov's OK. We got nicked together.'

The room relaxed slightly. Clearly my arrest counted as a creditable achievement with Pearly's friends.

'You know the rules, Pearly.'

'I shit on rules. I told you, he's OK.'

A bearded man, older than the others, came over to me. Looked me up and down insolently. Suddenly, he smiled, held out his hand with surprising formality.

'I'm Drew.'

I did not take his hand. Instead I stared back. This calculated rudeness, as I expected, completed my successful induction.

'He will be useful to us.' Pearly smiled. 'I know Dov very well.'

Drew crossed to his box, sat.

'Carry on, Drew.' Pearly indicated a chair for me, sat on a box.

'I am presenting our manifesto.'

A blonde girl in a jeans-suit spoke. 'If we're Anarchists why do we need a manifesto at all? Why don't we just go out and fight?'

'What's the point of fighting with our hands tied behind our backs.' Drew's soft voice commanded attention. 'We're engaged in politics, even if our methods aren't conventional. In any case, we agreed that we were going to issue a manifesto. We've printed it on the front page of the rag.'

This seemed to surprise the revolutionaries. Drew was clearly an impatient man. He bent down and opened one of the bundles. Took out a newspaper, began to read.

'Until today there has been no such thing as an Anarchist movement in Britain. There was a social scene made up of a few anarchists, pacifists, gays, lesbians, greens and a whole lot of others who were irrelevant to social revolution.'

'Gays and lesbians are running their own revolution.' A young teenage man with a crew-cut.

'Don't interrupt. I want to finish reading this. Then we'll discuss it.'

He read on. 'Now everything has changed. Street War is a growing movement dedicated to the overthrow of the State. We know our business. We know how to mount actions that bring the Capitalist machine to a grinding halt. We're totally in favour of mugging the rich, of breaking into Capitalist shops, of smashing posh houses, of cutting the tyres of scumbags' Mercedes and Rollers, of giving the police broken heads. Street War is going to put the boot in.'

His audience murmured their approval. The girl in the jeans-suit took a tobacco tin from her breast pocket, began to roll a cigarette. The young man sitting next to her, clearly her man, leant towards her and touched her shoulder with his. She smiled at him briefly.

'The State is not invisible. It is not untouchable. It is not just an idea. It is an organisation that can and will be destroyed. Street War is fighting to replace the State with a series of self-regulating groups.'

Drew threw the paper down. To my surprise, I began to feel at home.

'I want all these rags out by this time tomorrow.'

'How many are there?'

'Two thousand.'

'Christ.'

Before the young revolutionaries could appreciate the size of the task Drew had given them, he changed the subject.

'John is going to report on the Westminster action last Saturday. John.'

A blond man in military fatigues stood.

'We was on a pathetic student march against the Education cuts. That prat Benn was there and that silly establishment tart Shirley

Williams. There was plenty of Bill. Just as we was going into Trafalgar Square, me and Dave and Red saw a copper alone in an alley having a quiet fag. We jumped him.'

I had the extraordinary thought as I sat amongst these young revolutionaries that I had found a group of people who could all be my friends. I felt a comfort that I had never felt before.

'That got people going. Dave and I saw our moment. We shouted and jumped about and managed to turn the march round into Whitehall. The organisers tried to stop us, and the Bill tried, but it was a fiasco. We got about a thousand to march back up Whitehall to Parliament. Then we just stood outside shouting. Scared the shit out of the MPs who were trying to get in and out. It was a real revolutionary moment. The apoliticals were totally caught up in the revolution.'

I drank it in. Not the words. Not the naïve ideas. Being with these lovely young revolutionaries. Being with friends. It was the first time in my life that I had felt that I was among friends. People who saw the world in the same way as I did. People who wanted to change it. As I did. People who would resist the terrible pressure to conform that every crowd exerted on every individual.

I realised that day that friendship can bring great comfort, even to a free spirit. I realised why most people joined a crowd. This was a crowd after all. A crowd which wanted to assist the individual, but nonetheless a crowd.

'I say we should concentrate on meetings organised by the Labour fiasco. If we shout and jump about we can get the blacks and gays to support us. They don't trust Labour.'

I was so happy I could have burst into song. I felt as though I had come home at last.

It was the first Thursday in October. The Stock Exchange opened as usual. The bell rung. The frenetic activity began. Market-makers shouted into their portable telephones and waved their hands about. Prices flashed onto screens, red for lower, blue for higher. Dealers with portable telephones received their orders from fund-managers. Market computers made their calculations. Transactions were transacted. Large sums of theoretical money changed hands.

By noon, the Financial Times Ordinary Index was up eighteen points.

In the car-park opposite Spittalfields Market, small groups of young supporters of Street War began to assemble. At the back of the car-park, on the top deck of an old London bus, Drew, Pearly and Dov were studying a street map.

'We'll have to split into at least three groups. Pearly, you take yours up Old Broad Street. I'll take mine up Moorgate and turn left in Lothbury. Dov, you can take your people up Moorgate with me then split off round the Bank of England and down Threadneedle Street.'

Dov's promotion to a street commander had been rapid.

'If the filth ask you where you're going, tell them the Bank of England.'

'We want free samples.' Pearly laughed at his own joke. Drew looked at his watch.

'Ten minutes. Once we're there we want to provoke the filth into using force. Soon as they do, melt away. We'll put an announcement out to the Press Association an hour later. And Julie's been briefed.'

'Julie?'

'Drew's friendly journalist on The Guardian.'

'She safe?'

'As houses.'

'I'm calling it the Temple of Money.'

'Emotive.'

'Intended to be.'

I saw that Drew was an experienced political agitator. It occurred to me that he could well have been trained. I didn't mind. I was enjoying myself.

'Make as much noise as you can. We want to scare the shit out of the money bastards.'

By a quarter-past twelve, about a hundred supporters of Street War had assembled in the car-park. Young warriors with short hair and big boots. A few intellectuals in drab jackets with hoods and running shoes. Short-haired girls with grim looks.

Drew stepped out of the bus. Walked among his supporters giving instructions and directions.

We set off in one group, Drew, Pearly and Dov at the head. As we walked along Bishopsgate the warriors began to sing and shout and wave their hands. We walked along the middle of the road, an army on the move.

Two policemen stood near the junction of Bishopsgate and Wormwood Street. When they caught sight of us they hurriedly began to speak into the radios they wore on their lapels.

'Shall we scragg them?'

'No, John. Wait until we get to our objective.' Drew spoke with the voice of command. John dropped back and spoke to several of the warriors.

The officers stood in the doorway of an office building gabbling into their radios and looking nervous. As we drew level with them, one came over.

'Is this an authorised demonstration?'

'We don't recognise authority.' Drew's reply was greeted with a cheer.

'What is your route?'

'We're going to the Bank of England to ask for free samples.' Pearly couldn't resist trying his joke again.

'Very funny. All demos have to be notified to the City Police. Have you notified this one?'

'Why don't you run along.'

'There'll be trouble.'

'There will?'

'We've already radioed in for reinforcements. You'd better disperse.'

'Disperse yourself.'

The officer shrugged, stepped back, returned to his companion. He spoke into his radio again. He was greeted with more shouts and signs as Street War passed.

The Pound was up three fifths of a cent against the dollar when Street War split into two groups. Pearly and about forty others continued up Bishopsgate, as instructed. Drew and Dov and the rest turned up Wormwood Street.

Traffic was piling up in front and behind us. Passers-by hurried into doorways. Office windows flew open as their occupants heard our noise. One or two braver souls came up to ask what we were marching for. They were shouted and sworn at until they retreated.

Just before one o'clock, outside the Bank of England, a group of white police vans drew up. A superintendent and his officers jumped out and lifted crowd barriers out onto the pavement. They hurriedly errected them reflecting, no doubt, on the embarrassment to the City Police if a mob of anarchist hooligans managed to invade the sacred precincts of the Old Lady of Threadneedle Street.

Dov split away from Drew at the corner of Moorgate and Lothbury. I led my troop up Princes Street. Drew and his followers turned up Lothbury. It began to rain.

The Bank of England was entirely surrounded by crowd barriers manned at every few yards by policemen. The warriors behind me shouted and jeered. We walked on along the middle of the road, turned left, walked on up Threadneedle Street, past the ornate entrance to the Bank of England. As we drew level with it, we heard a roar from Drew and his troops. We broke into a run, charging up Threadneedle Street. We rejoined Drew and his group. The diversion had worked.

Pearly and his warriors were roaring down Threadneedle Street towards us. In a moment we all converged on the entrance to the Stock Exchange. We rushed the startled security guards and plunged onto the floor of the exchange.

Drew and Dov stood beside the entrance as Street War rampaged in that great hall, knocking dealers off their feet, kicking computer terminals to the floor, snatching telephones from the startled ears of brokers, tearing up their record slips. Pandemonium broke out. The market stopped.

The first police officers arrived a few minutes later. Drew spotted them, grabbed my arm.

'Come on, I know another way out.'

We picked our way through the chaos towards the south of the floor.

'It's worked. We've closed the Exchange. One up for Street War.'

We stepped behind a kiosk on the south wall and found a service door. Drew pressed the bar and it swung open directly onto the street. We stepped out quietly, began to walk slowly down Throgmorton Street. Police vans were screaming towards the Stock Exchange, too hurried to take any notice of us.

'Well Dov, it went well?'

'It went well.'

'Like Jesus, we've thrown over the tables of the money lenders in the Temple.'

'Hardly a temple.'
'Temple of Mammon.'
We walked on through the rain.

* * *

The Stock Exchange re-opened at four. Drew, Pearly, Dov and the closest of the warriors sat in the squat in Carter Street. All except Dov were elated.

'We stopped the fucking exchange.'
'They'll have to notice Street War now.'
'What a result.'
'Wait for the papers tomorrow. It'll be headline stuff.'
'Wonder if any of those money bastards had a camera.'
'Hope not.'
'Why?'
'They'll be able to identify us.'
'I didn't see any camera.'
'Anyway, we got a result.'
'Anything on the radio?'

Drew took the radio down from its nail over the sink. Switched it on.

... the damage is estimated at several million pounds. First reports suggest that at least fifty computer terminals have been damaged.

'Great.'
'That'll teach the bastards that we mean what we say.'

Many dealers have lost records of transactions made. It could take months to sort out who bought what from whom and at what price. The Chairman of the Stock Exchange has called the attack an 'outrage' ...

'Outrage ... is that all he can say. Twat.'
'They'll have to sell their Rollers and Mercedes.'
'Maybe some of them will go broke.'
'Too fucking rich.'

Despite the disruption, the market re-opened at four.

I looked at these happy young faces and felt a growing sense of sadness. I saw how they would, each one, soon grow older, soon drift back to obeying the social rules they hated so much now. I saw the blonde girl would get pregnant, and, in blind obedience to her biology, exert every effort to bind the father of her child to her. I saw her man responding out of the same blind obedience. I saw John helping his mother carry the shopping home from the local supermarket. I saw another, weak-looking, thin, straggly, man who had musician's hands, drifting away from his friends of today and ending up in a sleazy pub, playing the piano and drinking himself to sleep, night after night when the customers had gone.

Despite this astonishing attack the market is, at the moment, up twenty points. The Chairman of the Stock Exchange said that the performance of the market is a tribute to the stability and courage of the City.

Sitting in that damp, dreary room in Carter Street with those lovely young ones I realised that they were too young, too happy, too ingenuous to achieve any of their dreams. I saw them all, slowly, inexorably, as middle-age overtook them, buckling under the weight of the society that had created them and was rushing on past them. While they were mouthing their futile political slogans, dreaming their hopeless dreams of a better world, making their insignificant protests, the State, fuelled by the vast growth of international wealth, informed by the unstoppable march of technology, was rushing on ahead of them. Not one of them had the stature of a great leader. Not one of them would do anything to change the world.

I saw that these young anarchists were making the first and most grave mistake. They were creating a crowd and so defeating the principal object of their efforts.

I felt a growing sense of sadness. And anger. At myself. I had made a fundamental mistake. I had joined a crowd. It was time for me to move on and see what a free spirit could accomplish on his own. It would not be much, I knew. But it would, at least, be the work of an individual. If I was fortunate and my act was sufficiently startling it might make its way into the national mythology and, at least, point the way. Even if I was to fail I had no choice. For Dov the next step was inevitable.

W ATERY SUN-SHAFTS FELL out of tumbling clouds. A thin rain spattered onto the roofs of the Palace of Westminster and onto the uncovered head of Cromwell. The roofs smiled. Cromwell glowered. Further down the road, King Richard, remembering the obligations he was born to, wore an idiotic smile pretending to be impervious to rain.

My breath showed itself briefly as I waited outside Saint Stephen's entrance with a small group of Japanese students. All had the relaxed gawp of the tourist.

I stood among the brightly-coloured tourists, my rather drab appearance in stark contrast to theirs, my battered tweed jacket and beige raincoat utterly different from their orange and blue windcheaters, my cracked, leather, lace-up shoes in complete distinction to their gaudy canvas and rubber ones.

In due course a guide ushered us into the historic halls. We passed up the long stone steps and one by one were herded through the security machine.

Once checked, our group was re-assembled by our guide and ushered along the gallery that leads to the Central Lobby.

We filed slowly past the murals depicting England's finest hours. The guide intoned his habitual dirge.

'King Alfred's long-ships attacking the Danes at Swanage Bay in 877. Note his determined expression.

'King Henry taking the victory salute at Agincourt. It was the longbow, used for the first time against the French armoured cavalry, that won, not the impassioned rhetoric of King Henry, whatever you think of Shakespeare's interpretation. He was a playwright, remember, not a historian. The long-bow could penetrate armour at eight hundred yards. King Henry didn't make much of that when he was celebrating his victory.'

We passed on.

'Drake finishing his game of bowls at Dover. He wasn't going to be hurried. After all, the Armada was no more than a bunch of over-dressed, Spanish pirates.'

The guide smirked at his own joke. The Japanese tourists smiled with profound politeness, understanding the words but not their meaning.

Eventually we came to the great hall which is called the Central Lobby of the House of Commons, cradle of so much of what, Citizen, you please to call your history, although history belongs to no-one, just as it takes no notice of the present.

I looked around me. At the four Great Arches, at the Saints guarding them, at the carved stone figures of Kings and Queens, layer upon layer, foot upon head, higher and higher up to the glorious, gilded ceiling.

I was standing in an octagon. High on each of four of the walls, at the four points of the compass, four huge, gaudy mosaics masqueraded gaily as stained-glass windows. The first, on the west wall, depicted Saint George, patron saint of the Angles. He had just slain the poor, old, green dragon. Again. He stood, rosy-cheeked, projecting his heroic gaze into the middle distance, his foot on the unfortunate creature's head. Fortitude and Purity attended him carrying his helmet, his club, his banner and a bunch of white lilies, just in case the dragon managed to destroy him.

Saint David hung on the east wall, caught between earth and heaven. He had a dove on his shoulder, suitable angels in attendance. He carried the obligatory harp and a lamp, presumably against a failure of the lights. He had a soupy look.

Saints Patrick and Andrew, with companions holding appropriate banners, stood guard to north and south. Saint Andrew had just caught a salmon with a valuable ring concealed in its mouth, presumably stolen. Saint Patrick was accompanied by Saint Bridget holding another harp.

Eight benches stood below the saints, two beneath each so that not one of these holy warriors had the slightest cause for jealousy. The seats were covered with thick, green leather.

I had detached myself from my group of Japanese tourists. In a few moments the guide noticed my absence. He called to me to follow. The other tourists were waiting impatiently to pass beneath St Patrick's arch and gawp at the paintings in the Lower Waiting Hall. The guide called again.

The Japanese were eyeing me in a most unpleasant, self-righteous way. They were beginning to realise that I was not one of them, that I was not a self-possessed, well-scrubbed tourist, with an expensive reflex camera and an expansive, grinning gawp but a scruffy bird, intent on my own devices. They stared at me as though they had been deceived.

It is always thus, Citizen, even when there is no contract. If a man turns out not to be exactly as expected, members of a crowd summon up righteous anger and cry that they have been betrayed.

At last I permitted myself to show that I had noticed their attention. I smiled, offered them a tiny bow, in the oriental manner. They were unimpressed. They continued to stare unhelpfully, to glare unreceptively, to fidget and mutter.

I raised my right hand, offered them a tentative gesture of farewell. This they understood. They accepted it readily.

They exchanged words with the guide, who shrugged. The group passed on out of sight.

I crossed to the bench beneath Saint George, sat.

* * *

I sat beneath Saint George, settled myself, waited for the police to ask me my business. I didn't have to wait long. Within minutes an officer approached, asked me what I was doing. I said nothing. He asked me again. I remained silent.

The officer received my silence, contemplated it, turned it over in his mind. It was, somehow, inconceivable that this odd-looking man with the vacant expression, this strange man who kept glancing up at the ceiling and smiling, that this kindly-looking man, despite his aquiline face, could intend any danger to anyone. There was absolutely nothing in his manner that spoke of aggression.

Perhaps this was a vagrant who had wandered into the Palace of Westminster for shelter from the cold. It was difficult to tell. His appearance was so very confusing.

Superficially his clothes were conventional, beige raincoat, tweed jacket, grey, serge trousers, old school tie, black lace-up shoes. Superficially, the outer garments were made of the same mixture of cotton, wool and artificial fibres as all garments are, not much dirtier, not much more torn than many others.

In fact, my clothes, once smart, were, by then, on their last legs. Their continuing dedication to their task bordered on the miraculous. They proclaimed the extraordinary advances of modern technology. My raincoat, for example, though at least six years old, resisted stains without being asked. Even when I threw tomato paste at it, to try to convince Candida that I had been wounded one foolish afternoon, it kept the sticky mess at arms' length, on the surface, away from the tendrils of fibre so cleverly woven. Candida was not taken in. I was forced to admit defeat and sponge it off. One wipe and no trace remained.

Even though the officer thought that I was too scruffy, too weak-looking, too run-down to intend any harm he decided that he could not allow me to stay in the Central Lobby. However sympathetic an officer might be to the poverty of others, the authorities did not allow vagrants or other suspicious persons to assemble in the Central Lobby. The sight of them could give offence to the elected representatives. The smell of them could offend their delicate susceptibilities. Often they started to speak. Usually nonsense. Sometimes they begged.

Even though he looked harmless, this man might open his mouth. He might try to elicit sympathy from some soft-hearted member, try to extract money or tobacco from him. Worse, knowing nothing about the ways of Parliament, knowing nothing of the pecking-order, he might importune one of the great men. A Parliamentary Private Secretary. A Junior Minister. He might even be entirely ignorant of the status of his elected representatives and try to attract the attention of a Cabinet Minister. That would be a disaster. It was not to be contemplated.

The officer spoke.

'Oiyou ... '

I said nothing.

'Oiyou ... '

A sergeant arrived. He made a similar approach.

'Oiyou ... what do you think you're doing here?'

'I am here to lobby my MP.'

'You'll have to move on.' He spoke unconvincingly.

'Why?'

'You can't just sit here.'

'I am here to lobby my MP.'

'You can't do that.'

The officer was wrong. And he knew it. I knew it, as well.

It is an Englishman's inalienable, constitutional right to sit in the Central Lobby if he wishes to lobby his MP. No-one can prevent him, as long as he is a citizen of the United Kingdom. That's why, Citizen, it is called the Central Lobby. The place where people and rulers meet, the place where our democracy is supposed to be most sharply focused.

'I am here to lobby my MP. If you are in any doubt as to the view of the Constitution on my right so to do, you should consult the Speaker.'

The two officers retired, defeated.

I SAT BENEATH Saint George waiting to enter the national debate.
The people who passed through the Central Lobby that morning must have thought, if they thought at all, that I was a constituent waiting to lobby his member.

As I intended.

The morning unwound. People came and went about their business, about others' business. Business makes people busy. Too busy to take much notice of a scruffy man with a ready smile, sitting quietly by himself.

Even when they did take notice of me, because, for example, I was coughing, or sniffing too loudly, or blowing my nose onto my handkerchief, even then the conventions of a public place protected me.

Who would make a fuss because what appeared to be a battered old tramp had refused to give them the time of day?

Of course eyes did fall on me from time to time. When, for example, the odd passer, secretary, researcher, member, startled out of self-interest by some thought he didn't wish to confront, caught sight of the angular man with the swept-back hair. On first sight the passer considered me to be utterly conventional and so he closed his mind to me. It was only once or twice, when by some accident or because of some inconvenience, as when a man is forced to go to a stranger and ask him where he can find a place to piss, that any passer gave me a second glance. Then, my too-gentle smile was, perhaps, disturbing. Then, if by a series of even more improbable accidents the passer cast a third glance to reassure himself that the tramp with the piercing gaze was really a tramp, only then would he decide that I looked odd. Realising that Dov looked odd, the first thing the passer did was to put me out of his mind.

Despite my sitting in full gaze of all the people in the Central Lobby, my location, my persona, my status were all too improbable. People simply could not take me into their minds. The first beach-head.

And I was cut off from my past. The second beach-head. The moment I took my place beneath Saint George I realised that I could never again be Dov of number so and so, in such and such a street, in such and such a town. My address could not, like others', ever again be listed in directories, contained in the silicon memories of computers, be and continue to be a matter of record.

You, Citizen, live in a box that you sometimes please to call your castle. Inside, you feel secure, huddled behind tightly closed doors, thinking that you are afforded absolute protection by your four jerry-built walls, penetrated at more or less regular intervals by eight sheets of shoddy, thin glass. You think it is for you to decide when you will invite me to enter and when you will not. You lock your flimsy front-door, sit back and tell yourself that your house is a fortress against all invaders. But anyone who is determined to invade your space knows exactly where you are, Citizen, and precisely how to get at you.

I SAT BENEATH Saint George. Archie Moore sat in his office nearby and contemplated the advances in his political career.

After Edward's misfortune Lady Brompton had withdrawn into herself. She had begun to find the role of President of Great England too arduous. She wanted to continue to serve but in a less demanding capacity.

'We can't let such an opportunity pass even if the landed classes are a pain in the arse. Even if Lady fucking Brompton is the biggest pain in the arse of all.'

Archie Moore offered to relieve Lady Brompton of the burden. His offer was accepted with gratifying alacrity.

Once in charge, Archie Moore had applied the same dedication to organising Great England that he applied to his own career. After all, nothing in The Philosophy of the Middle Way forbade the ruthless creation of an efficient political organisation.

'Moderate in policy, fucking ruthless in application,' he told the dutiful Staines.

He realised that if the movement was to have real power it would have to broaden its appeal. The landed class, although influential, were by no means numerous. What he wanted was an extra-parliamentary movement that would advance his parliamentary career.

Archie Moore's greatest insight was to realise that Britain was sufficiently affluent to have created a class of *haves* that was much more numerous than the *havenots*. They owned their own houses or flats. They had new cars every two years paid for by their employers. They went to the Costa Brava for their holidays. They watched cricket or tennis on their colour televisions in the summer and football or snooker in the winter. They believed in the Welfare State as long as their taxes didn't have to go up to pay for it. They supported the police as long as they kept the *havenots* under control. They preferred suburbia to the cities and the South to the North. Above all, they had jobs and intended to keep them.

Archie Moore widened the exclusively landed class membership of Great England to encompass the *haves* by making jingoistic appeals to them.

'Great England will put the Great back into Britain.' 'Get your pride back with Great England.' 'Be an Englishman, join Great England.'

And he made sure that Great England espoused populist political policies. While loudly rejecting accusations of racism, Great England was strongly in favour of an end to any form of immigration, especially the immigration of blacks and Asians wherever they came from. Great England, while broadly supporting Conservative policies on Law and Order, made it clear that those policies didn't go far enough. Great England was in favour of longer prison sentences and wanted the government to use its majority to re-introduce hanging for terrorist offences and the murder of police officers. Great England was in favour of an increase in defence spending. Great England wanted Britain, if not to withdraw from the European Community, at least to re-negotiate the terms of its membership. Great England was especially insistent that Parliament should retain absolute sovereignty.

The *haves* joined in great numbers.

Soon Great England had offices in all rural constituencies and many urban ones. At each office volunteers were always available to put leaflets through letter-boxes, to sell the movement's news-sheet, to write letters to the local newspapers, to collect money at supermarkets, to engage in street politics of all kinds.

'With our organisation we'll put the fucking heat on the colleagues until the kitchen's too hot for their pale political skins.'

Staines smiled wanly. He wasn't feeling well that day. He had eaten oysters the night before.

Archie Moore's methods soon achieved the desired result. Even though the Conservative Party was in government at that time it was not popular. An election was due within eighteen months. Party leaders were determined not to alienate any significant part of the electorate. It became clear to them that the membership of Great England constituted just such a significant part. They accepted that any attempt to oppose Great England would be politically suicidal. And so they joined forces. Great England became an adjunct of the Conservative Party as Archie Moore had always intended.

It was not long before the chairman of the Party's candidates' list was an Archie Moore nominee, the president of the Party's youth wing was an Archie Moore appointment, the officers of the Party were all appointed by the Chairman, but only after he had consulted Archie Moore.

The movement had by now lost its original aim. Under Archie Moore it had discovered a simpler one. The uninhibited acquisition of power.

'Let's not fucking confuse ourselves about what we're after. The top job. No messing.'

'What will we say to our supporters?'

Staines was troubled by such a naked appeal.

'We'll tell them we need power in order to protect them.'

The great idea that had become Great England had not disappeared. It remained intact. But Archie Moore had pushed it farther away. On purpose. So that its aims could not be attained in the too-near future. As with salvation, if it was readily and credibly available people would realise that there was no purpose in the practice of the religion that offered it and the priests would become redundant, so with Great England, Archie Moore realised at an early stage that if the *haves* lost their fear of the *havenots,* that if the propertied and monied lost their fear of being dispossessed, there would be no reason for the movement to continue and his political platform would evaporate.

That year, the Party Conference had been entirely dominated by the Great England faction. The Party Chairman consulted Archie Moore on the selection of motions to be debated. He consulted him on which speakers were to be called and which were not. Archie Moore sat on the platform for every important debate. He addressed Conference on three separate occasions. An unprecedented honour.

The press joined in the game. Reports of the Conference were full of Archie Moore and Great England, their reaction to debates, their policy plans, their political vision.

Archie Moore sat in his office in Westminster contemplating his success and considering how he could supplant his Party leader.

Although he had never seriously doubted that he would succeed, he was surprised at how well things had gone at the Conference. Politics, he knew, was a chancy business and the Conservative Party did not often allow its highest citadels to be assaulted. Senior Party managers had not liked his success. He did not doubt that. But he could not for the life of him think what they could do about it.

* * *

As Archie Moore sat in his office, in a splendid house presented to the nation for the exclusive use of the Prime Minister of the day, Prime

Minister Blunt and five colleagues sat in the grand dining-room beneath the paintings by great masters that had been lent by the National Gallery. All except Blunt were smoking cigars.

'But if you call an election, now, we'll be slaughtered,' the Chief Whip said.

'I've done my duty to Party and State,' said Blunt, smiling. 'I've been in the job for six years. That's enough for any man. Besides, Emily's tired of it.'

'I am sure, Prime Minister,' Lord Wambaugh took his cigar out of his mouth, 'that you would not want to do anything that might injure the Party.'

'It's not the Party I joined any more. It's been hijacked by that dreadful upstart, Moore.'

'If we were to let it be known,' said the Scottish Secretary, 'through the usual channels, you know, that senior Party managers were displeased with the advance of Moore?'

'There is no honour in leading a Party that espouses principles that one doesn't believe in. And no profit.'

'Forget principles.' The Chancellor was a blunt man. 'Let's just keep our minds on practice. The displeasure, however great, of senior Party managers, won't stop Moore.'

'If I let it be known, in the right places,' the Chief Whip suggested, 'that we're thinking of calling an election unless Moore is dealt with?'

'That might work.' The Chancellor scratched his nose. 'Back-benchers are windy as hell. They might lose their nerve.'

'Exactly.' The Chief Whip smiled at his own cunning. 'I'm sure of it.'

The six men sat and smoked and contemplated this strategy. Finally, Blunt spoke.

'Well do it then.' The others sighed. A decision had been reached. Blunt smiled, stood. 'We must go to the House.' He walked swiftly from the room.

The mysterious cabal that ruled the Conservative Party, had ignored Archie Moore and all his works for several years. Now, at last, it had permitted itself to notice him. It did not like what it saw. It did not like outsiders and Moore was an outsider. It did not tolerate upstarts. Moore was an upstart. Above all, it did not like men who tried to undermine its power and control.

If other events hadn't intervened the Conservative Party would have made sure that Archie Moore's sun would have been eclipsed by its authority. But matters were taken out of its hands.

THE AFTERNOON WORE on. I sat beneath Saint George growing angry as I contemplated Parliament. Although it is widely advertised as the guardian of our liberties I realised that it is nothing of the sort. It could be. But it is not. It is, instead, the clearing house for the lie. The exchange where the lie finds its most potent expression. The auction where those who enter it intending to tell the truth are soon won over and converted to the use of the lie. Those few who do, despite everything, insist on telling the truth are treated as outcasts, eccentrics, fools.

Over and over again, like a parasite, the lie has made men its own.

The lie falls from a man's lips, takes root, shoots up, reveals its tempting stems, its delicate flowers, bears its poisonous fruit. Not just one plant, many sub-species have evolved from the one species so that nowadays the lie manifests itself as a plant, as a small bush, as a tree, as a great orchard of trees, all bearing all-too-tempting fruit.

Where there is fruit fools will eat, even if it is poisonous, even if many corpses lie rotting all around with half-eaten fruit in their gaping mouths, still fools will be tempted.

The lie knows the same sadness as man, the same heaviness of heart, the same longing for the sweet release of night. The lie has seen the same stranger's stare, the same cold eye of the unknown watcher, the suddenly perceived aggression. It has felt the unexpected sensation on the skin at the back of the neck, the sweat on the scalp, the inexplicable sense of malaise that clouds the minds of men. The lie has known the same cheerless trembling of the limbs, the winter frost of the heart. It has seen the sudden flight. Yes, the lie has felt the desperate thundering of the heart in the breast, the draining of colour from the cheeks, the leaden steps, the fear of death.

The lie has known the terrors of night, those nights of suffocating darkness. It has felt the same rasp of time as men feel. It has seen the blood shoot out into the startled air, heard the cries of the dying, the screams of the disintegrating dust of men. The lie has seen the silent, stupefied agony of a child watching the murder of his parent, the uncomprehending hurt of a child when his father whose hand he is still holding suddenly becomes pieces of flying flesh, spurting blood, splinters of white bone.

The lie has seen all this and whispers to its adherents that it too is experienced in the ways of the world. It whispers in its tired voice that the only protection for the individual is to join a crowd.

The loving lie persuades the individual to lower his guard. The family lie lulls the individual into dreams of immortality. The money lie takes the individual's eye away from his own internal truths and prevents him from preparing himself for death. The relativist lie confuses the individual and prevents him listening to the truth in his heart. The egalitarian lie confiscates the individual's freedom and stifles his soul. The political lie deceives the individual into thinking that he has a share in the power of the State. The collectivist lie confiscates the individual's responsibility in favour of State Welfare and destroys his moral strength.

The lie takes many forms and many disguises. It cannot be simply defined. One single sentence cannot be spun out and thrown around it even if it were to be as long as the circumference of the world. Even if as much breath as there is in all the world were shouted out to deny it, still the lie would reappear.

But we all know what it is. All of us can point a finger at it if we want to. For the lie is so bright and shiny that it cannot be missed.

When it is accepted, it is not because men have failed to identify it. It is not because it has slipped unseen into their consciousness. Oh no, we all recognise the lie. We all know it. All the time.

When men accept it, they do so knowingly, determinedly. They set their faces hard against the truth and allow themselves to be intoxicated by the lie and its promises.

But they soon discover its action. They feel their spirits shrink. They feel their freedoms diminish.

Nonetheless, far too often, whether from weariness of spirit or from other laziness, men allow the lie to dazzle them.

Even though they know that it is wrong to let the lie go unchallenged, most people are too afraid to challenge it. It has so many supporters, judging by the number of mouths from which it escapes, it has such a great army of supporters that only the foolhardy challenge it.

Yes, Citizen, we who love freedom are foolhardy. It is our mark of Cain as well as the light of a certain kind of laughter that guides us through the darkest, deepest, blackest nights of our troubles.

Yes, we free spirits know troubles. Who but a fool would give up the comfort of belonging to a crowd? Who but a madman would willingly throw over the chance to belong to that exalted, shining crowd of smiling faces turned up to the sun, faces that have given in and decided to accept the lie?

MR SPEAKER SITS in his chair, his black stockinged legs dangling over the seat, his wig perched on his bald pate. He is whispering to one of his clerks, while the Member for Walstead East is on his feet attempting to delay the proceedings of the House with a Point of Order proposed not so much to discover if he has a point but rather to draw attention to himself.

The Member for Walstead East concludes his speech and sits. Mr Speaker stands, tells him testily, that if the Honourable Member had been present last Tuesday, I think it was, he would recall that I have already ruled on the very same point raised by his colleague the Member for Walstead West. I ruled that it was Out of Order then and I see no reason, compelling though the Honourable Member's arguments are, to change my mind now. The Prime Minister.

Mr Speaker sits. Blunt slowly gets to his feet, steps to the despatch box. He leans impressively on the table and waits for silence. Presently, he tells the House, in his most pleasing tones, that after that amusing little piece of business we must now turn to a more serious matter, a matter indeed of grave national importance.

It is three thirty-two in the afternoon. Blunt looks round at his colleagues sitting behind him and then across at the members of Her Majesty's Loyal Opposition.

Prime Minister Blunt says I am grateful to the Opposition for supporting the government's position without criticism so far and I hope that the government will be able to call on that support once more when I have finished my speech.

The Member for Nortonside rises. He asks the Speaker, will the Prime Minister give way? The opposition has not been uncritical. Some of us don't support the government at all.

Blunt remains standing. The Member for Nortonside falls silent. Both men stand and glare at each other.

Mr Speaker stands with a sigh. Both men sit. Mr Speaker tells the House that it is clear that the Prime Minister is not going to give way. Mr Speaker sits.

Blunt and the Member for Nortonside stand at the same moment. Cries of sit down erupt from the Conservative benches. One or two opposition members shout unconvincingly that they are being gagged. The Member for Nortonside is eventually persuaded to sit. Silence falls, Blunt clears his throat.

Blunt tells the House that the dockworkers' strike does not just present the nation with a grave challenge to its essential supplies but also a challenge to the authority of the government itself. The violence on the picket lines and the intimidation of those dockers who want to go to work are both to be deplored. Although the leaders of the Opposition have condemned this violence we haven't heard anything like enough from some of the Opposition's more usually vocal supporters.

The Member for Earlsden rises, exclaims that I have never heard such a travesty of the truth. There is no-one on this side of the House who doesn't condemn the violence. The police too have been violent. Above all, we condemn the man who created the violence. This strike was quite unnecessary. The government created the strike. I wouldn't be surprised if they didn't welcome it, at first.

This intervention is greeted by cries of Hear, Hear from the Member for Earlsden's colleagues mingled with shouts of disgraceful, sitdown, shutup, from the government benches and laughter from all sides.

Mr Speaker stands. The Member for Earlsden sits. Mr Speaker sits.

Blunt, who has remained standing, suggests to Mr Speaker that the Honourable Member should withdraw his disgraceful allegation, an allegation that casts serious aspersions on my honour. To suggest that I created and welcomed the strike is utter nonsense. It is to suggest that I welcome the violence.

Blunt sits. Mr Speaker stands and tells the Member for Earlsden, I have had cause to speak to the Honourable Gentleman before. I know that passions run high over this issue but really I do think that the Honourable Member should withdraw his remarks. His language was unparliamentary as well as silly. It is preposterous to suggest that the Prime Minister deliberately organised any strike, certainly a strike that could have such deleterious consequences for the nation.

The House voices its feelings. Conservatives cry withdraw. Opposition members shout butitstrue. Mr Speaker calls for Order. The Member for Earlsden is persuaded by his more senior colleagues to mutter a retraction. Order is restored.

Mr Speaker sits. Blunt stands, explains that I will come to the level of essential supplies in a moment but before I do I want to deal with some more general matters. The dockers' leaders, I must assume, are reasonable men. The government is also reasonable.

The Honourable Member for Nortonside mutters, not this one, from the sedentary position and achieves a frisson of laughter from his colleagues.

Blunt tells the House that it is a great pity that some of the Honourable Members opposite cannot join their more senior colleagues in behaving responsibly. And it is a pity that the proceedings of this House are regularly debauched with unfunny jokes, childish japes and frivolous jollities delivered from the sedentary position by a clique of undemocratic and un-parliamentary members opposite. No doubt the Honourable Member finds facing the truth as difficult as telling it.

The Member for Nortonside rises. Conservatives shout hear, hear, sit down, let the Prime Minister be heard. Blunt remains standing. The Member for Nortonside remains standing and asks Blunt are you calling me a liar? Mr Speaker I demand the Prime Minister withdraw.

Mr Speaker stands. Blunt and the Member for Nortonside sit.

Mr Speaker tells the House that I will have to rule although I would rather not. There are many Honourable Members who I know will try to catch my eye after the Prime Minister has spoken. I really think that Honourable Members should restrain themselves and allow this most important debate to proceed in an orderly manner. The Prime Minister, on reflection, will no doubt agree that he was provoked by the continual interruptions into going a little too far.

Mr Speaker sits. Blunt rises. He looks at Mr Speaker, tells him that if it would assist the House, I will gladly say that I did not intend to convey the impression that the Honourable Member for Nortonside was a liar. It is, of course, quite unnecessary for me to comment on the veracity or otherwise of the Honourable Gentleman. Those who know him know exactly what he is.

The Member for Nortonside rises. That's not a withdrawal. Blunt remains standing and glares at the Member for Nortonside.

Mr Speaker rises. Blunt and the Member for Nortonside sit. Mr Speaker tells the Member for Nortonside, pipe down, the Prime Minister has withdrawn.

No he hasn't, shouts the Member for Nortonside and some of his colleagues from the sedentary position. This is greeted with Conservative cries of shutup, be quiet you silly ass. One rural Conservative roars letthedogseetherabbit.

Mr Speaker shouts Order. I have ruled. Let's get on. The Prime Minister.

Mr Speaker sits. Blunt rises.

Prime Minister Blunt tells the House that the government is best advised to give the dockers' leaders the benefit of the doubt and assume that they are reasonable men.

The Member for Hungington rises behind Blunt, tells the House that my Honourable Friend can't rely on our support if he comes out with idiotic statements like that. If they were reasonable men they wouldn't try to hold the country to ransom. If they were reasonable men they wouldn't intimidate their fellow workers and orchestrate such unprecedented violence. The Member for Hungington sits.

Laughter and cries of hear, hear volley from the opposition benches.

The Member for Dovehouse rises, tells his opposition colleagues that the Prime Minister should ask his Honourable Friend to withdraw as he did the Member for Earlsden, or does he agree with his colleague? We on this side of the House are prepared to accept that the Prime Minister is not an idiot. He may be a charlatan but he is not an idiot. The Member for Dovehouse sits.

Blunt, who has remained standing, tells the Member for Dovehouse that I am trying to get on with important business and I choose not to have heard the remark of my Honourable Friend or the remarks of the Honourable Gentleman.

The opposition benches erupt with cries of not good enough, make him withdraw, coward.

Mr Speaker rises. Blunt sits. Mr Speaker explains that if this unseemly behaviour doesn't cease I will suspend this sitting. This House is not a kindergarten. The Prime Minister.

Mr Speaker sits. Blunt rises, explains, Mr Speaker, we believe that the dockworkers' leaders are reasonable men. We give them the benefit of the doubt. That is why I arranged a meeting with them yesterday evening to see if any common ground could be found.

To give them a bollocking, more like. The northern accents of the Member for Worlsden emerge. He too is sitting. Blunt looks at Mr Speaker. Mr Speaker, for the sake of propriety and the good name of the House decides to ignore this intervention.

Blunt clears his throat again and tells the House the dockers' leaders came to Downing Street yesterday evening. Our discussions lasted several hours.

WHILE THIS FARCE is making its stilted progress I sit beneath Saint George, dreaming of the English countryside. I dream of its plenitude, of the meadows and moors, the woodlands and hedges. I dream of the warm summer secrecy at the end of unthought paths, of the poplars and willows that stand quietly beside secret lanes and ghostly fens, of the oak trees and ash trees that give their shade without thought, of the cattle that graze beside slow, weedy streams, of white figures playing cricket in the peace of summer Sundays.

I dream of the east-coast sand-cliffs facing the ozone sea, home for tunnelling martins and yellow-horned poppies, rarest of rare flowers.

Here, on autumn nights, the wild geese call to each other from the stubble ponds.

Near here, I began.

I dream of the place where I began. Of the house of my father and my grandfather and my great-grandfather, of Isaac, Nathaniel and Jacob. I dream of its peaceful bricks, of its quiet roofs, of the red carpet that was such a friend to my bare feet.

It is proper, from time to time, for a man to consider his birthplace, to take himself to walk again in the fields and meadows of his childhood.

I dream of the room where my mother kept her counsel for so many years, of the blue curtains of her fortress bed, of my disappointment in her, still bitter. I dream of the gentle peace of my father's study. I see his papers tidily arranged, belying the untidiness of his business affairs, the friendly water-colours he painted and then hung on the walls, the cracked paint, the faded Afghan rug, his figure standing at the window, back to me, looking out over the park. Whenever I think of him he always has his back to me.

I dream of kind Wendy who always had time for me, of friendly Austin, who played the role of uncle at the top of his voice, in his poshest accents, as though he were on the stage in a music hall, of Daphne, perhaps the only woman I ever truly loved. Until she betrayed me.

I dream of school, of the smell of polish and disinfectant, of the extraordinary day when the white marble eagle took me right out of my body and up into the air, of Grania the gardener's daughter, my first physical love.

I dream of Candida, of her lovely body walking along the strand while the sand-martins wheeled and screeched above us. I dream of that summer of being-in-love, of delightful irresponsibility. I dream of Lady Brompton and smile to myself. I dream of Cohen and laugh to myself. I dream of Flowerdew and feel sad that I will never see the house of my childhood again.

It is proper for a man, from time to time, to look back at the morning of his life and it is proper for him to look further back, to consider his tribe, the tribe that created his understanding. His tribe, after all, is the human landscape from which he comes.

My tribe, Citizen, when they had finished their long apprenticeship as predators, when pre-history became history, my tribe became desert people.

The desert was hard and dry and cruel.

My people were, first, the people of the desert. Herdsmen. Their wealth was in sheep and goats. They moved. Always, they moved. And they killed. They killed where and what they pleased because they believed that all things that fell beneath their gaze belonged to them.

Fierce, wild, merciless, their war banners embroidered with the graven images of the gods that they worshipped, the bull, the lion, the snake, the unicorn, oh yes, Citizen, the unicorn of England was invented by the Jews three thousand years before the English Monarchy. As was the English God.

Yahweh the thunderer.

Yahweh the name that can never be spoken.

Ehyeh-Asher-Ehyeh. I am-being-I am.

Yahweh, the Great I Am.

It is not only your God that my people give you, Citizen. We offer you a vision of freedom that only a diaspora Jew can know. It's there. In our holy book. Pentateuch to us. First five books of the Old Testament to you. Testament to our love of freedom.

What other race offered each and every individual a personal relationship with God? Prophet after prophet we created, step by hundred-year step, for each individual of the tribe, his own unique and uniquely personal relationship with God. This is the root of all Western concepts of personal freedom.

This great affirmation of the rights and freedoms of the individual found its greatest assertion in our greatest prophet. Jesus showed the world that each and every individual is the son of God. That is the essential symbolic truth of His life.

No other life, nothing in the history of human thought has more clearly, more effectively, more permanently affirmed the right to freedom of the individual.

* * *

A distant muttering. Prime Minister Blunt steps out of the Chamber. Begins his customary slow, stately walk across the Central Lobby. The great man is accompanied by two private secretaries. Looking neither to his right nor to his left he strides slowly over the fine, Venetian mosaics. His acolytes do their best to imitate his manner. They look neither to their right nor to their left. They stride slowly.

Perhaps it is the tension of the moment. Perhaps it is simply caprice. Perhaps Dov is willing it. As Blunt reaches the centre of the Lobby he stops walking, looks up, finds himself staring at a scruffy man sitting on the bench beneath Saint George.

He is staring at the man. The man is staring at him.

Under these circumstances he habitually looks away. It doesn't do for great men to allow themselves to look too closely at lesser mortals. Certainly not in front of others. When an individual tries to catch their eye they must look away in order to demonstrate their greatness. But today Blunt forgets himself. He forgets his greatness. He forgets his acolytes to whom he usually tries to set a good example. And he forgets to look away. Instead he discovers himself staring at a tramp of a man sitting on the bench beneath Saint George.

Not just at the man. At the man's extraordinary eyes.

Prime Minister Blunt caught sight of a man sitting on the bench beneath Saint George. He hesitated as though he recognised him. For a moment it looked as though he was going to cross to the man and speak to him.

A scruffy, angular, tall man with extraordinary eyes. A man he thinks he has met before.

Where?

He cannot remember.

At this moment he cannot remember anything. At this moment all trace of memory has departed his consciousness, for the man who has caught his gaze is taking irresistible and successful steps to dominate his entire attention.

With his eyes.

Eyes unblinking. Eyes staring with the deep penetration of a predator. Eyes that proclaim the implacable gaze of generation upon generation of the solitary hunter.

Blunt cannot take his attention away. He comes to a halt, stands rooted to the spot beneath Hardman's great chandelier.

Those who were with the Prime Minister, notably his political secretary, later confirmed that it was not customary for him to stop when on his way into or out of the Chamber. They said that he appeared to catch sight of the tramp and was somehow arrested by what he saw. They said that the man had fiery eyes as though he had been drinking.

Fiery eyes.

And behind the eyes a terrible calm. A dispassionate certainty.

Prime Minister Blunt feels himself being drawn towards those eyes, towards that sea of calm.

The sea of calm is white, without end, all-encompassing.

Blunt feels the sea beckoning. He feels its peace. He knows that if he goes too far he will never return.

Is it the sea of death? The thought presents itself to his mind. He shakes his head. But he cannot shake the thought away. The eyes insist.

Then he hears a distant, weighty sound. The sound of huge volumes of air being beaten by ... wings?

What wings? Blunt knows that there cannot possibly be any wings in the Central Lobby. Nevertheless, he hears the pulsing, drumming, rushing sound. It seems to be coming from the eyes.

He feels a wedge of thick air pushing towards him, palpable, heavy, pressing. Blunt knows that there cannot be such air, nonetheless the air surrounds him.

Blunt senses a towering space opening up above and about him, cutting him off from himself, from his sensible self that is still telling him that his feet are on the ground.

His sensible self. He tries to find it. To return to it. But he cannot believe in his sensible self. For other of his senses have taken over and are insistently giving him other information.

For example. That the walls of the Central Lobby are disappearing. That the fine, gilded roof of the great hall is lifting away. That he, Henry Blunt, that he, the Prime Minister of England, Scotland, Wales and Northern Ireland, is slowly being sucked out of himself.

Everything is in the eyes.

The Prime Minister suddenly stopped in the centre of the Central Lobby and stood staring at a poorly dressed man whom his political secretary assumed was a constituent waiting to lobby his MP.

Blunt tries to resist the eyes. He tries to blink. The eyes sense it. The eyes sense that he is trying to escape. They respond.

In the vast, timeless space of the eyes a small speck appears. A small, flying speck. It grows rapidly, rushing silently and without effort over vast distances of time and space.

I am an eagle over England at last. In my highest flight. I look down and know that the Prime Minister is mine.

The Prime Minister seemed to be in pain. He put his hands to his ears. The Prime Minister's political secretary said, afterwards, that he had heard no sound at all. He assumed, at first, that the Prime Minister had had some kind of a seizure.

Blunt knew that he could not resist. He realised, to his surprise, that he was not at all surprised. He realised that he had been expecting this all his life. Now that it was upon him it was, somehow, a relief. He was deeply weary.

According to one eye-witness, at one moment in this extraordinary encounter the Prime Minister began to step towards the man.

Blunt realised that in an obscure way he welcomed this moment.

Suddenly, the tramp fell upon the Prime Minister and, before those present could act, he started to shower him with slaps and blows. The Prime Minister made no attempt to escape or to defend himself. He stood quite still, as though paralysed, and allowed the man to assault him.

At last, a huge peace closed around Blunt and joined with the peace that had always been inside him.

The Prime Minister was taken to the King Edward VII Hospital for Officers. A shocked nation waited for news of his condition. During the night it was rumoured that he had died. But this morning at ten-twenty am, his doctors issued an official bulletin.

The Prime Minister has suffered a mild heart-attack, probably induced by his encounter in the Central Lobby. No date can be given for a return to his duties.

A LEXANDER IS TROUBLING me more and more. This morning, he brought me a small pot of honey to please me. I decided not to eat it even though I like honey as much as anything. I was trying to keep the upper hand. But he looked at me quite sternly and said that there was no point in such a demonstration, I was merely cutting off my nose to spite my face.

Alexander is obliged to write a report about me. It is clear that he is getting nowhere with it.

He can't decide if I am a dangerous anarchist who went to the heart of the nation intent on destroying the pillars of the State and failed or a penniless idiot who was and apparently remains happy to lie on his arse all day and all night and stare at the ceiling.

His problem.

As is my stillness. He is deeply troubled by my stillness. He finds it impossible to come to terms with it. I lie here, hours on end, head bent back, staring at the empty, white ceiling of my room. No sign of motion. Functions indicating life, but at a minimum. Smiling inanely, so Alexander thinks. Quite inert, so Alexander observes.

He has to make decisions for his report, as he has to make a show of kindness for his self-esteem. He can't quite kick the habits of his profession. This show takes the form of repeated protestations concerning the good will he feels for me.

He tells me, 'You're ill. That's why you're here. And I'm here to cure you.' He offers me a sickly smile which I reject and says, 'I'm experienced in these matters.'

Then he takes out a pad and a pen, begins to ask me silly questions that he must have been put up to by his superiors. He asks me, 'Do you get giddy spells? Are you afraid of heights? Do you get sudden sweats at night? Did your father beat your mother?'

If only he had. I manage not to laugh.

Then trick questions. Also, doubtless provided for him by his superiors. He asks me, 'Did your Father kiss you goodnight? Did your mother undress in front of you or behind locked doors?' presumably hoping that he will be able to latch on to my answers and so demonstrate my mental instability.

My stillness offends him. Offended, his desire to treat me with his potions and pills, his anti-depressants and his tranquillisers, his pick-me-ups and his put-me-downs increases. I can see that his fingers are itching to slip me his intra and extra venous, oral and anal, potions. I can see it in his eyes. I don't have to look far into them.

I'm not going to bend down to Alexander.

Sometimes, when he realises that I will not co-operate in any treatment that he or his colleagues have in mind for me, he confesses his failure. Without, of course, realising it.

He leans over towards my bed to put his lips closer to my ear and tells me in a low voice, 'You're not trying to get better. You just want to escape responsibility. You can't face the real world. If only you'll let me treat you, I'll soon get you well.'

Well. Wellness. The state of being he'll get for me . . .

Hear these words, Citizen, and recognise them for what they are. I'll get you. That's what Alexander means. One way or another, I'll get you, you inconvenient bastard. That's what he really means. Get you to see it my way. Whatever it costs you.

Then he asks me, 'Where do you really come from?'

I say nothing. Of course. Except to myself. To myself I say, I will tell you, Citizen, but you won't like to hear. I will tell you that I come from uncounted generations of survival, from unnumbered generations of gazing without fear, from numberless generations of inner silence, the inner silence of the seer.

I will tell you the truth, Citizen, but you won't like it. Between my appearance and your reality is a fathomless gulf of misunderstanding, as is always the case between a free spirit and a member of a crowd. I will tell you that, exactly obverse to the way that you and all like you think things are, it is not you who is seeing over me but I that am seeing over you, for I have the gaze of an eagle and you do not. Whatever my circumstances, I am an overseer and you are not.

November 1987